spin cycle

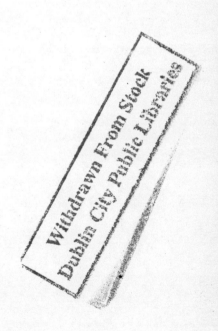

also by zoë strachan

negative space

spin cycle

zoë strachan

PICADOR

First published 2004 by Picador
an imprint of Pan Macmillan Ltd
Pan Macmillan, 20 New Wharf Road, London N1 9RR
Basingstoke and Oxford
Associated companies throughout the world
www.panmacmillan.com

ISBN 0 330 48632 2

Grateful acknowledgement is made for permission to reprint the following:
excerpt from *Bible John and Such Bad Company* by George Forbes copyright
© 1996, published by Lang Syne Publishers; excerpt from *Bright Colors Falsely Seen:
Synaesthesia and the Search for Transcendental Knowledge* by Kevin T. Dann
copyright © 1998, published by Yale University Press; lines from 'Lack of Evidence'
from *Swimming in the Flood* by John Burnside copyright © 1995,
published by Jonathan Cape.

1 3 5 7 9 8 6 4 2

A CIP catalogue record for this book is available from
the British Library.

Typeset by IntypeLibra, London
Printed and bound in Great Britain by
Mackays of Chatham plc, Chatham, Kent

To
my parents
Hazel and Stuart
with love
x

It was on the night of Friday February 23rd 1968 that a vivacious 25-year-old brunette in a sexy black dress called Pat Docker was gyrating to the music and letting herself go after a busy week at the Victoria Infirmary where she worked as a nurse. She danced with several young men in the semi-darkness that night but no-one could later recall in whose arms she enjoyed the last waltz.

George Forbes, *Bible John and Such Bad Company*

For Edgar, the whirring of electric fans was orange, the humming of vacuum cleaners black, the rhythm of a moving streetcar yellow. Alone in a room with a piano, he tentatively touched the keys, crying out with delight the different colors they produced – middle C red, bass notes black, high notes white. One day, upon seeing a rainbow, Edgar exclaimed, 'A song! A song!' (Whitchurch, 1922)

Kevin Dann, *Bright Colors Falsely Seen:*
Synaesthesia and the Search for Transcendental Knowledge

There's something in our lives
will not be eased:
a flow in time, a blemish in the air.

John Burnside, 'Lack of Evidence'
Swimming in the Flood

Opening

Down the back lanes behind the long, straight terraces ambles Siobhan, tripping over the uneven cobbles as her ear catches a frenetic shower of birdsong. City birds trilling mobile ring tones, but the sound of pure nature is never far from the surface. She glimpses it, every now and then, red in tooth and claw.

Myrna is also walking, though she sticks to the main road. Fast, late, smiling to herself; a cunning, secret smile born of the night before, full of the promise of the night to come. Yes, there's something in the air, not love – she's far too worldly wise for that – but something nonetheless. Her feet fit a rhythm as she plays a childish game. Don't step on the cracks, the bogeyman is waiting.

Agnes is on the tube; so much quicker than the bus. With her is Vina. In memory only but no less real for that. Agnes thinks of a summer distantly past. The warmest August in years, but muggy, not a pleasant heat. The air of the city weighing heavy with pollution. Saturday night, and Vina, all dressed up, dancing in the arms of a stranger. Heels light on the sprung floor, she is smiling. Having the time of her life. Her partner is a skilful dancer, moving quickly and smoothly. He later turns out to be nondescript.

Everyone and no one recognize the photofit circulated by the police.

Within ten minutes of each other they'll arrive here, at the launderette.

Next door, the plastic UNDER OFFER sign has yellowed with age, and the metal shutters are thoroughly fly-postered and graffitied; it used to be a newsagent and grocery, but there are plenty more of those nearby, well stocked with stale scones, fizzy juice and Rizlas. This old place, the launderette, only survives because of the area, its transient student population, the abundance of bed-sits, DSS B&Bs. Shiny new premises have opened on the main road, offering dry cleaning, ironing, vending machines full of cans and chocolate, and a good view of the passing talent. But it's further away, and here the customers are faithful, favouring cheap over cheerful any day, not caring how many dress shirts can be starched and pressed for ten pounds. Siobhan once brought in a newspaper article about young professionals finding love in their local laundry. Agnes, tickled by the idea, pinned it up on the wall, but it tore, fell down, ended up in the bin, and still nobody showed any sign of finding love. It isn't that sort of place. Not yet. Occasionally a spate of new customers come over all *Tales of the City*, but they never stay long.

Silver script on a faded blue sign, the same in any city:

Coin-Op   Fully Equipped   AUTOMATIC   self-service

Somewhere to take all those little domestic emergencies, the wet or bloody bedclothes, the soiled undergarments of children and alcoholics, the dog's blanket caked in mud and hair, the garment spattered with evidence of crime or infidelity. An establishment without embarrassment, discretion assured.

Yes, it's seen a few sights over the years, heard a fair bit too. Rows, propositions, knockbacks, reconciliations, drug deals, there have been some humdingers. The man arrested for making dirty calls on the payphone, caught in the act by a plainclothes police officer who had been washing the same load of t-shirts all afternoon. Agnes had previously commented on the customer's smart clothes and lovely manner, as he stood with the paper, pretending he was phoning about jobs. After the event she was undeterred by her error of judgement, and confirmed with relish that those were just the type you had to watch. Didn't she know that better than most? Never trust a man in a wide pinstripe, she told the girls, that's my advice.

This summer is sultry, warm, but rainy. Moody. A curious summer altogether, and one in which the most ordinary of exteriors conceals some extraordinary secrets. And how much more ordinary can you get than a launderette? A place where women are paid to wash the clothes of others, to remove the dirt and grime of day-to-day life, to return everything cleansed, pristine. Whilst remaining themselves unsoiled, now there's the trick.

These things can stay

It was the article in the paper that started her off. A murderer caught, the happy ending to an unhappy tale. A semblance of peace at last for the parents of a fifteen-year-old schoolgirl, missing then found. Abducted walking home one afternoon. A man in his late thirties charged. Not his first offence.

Agnes thought of a favourite Agatha Christie, in which a schoolgirl was lured away with promises of a film test. Her hair done with peroxide, she was all made up and given a dress to wear, but her future was short, and nothing to do with movies. She was a body double, for one key scene. Her last. Miss Marple got to the bottom of it, naturally, and the murderer was soon brought to justice, the required resolution achieved. Agnes usually felt a similar catharsis at a real-life crime solved. But today, she read the article, looked at the picture of the girl and started to cry. She was too young this one, far too young. Agnes had to lock herself in the toilet so the customers didn't see her. As the tears kept coming, she realized that she wasn't just crying for Joanne from Solihull, she was crying for Vina from Glasgow, who had been three years older, but perhaps no less of a child.

All of a sudden, Vina is not dancing. She is dying. Who would have thought 15 denier strong enough, to twist and squeeze and expel the life from somebody? Her eyes grow bulbous, and mascara powders onto her cheeks like soot, while her manicured nails clutch at her neck, her assailant, thin air. Nails which are later discovered to be broken and chipped, skin and blood and dirt lodged beneath them, bravely but pointlessly, for this is before such remnants can be scraped out and analysed to lay a path to the door of a killer.

Her mind, grasping for oxygen but still functioning, just, is a tangled mass of denial. Not real, not happening, not my fault, not true, and most of all, not me. Not me.

Vina shudders as her heart gives a final lurch, then stops, and she sinks to the ground. Her killer stands for a moment, looking, then walks away. He stops for an awkward, half erect piss, smoothes his hair and continues along the alleyway. He has done this before, he knows the value of his composure. Behind him, the pleated hem of Vina's eau de Nil dress dips into an oily puddle, and, as if in exchange, her lifeless body allows its last fluids to seep slowly into the earth.

Agnes? Myrna's voice had that unnaturally upbeat tone

which suggested she was about to try to wheedle something out of her boss.

Uhuh?

I know Siobhan's still out, but can I take my lunch now? I'm starving.

Are you going out?

No, I've got a sandwich.

Oh well, I suppose so. I'll give you a shout if it gets busy. Are you not wanting to get out into the sunshine?

Not really, thanks. Bit of a late one last night. Wouldn't mind a quiet moment.

Oh aye. Serves you right if you're paying for it today. What were you up to?

Went to see a band at the Barras.

There's a coincidence, I was just thinking about that place. An old haunt of mine. I take it you had a good time.

Fantastic. Hadn't been there in ages, and last night, it was as if nothing had changed. Peeing down when we got out though, and you never get a taxi on that side of town, must be the law. That's how I'm so tired, had to walk home.

You've got to be careful though hen, especially over there. You can't go wandering about on your own. It's foolish.

Och, Myrna tutted, with vital insouciance. Washes off the concert sweat at least. Was the sign still the same, when you went?

The shooting stars? Oh yes, they were there.

A hundred thousand indie boys' dreams are written in

those stars, of being up on that stage, playing to a sell-out crowd. As if.

Oh well, what's life without aspiration?

Content, I suppose.

Myrna sat in the kitchen, flicking through a magazine, looking at page after shiny page of things she couldn't have, people she didn't know and places she wasn't. A celebrity chef cooked for an intimate gathering of friends at the beautiful apartment of a model and her famous-for-nothing-except-he's-shagging-a-model boyfriend. They wore clothes that made her sick, it would take her a week's wages just to buy that belt, a month's for that handbag. Ostentatious, tacky even, but she coveted it nonetheless. She glugged her tepid Tetley's greedily as they sipped from champagne cocktails adorned with fresh berries, their exquisite hors d'oeuvres showing up her sweaty sandwich as the nasty lunch it was. Beautiful, stylish, rich, successful, and some of them younger than her. Myrna wondered how you made that leap, from where you were to where you wanted to be. Did you have to be born that way? Bastards, each and every one of them.

She wasn't stupid, she knew money wouldn't necessarily make her happy. Of course it was who you were that mattered, not what you owned. But she wasn't sure she entirely liked who she was these days, and a swift injection of cash would help. If she cleared the debts, she'd be able to make some changes. After that hurdle, she'd be heading for the finishing line. Money, quick, easy money. It didn't seem so unreasonable. Other people managed. She could do it too. And then, and then . . . a lone shopper, she loved that feeling of entering a store, the smell of new clothes, of leather shoes, the trying on, the tissue wrap of the purchase. Followed by getting ready, dressing up, looking good, going places. Which in turn led to having fun, to meeting people, to sex, who knows, perhaps to love. Like it or not, the road to happiness was paved with gold.

Myrna turned to her horoscope, read and forgot her key career date of the 25th, because – hallelujah – the earth was going to move on Saturday, and she was going out on Saturday night. She scrutinized the advice. *Playing it cool wins hearts*. She could do that. Generally, she was attracted to people who smiled and laughed, but what was there to be so happy about? The effort involved would be minimal: adopt an impassive face. Look deep. She could carry it off no problem; honestly her talents were wasted in the launderette, she should've been an actress. And it was a popular look. She had friends who had fallen for it. I'm always trying to guess what she's thinking, they'd tell Myrna, like a favourite track on repeat. Myrna – who rarely succumbed to the desire to suggest that perhaps the object of their affections wasn't thinking at all, or else was suffering from constipation – privately thought she'd figured out the real appeal of the blank, mysterious look. Men wanted to break the facade, to see the woman flustered. And, typically, they suspected this could only be achieved through sexual means. Which was fine by her.

Much cheered, Myrna decided she'd pop into town

after work, just in case she saw anything. Playing it cool might win hearts, but you could never underestimate the power of a new outfit.

Agnes, happy to have her own quiet moment, blew her nose luxuriously, lit a cigarette and walked to the front of the shop to look out of the window. The first day of the year she'd been warm enough without her jacket. Disregarding the auld wives' advice, it wasn't just clouts that were cast but jumpers, tights, socks. The street abounded with winter limbs, projecting palely from vests and t-shirts, and even, in the case of a foolhardy few, shorts. Many carried plastic bags which Agnes knew would clink with carry-outs. Heading parkwards she guessed, to find a spot out of view of the police cars which would be patrolling, ready to make people empty their bottles, to lift those who argued too vociferously with the council's bylaw.

Although it was close by, Agnes hadn't passed through the park since last summer, when she went to check out the prices at the Laundromat on the other side. Lots of young people, sitting in pairs or little groups, on a slope beside the big path. Some had music playing. She'd felt awkward walking past them all, though she knew they weren't looking at her. She was too old for that now, and besides, she'd never been a head turner. No, they wanted to see each other, wearing less clothes than usual, more relaxed in the late afternoon warmth. Great bundles of girls and boys, all mixed up together. Agnes could practically smell the hormones. Not like when she was a youngster, though she hadn't had many friends. Except for Vina, she thought. Vina really had been her friend.

They'd been taken to the park as children, by her mum and Auntie Maureen with wee cousin William in tow. Maybe they'd been going to visit someone in Partick, she couldn't quite recall. It had been out of the ordinary though, that she did remember, both the outing and what else happened that day. Willie got plonked on the roundabout, left to the mercy of the other kids while Frances and Maureen sat on a bench and chatted. Agnes and Vi went to feed the ducks. Vina's hair glinted blonde in the sunshine, a precursor to the rinses she would put through it when she was a few years older. She kept stooping to pull up her over-the-knee socks. Agnes thought they looked very grown up, like stockings. She'd been eight, so Vina must have been about twelve.

Their supply of stale bread exhausted in minutes, they walked around the pond, along a quieter path, where it was cool and dank under the trees. Out of the corner of her eye, Agnes saw a man standing still, thought nothing of it, until suddenly Vina had her by the hand and was pulling her along, hissing under her breath,

Run! Come on, run!

Then she looked back over her shoulder and screamed, shrill enough to burst an eardrum and for no reason Agnes could see,

Filthy pig!

They'd been taken for tea in the Coronation Cafe, told

to put extra sugar in for the shock. Auntie Maureen had mentioned the police, but agreed with Agnes' mother that it wasn't worth the risk.

You've got to be careful, Agnes remembered her saying. These things can stay with a girl.

Vina had been allowed a butterfly cake, while Agnes chose an éclair, and wondered what the fuss was about. Everyone was nice to them though, and it wasn't often you got to go to a tearoom and have anything you wanted. Even if they didn't get to try out the jukebox.

Agnes returned to the desk, licked the tip of her pencil and tried to get back into the accounts. The taste of the graphite kept her locked in the past, when boys and girls had separate playgrounds and children were afraid of their elders, because they knew it was no joke when they were told they'd be sorry.

Siobhan, meanwhile, was in her favourite lunchtime spot, the humid glass cupola of the Kibble Palace. She could feel the sweat welling in her pores, imagine the plants growing, blooming, around her, as she walked towards her preferred bench, JEMIMA MCDONALD, 1937–1969, next to a statue she especially liked, a figure naked save for a turban and a necklace of three dangling coins, with snail trails of green trickling over her breasts from the leaking mosaic of glass above. And yes, Jemima was free, waiting for Siobhan to settle and examine her latest purchase. She disliked having to sit elsewhere; the undedicated bench in front of a crouching, Medusa plaited nude, for instance, where more than once she'd been dripped on or swished by a springy branch, as though the statue was trying to shoo her away.

Siobhan poked her finger through a hole in the shrink wrap, slitting it carefully along one side to free the seductively weighty hardback it contained. It had been expensive, two days' wages, but worth every machine loaded, every garment folded. Siobhan's current passion was Paris, from the belle époque to the twenties, and that evening Atget would come home and join Brassaï, Man Ray, Beach and Monnier, Toulouse-Lautrec, Kiki, Rimbaud. (The last had made it in by the skin of his teeth, largely on account of his *Voyelles*, though she sympathized with him deeply over his relationship with Verlaine.) Rubbing her thumb along the edge of the book, Siobhan opened it at random and peeked in, at the glorious, dusty stairway banister of the Hotel d'Eperon. Page after page spread under her fingers: elegantly abandoned salons; tantalizing glimpses of dark wood panelling; the twisting cathedra of an empty church; shadowy reflections in fireplace mirrors.

She loved art books, especially collections of photographs. Pictures in books were true, uncomplicated by the colouring of the letters that flashed up like the bright keys of a child's xylophone when she read a sentence – whereas a fast-paced thriller could land her with a migraine within a few chapters. Nevertheless, Siobhan knew there wasn't time to savour Atget's images and have her lunch, so reluctantly she returned the book to her bag, away from greasy fingerprints and crumbs. Instead, she ate her sandwich, listening to the quiet tinkle of water in the pond: soothing curves of gold in her mind if she chose to focus on them, unobtrusive if she didn't. Atget would have appreciated the glasshouse, she thought, with its architectural greenery and umbelliferous ironwork. As she looked up, a sudden phalanx of black shapes flashed across the windowpanes. Not a flock of birds, not quite, because the glass although grubby was transparent. Siobhan had observed this phenomenon before. Shadows cast by the ghosts of birds, she'd decided, wings beating endlessly across the sky.

Time to return to work was pre-empted by the arrival of toddler twins, high voices ricocheting around the enclosed space, bouncing sharply off the glass. Shrill echoes became shards of noise, ready to plummet down and impale her, *Exorcist* style.

Siobhan left quickly, then dawdled back through the botanical gardens. It was said, and she liked to believe it, that an attack on the Kibble in 1914 was the act of militant suffragettes, trying to draw attention to their fiendish cause.

In the early hours of one Saturday morning, at the end of January, the night attendant was startled by a loud bang. At first he thought there had been an accident at the gasworks, but then he heard the sparkling shatter of glass, and realized that something was afoot closer to home. Siobhan imagined him edging out into the night, torch in hand, and wondered if he took refuge in his military training. The culprits had made good their escape, but several pieces of evidence were later taken down by the investigating officer:

1 prints in the soft ground, such as would be left by a lady's high-heeled shoe
2 one black veil, silk
3 several fragments of cake
4 one champagne bottle, empty

They did it in style, whoever they were. Suffragettes, pranksters, perhaps it didn't matter; Siobhan loved the idea of the two of them – though nowhere had it said that there were two.

To be in the glasshouse at night, that would be good enough. But to be there eating cake and drinking champagne, straight from the bottle. Kissing between swigs, perhaps, tongues fizzy with demi-sec. Then the icing on the cake (and Siobhan assumed the cake in question was iced), a homemade bomb! The schoolboy favourite, salt and sugar, or something more professional? Whispering, creeping, through the flimsy filmy ferns. Lighting the short fuse and running. And perhaps one of them stopped, swiftly plucked a flower, tucked it inside her jacket; a voluptuous, foreign orchid, to press between the pages of a book, to smile over in years to come, a keepsake. Stifling giggles as they clutched at each other, shoes sinking into the grass outside, clattering on the frosty path, running until they thought they were out of immediate danger and then, seduced by a secluded spot, stopping. A bench, the shadow of a tree, a gateway. Fingers nimble despite the icy air, finding routes to champagne-warm skin, even as the clanging of the police van rang out over the wrought-iron fence and into the verdant, velvet darkness of the park.

The launderette was quiet that afternoon. Myrna finished at three, with a cheery toodle-oo as she buggered off for a quick snifter on her way to the shops, while Agnes got a cancellation at the doctor and wasn't far behind her. She thought her HRT was all wrong – up here, she explained, tapping her head; not down there, pointing vaguely south of her waist – and indeed Siobhan had heard her on the phone, complaining of mood swings and weepiness.

Okay, that's me away Siobhan dear. Remember to check the back door before you go, and put both the padlocks on, will you?

Yes Agnes.

Siobhan had locked up the shop often before, and never yet forgotten.

And sweep up before you leave.

Will do.

Bloody hell, it's pissing down now, would you look at that? Grim.

Never mind, Siobhan said, it'll keep the customers away.

Well, if you're stuck for something to do, check the machines for oose.

Okay. Hope you don't get too wet.

Aye. Cheerio then.

Siobhan had no intention of scooping out the balled

residue of hundreds of jumpers and socks, which assumed a uniform dirty grey colour, then escaped and drifted across the floor like tumbleweed. She stood for a moment after Agnes had gone, watching the impact of raindrops against the glass. Each one burst with a ripe slodge of burnt umber. The colour of her name, she'd always thought, even when she was too young to know the word itself. The drops were so full and tantalizing, she was tempted to go out and open her mouth, catch them on her tongue. Thoughts of acid rain quickly deterred her, and besides, her book was gently and irresistibly reeling her in.

So: the Jardin du Luxembourg at dawn, the damp chill of Spring on her bare arms. Occasional cascades of early birdsong, not yet swallowed by the noise of the day, each cheep distinct, a tiny, glinting bead on the end of her eyelash. The tone of the photograph changing from sepia to the greenish grey of mossy grass, leaves on the verge of sprouting. The launderette gone, the clean smell of powder replaced by the last dryness of dusty paths gathering dew. The simple act of walking sharpened by the beat of her heart, anticipation in the pit of her stomach. A statue up ahead, and her moving towards it, not yet able to make out if there is one white figure or two on the plinth . . .

The bright ring of the bell on the launderette door collapsed her imaginings. After a moment Siobhan realized that there was a customer waiting at the desk, a girl with drookit hair and wet clothes, quietly dripping. Closing the book, Siobhan rose from her corner position on the bench by the window,

Hello?

The girl twitched, Siobhan's voice, unexpected behind her, spoke just a little too loudly.

Oh, I didn't realize there was anyone here. I didn't see you when I came in.

Could she have been so deep in her fantasy world that her real outline had faded and blurred? Siobhan flapped the book in her hand,

I was just . . . reading.

I'm sorry I disturbed you.

There was a slight accent in this girl's voice that Siobhan recognized, a tumble of little shapes that fell from top to bottom of her vision.

That's okay, it's just a picture book. Photographs. Atget, you know? Paris. I only got it today. Better to look at it at home, in peace. Not that you've disturbed me, of course.

She drew breath. The girl was very pretty, Siobhan realized. Even with sopping wet hair. Marble legs stretching down from the plinth, toes wriggling as they felt the dew, white stone warming into flesh and spreading across the ankle and upwards, like fire licking a piece of paper . . . Where had that image come from? Belatedly, Siobhan remembered what she was supposed to say:

Can I help you?

The girl held out a brightly coloured laundry bag,

Yes, please. Can I get these washed?

A service wash?

I don't know. I've just moved here and I don't have a washing machine yet.

Well, for £5.20 we can do it for you and you can collect it tomorrow, or I can give you a token for £1.80 and you can do it yourself now. Then it's 10p for the spinner and the dryer takes twenties. Take a bit over an hour, altogether.

I'd rather leave it, if that's okay. For a service wash.

Of course.

What time will I come back tomorrow?

Lunchtime? It's not busy.

Siobhan grinned, indicated the empty launderette, one machine chugging away on a slow rinse.

Okay then.

Siobhan grinned again, weakly this time. She felt she had botched the conversation, that it hadn't been a shop transaction, but some kind of test which she had failed, and failed ignominiously at that.

See you tomorrow.

Yes.

Pausing as she reached the door, the girl turned and said,

I saw some of his photographs once. Atget's. In a gallery, in Paris.

Oh.

The girl smiled, briskly, and let the door swing shut behind her. Dear God, Siobhan thought, could she not have said something better than Oh? In her head she was capable of witty, intellectual conversation, but then in her head she had time to think, to plan and edit.

When Siobhan looked back at her book, it didn't seem quite so captivating. The pictures had lost their stereoscopic quality, become one-dimensional. A new customer and she hadn't even taken her name. Agnes would make a fuss about that, for sure. Siobhan sighed, and opened the door of the first machine to check for oose. She would have liked to have known what the girl was called, just out of interest.

Later on, at home, Siobhan looked at a photo of a man, made small by a huge, dilapidated building. The day of its demolition, though it was impossible to tell from the image how the man felt about this. He was alone in the frame, save for the ghost of a person on the far left, someone who had paused in a long exposure, then walked on and disappeared. Siobhan didn't know exactly when she herself had become so solitary. She had always liked being alone, certainly. Reading, watching films, thinking. Her synaesthesia had helped her reject invitations to busy bars and noisy clubs, but nevertheless she did remember a time when she had gone out, socialized more often. Gradually though the friends moved away, got jobs, got boyfriends, and she had retreated into herself. Meetings became awkward. She could talk about her work at the launderette, the customers who came in, but it seemed to make people uneasy, as they celebrated projects and promotions. She had tried sharing her obsession of the moment – a book, an artist, a period in history, a city – but this last was the only one to meet an enthusiastic response, and Siobhan, who had never actually visited Paris, or Berlin, or Florence, was at a loss when conversation turned to the reality of these places. What to do and where to stay. As for fashion, current affairs, television, shopping; her disinterest had slowly weakened her connection with these, until she regarded them rather as distant relatives, not actively disliked but seldom visited. A couple of made-up excuses, some invented prior engagements, a few calls which she forgot to return, and slowly people stopped asking. She would still get the odd friendly phone call, a fluttering of Christmas and birthday cards, but apart from that her life was all her own, free of social obligation, and she had grown to prefer it that way. And the less she did outside home and work, the more time it took to do it, so that cleaning alone could fill a day, even in her tiny flat.

Siobhan shut the book. The girl had been to Paris, seen some of these photographs for real. She wondered if that would be better than looking at reproductions in a book, if it would bring you closer still to the place they portrayed. After you'd been to the gallery, you could go and look for the streets or buildings themselves – those that hadn't crumbled slowly away. If you dared test the illusion, that is, and risk the disappointment. Siobhan had not yet found the courage.

8.17 a.m. – Jay

Myrna thinks his name suits him. Jay. She doesn't know what the other one's called, though sometimes they come in together, to do their washing. Jay's hair is razored choppy about his face, dyed L'Oréal red, roots showing brown. His friend's is blue-black, short and spiky. They wear alt-punk clothes, dog collars and skinny t-shirts over stripy long-sleeves, a little kohl lining the eyelid, maybe a flash of mascara. Both are very thin. Never the baggy wide-legged trousers, crotch down to the knees, favoured by other boys their age. That would be bad for business. Instead, dirty denims, tight as you like. Jay wears sneakers with holes in them; his friend, black leather motorcycle boots, soles cracked open, leaking tiny pebbles and fragments of broken glass as he walks.

Myrna was in a bar once, saw the one with the black spiky hair being thrown out. It only took one bouncer to drag him from the toilets to the door,

If I ever catch you renting in here again, you've had it. And the same goes for your wee ging-er pal.

While on the bar stools the older men sat quiet, the ones who usually spoke loudly of their work at the paper, the agency, the BBC. Studiously ignoring the hoo-ha,

21

checking out the sport on the telly, the bar menu, the newspaper. It was something to be talked about later, when they'd progressed from pints to the better single malts. When their voices had taken on a queen-y intonation.

Jay asks for his token in a polite, soft accent, which makes Myrna think he might be from one of the islands. He sounds like a girl she used to know, who had to go home every Easter to help with the lambing. The voice must be part of the charm, she decides. Along with that distinctive look, which makes them both stand out amongst the keep-it-Kappa and le coq sportif.

His dark-haired friend seems more resilient. Gallus wee bugger, Agnes called him once. Not quite so frail-looking, nor as softly spoken. While he waits for his washing he looks out the window, winking at familiar faces and closet cases, tongue touching teeth, insolent as fuck. He acts like he can look after himself. Just about: she's seen him with bruised knuckles. She hopes he looks after Jay too. And she really, really hopes that this is all some kind of bizarre phase. Too much Genet, too little cash. Something they have half a chance of outgrowing, if they make it past twenty. Myrna doesn't know, doesn't much want to know, what happens to rent boys when they stop looking like boys.

She can't make out the title of the tatty paperback Jay is hunched over this time. So thin that he'll slip through the cracks in the pavement one day, she thinks. His hair hangs in uneven shards over killer cheekbones, split ends frizzing in the afternoon light, small sparks of electricity against pale, greyish skin. She imagines that his friend cuts it for him, that sometimes Jay catches his hand and holds his wrist, just for a moment, finger tight against the veins until he feels the life in them. They look at the razor, then look each other in the eye. She's sure they're in love.

Real-life story

Agnes bustled into the shop, in that sweaty-backed, not enough hands for umbrella and carrier bags kind of way that she hated. Just as she'd dumped everything at her feet and shrugged off her summer waterproof, she noticed Myrna look at Siobhan with what she recognized as a 'do we tell her?' expression.

Okay, what's happened now? Can't leave you pair alone for two minutes. Spill the beans.

Myrna hesitated, then beckoned Agnes over into the doorway that led to the kitchen,

See that guy over there?

Reading the paper?

Yes. Well, he's got a porn mag behind it.

A redness started somewhere around Agnes' neck, and quickly spread to her ears, until her lobes felt like they were burning up.

What did you say?

Siobhan, who had moved closer, explained,

We saw it through the window. It's hidden inside his newspaper.

Agnes took deep breaths from her abdomen. She had read in a magazine that this was meant to help in anxious situations. It didn't. Images went through her mind: clearing the wardrobe, sitting on the bed; a bleak resignation, long familiar. She glanced back at the man, older than he looked but not old enough to know better, for age was no guarantee of wisdom – not when it came to that kind of thing, as Agnes knew only too well. A flat gold signet ring against the back page crossword. She'd never liked jewellery on a man.

He doesn't stagger, drunken, like the others who have left the dancing early. His arm is steady, more so than Vina, whose heels catch in the cobbles at the edge of the street as they walk away. Her legs are tired from her exertions, and she feels a twinge of cramp deep in her womb. Thank God she is with somebody quiet and undemanding. She realizes that she hasn't asked where he lives, but assumes he is the taxi type. His shoes look scarcely walked in. Home to bed for her, and no hough ma gandie, as Teri laughingly warned, before complaining that she hadn't even got a proper look at Vina's lumber.

As they pass under a streetlamp, Vina extracts a cigarette from her purse, and pauses, expecting him to light it for her, but he walks on, patting his pockets and saying he thinks he may have lost his Zippo. By the time he finds it, they are further along, beyond the bright artificial glow.

Agnes turned back to the girls, fearful suddenly that they were winding her up. That, inexplicably, they *knew*. But

Siobhan's expression was of concern, though the warmth in her usually pale cheeks could have been anger or embarrassment. She wasn't lying.

Behind his paper, you say?

It was Myrna who answered,

Yes, he must still have it. We've been watching him and there's nowhere he could have put it.

Right then, Agnes said, in her most not-to-be-argued-with tone. The one that could send recalcitrant customers ducking for cover: What do you mean, you're here to do a wash? Do you know what time it is?

For a second Myrna thought Agnes was actually going to roll up her sleeves, and box his ears. Instead she stalked along the aisle of the shop, between the banks of machines, getting closer and closer to the bench at the end. One still, silent second and then she lunged, snatched the paper away, sent the magazine flapping to the floor in a heavy sloosh of glossy pages.

Get out.

The man rose to his feet, as if to argue. Myrna and Siobhan quickly came forward to stand behind Agnes, who said,

No, none of your shilly shallying, I said GET OUT.

My washing's still in the machine.

Tough, Agnes snapped.

You can't stop me getting it.

I can, and I will. I've the right to bar anyone I want from these premises, and I'm barring you.

That's theft.

That's the least of your worries, sonny boy. I'll leave your stuff outside the door.

The shrill spinning of the machine suddenly stopped, and with a last, weary clunk it switched itself off.

There, you can take it yourself, Myrna said, suddenly nervous.

This is a fucking disgrace, the man started, but Agnes quickly interjected,

Siobhan, phone the police will you?

All right, I'm going, he said, then muttered, picking up the magazine, Fuck's sake, it's a free country.

He pulled his clothes out of the machine and stuffed them, sodden, into a large supermarket bag-for-life. Agnes held the door open for him as he left,

Good riddance to bad rubbish.

Might learn something, you frigid old bitch, he shouted, throwing the magazine back at her.

Agnes watched until he rounded the corner, then shut and locked the door, standing with her back against it. Her heart was trampolining in her chest.

Go Agnes! Myrna said, and Siobhan quickly added,

Well done.

After her breathing had returned to normal, Agnes smiled at the girls, then looked down at the magazine, which lay spread at her feet like roadkill. She stooped slowly to pick it up.

Every shop gets its nutters, that's just the way it is, she said, holding the magazine by the corner, at arm's length. And this piece of crap can go straight in the bin. If there's one thing I cannot stand, it's disgusting, vile things like this. I go to the shop, and there's three shelves of the bloody things, and the newsagent seems like a nice man but somebody's ordering them in, and there must be hundreds of folk like that – she gestured towards the street, as though it might be louping with perverts – that keep the filth merchants in business.

Shaking her head, Agnes marched through to the kitchen, still holding the offending article between her fingertips.

I've never seen her like that before, Siobhan said.

I guess she's not into porn then, said Myrna (who believed in absolute sexual freedom yet wasn't quite able to suppress a small sense of triumph). Though it was pretty tame stuff, as far as I could see. What about that magazine she buys, with all the murder stories in it? If that's not obscene I don't know what is.

They heard running water, then vigorous lathering of the squeedgy soap.

I'm going to see if she's okay, Siobhan said. Must have been a bit frightening, standing up to him like that.

Imagine reading that in public. What would have come next, eh? But Aggie can handle herself all right.

Still, I can make her a cup of tea. Want one?

Aye, why the hell not? Might as well live a little.

Agnes was sitting at the kitchen table, looking slightly dazed. Siobhan insinuated herself into her line of vision,

That was great. Do you want a cup of tea? I'm making one for me and Myrna anyway.

No response. Siobhan waited a second then asked, in a louder voice,

Are you okay?

I'm fine hen, honest. A cup of tea would be just what the doctor ordered. I'll just make it while I'm through here. You'd better go and unlock the front door, there's people who'll want back in to empty their machines.

What was she meant to say? For a second she was tempted to confide in Siobhan, who always seemed so calm. So modern, in a funny way. But no, some things were private, and Agnes had not yet managed to figure out what her little discovery said about her, let alone him. Although eased by the weeks passing, at the time it had felt as if a favourite pet dog, on being scratched behind the ears, had turned and bitten her.

Speed Queen

Looking through the window of the launderette, Siobhan saw that Myrna (unusually, for she was in on her own, no Agnes to spur her on) was already hard at work on the Friday morning rush of service washes. People liked to get clean for the weekend, the hairdresser always needed towels for Saturday, the rank gear of the Thursday night rugby team had to be done before it stank the place out.

Myrna seemed to be dancing away to herself as she fished shirts, shorts and socks out of one of the big Wascators, her head bobbing from side to side and a shoogle in her hips as she moved. Inside, Siobhan was surprised to discover that the radio wasn't on. As the door clumped shut behind her, Myrna turned, puzzled, then stretched her face into a smile as she too noticed the absence of music. Last night's make-up clung to her face, and her hair was twisted up in a lopsided top knot, but her eyes were as bright as new twenty-pence pieces in a Christmas pudding.

Fuck, can you believe that? I was dancing to the noise of the machines. Thought it was music coming from the flats upstairs.

Siobhan struggled for the right phrase, suddenly

worried about sounding fuddy duddy, which proved her very point. Who even said fuddy duddy these days?

Heavy night? she attempted.

Oh, you know me. Too much is never enough. Drowning my sorrows, or at least it started out that way.

What about?

Tell you later. Cannae bear to go into it just now. I'd forgotten about it myself by halfway through the night.

Looking at Myrna's saucer eyes, Siobhan remembered learning as a child that the pupils were holes, and wondering how you could have holes so big in your eyes, how it could be that sometimes she saw things which weren't there even more clearly than things which were. Myrna finished pelting the strips into the dryer, slammed the door shut and counted 20, 40, 60, 80 pence into the slot, turned the handle. As she held down the button to start the machine she nodded at the name written in silver script next to her hand,

Speed Queen right enough.

Want a cup of tea?

No thanks. Still on the Red Bull. Give us another one through, eh? Trying to keep the agony away until high noon, then I'll go to the chemist and get some supplies.

Siobhan went through to the kitchen and stuck the kettle on, opened the table top fridge and chucked a can over to Myrna, who caught it with undulled exactness.

You don't look too bad, if it's any consolation.

Cheers m'dear. Always feels better when you're getting paid to have your hangover. When's the auld bitch in today?

She's not so bad.

She is when you've got a hangover.

Siobhan didn't mind Agnes, largely because she found it easy to let the background noise rub out the harsher visual elements of her voice, like an eraser on soft pencil. Besides, in a rare moment of confidence Agnes had told Siobhan that when she was younger, she used to pretend to be called Rita. Just sometimes, when she went to the dancing.

Got used to Agnes eventually though, she explained. You have to, don't you? And that's what Donald knew me by, so I gave up on Rita when we started courting. Silly notion, really.

Siobhan would occasionally find herself looking at Agnes, trying to figure out whether glamorous Rita was still lurking in there somewhere. A funny expression, a lapse of concentration, and she suspected that Rita had taken over for a second, was having a quick shifty at the life she had been denied.

Anyway, Siobhan said to Myrna, she's off today.

Excellente. Couldn't face her in this state. So, do you want to hear what's happened then?

Uhuh.

Siobhan braced herself, expecting a variation on the Myrna's sex life catechism. She had her responses off pat: No! He didn't? Really? But how did you feel?

You know my bar job, that I was doing in the evenings?

That place in town? Siobhan couldn't remember the name of it, or where exactly it was.

Yup. Well, last night I went in, quite the thing, twenty minutes early as it happens. And I got called up to the manager's office. Now I've been there for months, and I've hardly ever missed a shift. And I work hard too. Honestly. Nobody likes waiting at the bar, so I go fast.

Myrna paused for breath and Siobhan nodded encouragement.

Anyway, Marcus-the-supervisor's leaving, and I thought maybe they were going to sound me out for his job. But no, in I go and that bastard hands me an envelope. So I goes, pay day's not till Friday, is this a bonus? And he tells me to open it, and there's my P45.

They sacked you? Why?

Search me. They didn't go into details. It wasn't just me, it was Scott as well. He was a good laugh. We used to volunteer to do the clear-up at the end of the night, because then you could have a drink while you worked, get in the mood for going out.

Isn't there something you can do? Someone you can complain to?

Nope. Bugger all. Casual staff.

That's terrible.

I don't know how I'm going to manage, I mean, I'll need to find something else and pronto.

Maybe you could get extra hours here. You should ask Agnes.

Suppose it's worth a go. Until I get another job. Fucking hell, just when you think you're getting somewhere, eh?

Myrna made a remarkable recovery as the day progressed, although Siobhan wondered if this was as chemically aided as her enjoyment of the night before. Either that, or she could be the new face of Alka-Seltzer. Regardless, when Myrna came back after lunch, she professed herself brand new.

Siobhan, on the other hand, was suffering. A burst water main in the street perpendicular to the launderette meant double the number of cars and vans. Usually the noise was filtered through the thick glass of the shop window, subdued by the muted bluegreen hum of the machines, but not today. Ineffectually, Siobhan fluttered her hand in front of her eyes, trying to chase away the angular forms which were plaguing her, until finally a noisy motorcycle chased her into the back shop, strident hexagons of burnt sienna scatter-gunning her irises as she scurried away. She turned the radio on, and the proximity of a new sound seemed to cancel out the noise outside, soft accents merging in discussion. Soothed, Siobhan let herself slip into an imaginary conversation, running the words through her mind.

She would be more interesting, more fluent, this time. Having studied the introduction, she could describe the matt paper used by Atget, how she thought it made the photos look older than they really were. She'd talk about movement – and by now The Girl would be sitting next to her on the window seat – pointing out instances when a person had glanced from a window, when a dog or even a parrot had shifted slightly during a long exposure.

They'd giggle at strict corsets on fixed mannequins in a lingerie store window, compared to a single, free-floating shift catching in the breeze outside. Then press close to keep the book held open between them, until The Girl's heavy hair brushed against Siobhan's cheek and she picked this as the moment to ask if she wanted to have a drink somewhere. Preferably Siobhan's own flat, as she wasn't big on pubs, but of course that would be far too tricky. There had to be an intermediate place, and it would help if it was licensed. Lower The Girl's inhibitions. Not to mention Siobhan's own.

Oh, Myrna said, sticking her head round the door of the kitchen. I forgot. Got you a present.

What?

Here you go.

She handed over a lucky dip lottery ticket.

Thanks, said Siobhan, thinking, you shouldn't have.

Well, I got a runners-up prize in the lunchtime radio phone-in yesterday, thought I should share my luck.

What did you win?

Don't know yet. They just said congratulations, it'll arrive recorded delivery tomorrow.

Nice to get a surprise.

Well, mind and check your numbers tonight.

I will, Siobhan said, crumpling the ticket into her pocket and turning away, glad of the distraction of a customer approaching the desk.

9.10 a.m. – Esther

Siobhan likes Esther, always finds her friendly, though she's easily thrown by unfamiliar things. Changes in routine. When the prices went up it took her weeks to adjust. Sometimes Siobhan still has to slip in twenty pence of her own, so as not to skew the cashing up. She's seen Agnes do the same, neither of them wanting to face the confusion in Esther's eyes as she looks at the coins in her hand, not quite understanding why she doesn't have enough now, when she did before. Bring it in next time, dear, Agnes said once, but the expression lingered on Esther's face longer than it took to do her wash. God knows how she manages in the supermarket, all those prices fluctuating, dancing away from her weekly food budget; she doesn't like to carry more money than she'll need, for fear of muggers. Every day she counts out her allowance,

That way I'm never profligate. I always have a day to think about anything I buy. No expensive mistakes.

But shouldn't you take some extra, in case of emergencies? Siobhan once asked.

You don't have to pay to ride in an ambulance or a

36

hearse. If anything else crops up, well, I'll cross that bridge when I come to it.

She's well known in the Cat Protection, or so Siobhan has heard from Agnes (via Margaret, who works there). Esther goes in nearly every day, always asking for things to be put aside. Then she can sleep on it and, if she still likes the garment, come in the next day with the three pounds for a blouse, two-fifty for a cotton top. It wasn't always like that. There was a time when she had cream melamine wardrobes full of clothes with hand-stitched labels. Colour-coordinated, of course, with shoes below, hats, scarves and bags above.

Easy come, easy go, Esther says as she hands over her washing money, in a small brown envelope with WAGES scored out and *Launderette* written instead, the sum neatly filled in. Underneath she always writes, *With Thanks*. Every time Siobhan wonders where these envelopes come from. They're much older than the ones Agnes dispenses every second Friday, she can tell by the musty aroma and the ancient stickiness of the gum. Esther must have a drawerful of them at home, left over from some day long gone when she was the bookkeeper or the boss. Maybe, Siobhan thinks, there's a correlation between the envelope supply and the length of Esther's life.

Today she's all in green. Headscarf matching anorak matching shoes matching eyeshadow. Siobhan imagines her at home, at her dressing table, opening a huge compact with a myriad palate. Greens, blues, browns, pinks, lilacs, peaches. One for every outfit. She always smells of parma violets, but whether it's the sweets themselves, talcum powder or the make-up Siobhan doesn't know. When Esther is leaving, she calls after her,

You look nice today. Nice and colourful.

A smile crinkles Esther's pearly eyeshadow as she replies,

I like to make the effort. No harm in showing a little self-respect.

Peach crimplene

Agnes walked briskly from the newsagent, *True Detective* rolled into a satisfying bulge in her handbag, ready to be unfurled and savoured later. This issue looked especially lubricious. Things were taken too far, sometimes, though. Agnes preferred the *News of the World* approach, that some matters could not accurately be described in a family newspaper; serial killers as celebrities appalled her, not to mention the dafties that married them in prison. No, Agnes was concerned only with criminals getting their comeuppance, justice being done. Always shocked when she read of a real-life crime, she told herself that – despite what had happened to Vina – these things happened to other people. And in fact Vina proved it. She was certainly other. Her face on the front page of the paper was like her coming into her inheritance. Her early teens had been a rehearsal, by age eighteen she was ready for the real thing.

As usual, Agnes walked the long way back to the launderette, past the vintage clothes store. Window-shopping: taking a trip down memory lane, acknowledging what she might have worn – during that brief time spent playing at being Rita – before she'd settled down. Nowadays Agnes favoured more comfortable clothes, and the Cat Protection shop was more her scene. Trousers with semi-elasticated waists, loose blouses, cotton lycra tops. Nothing with scratchy fabric, or which crackled with static when you pulled it over your head. She still took good care of herself – had her hair done regularly, plucked her eyebrows – but her days of suffering to be beautiful were over.

When she was a girl, she had imagined that when she left home she would wear neat little suits and stilettos, and paint her face like Vina's. She had coveted peacock blue eyeshadow, until finally Vina bought her some for her birthday. Agnes never showed her mother, who disapproved of that coloured muck, and the eyeshadow eventually shrivelled and spilled out into her drawer, its gorgeously grown-up scent turned dry and powdery. Then after she was married, Donald said she didn't need so much stuff on her face, she was beautiful without it. Agnes knew that wasn't strictly true, but if he preferred it, well, she was a sucker for his praise and it seemed a fair trade for the gold band on her wedding finger.

There in the window was a dress she could imagine Vina in, peach crimplene with short sleeves and a round collar, three white buttons and pocket details. In fact, hadn't Vina had something very similar but in pale blue, that she'd got in Reeta's down the Gallowgate? It had been quite pricey, that frock. But then, it seemed to Agnes that everything Vina had worn was quite pricey. Their families had been competitive that way, and there was never any question who was winning. For her part, Agnes had admired her cousin with an intensity that occasionally came close to hatred, and remembering that could still make her feel guilty.

He's a fine one, Vina thinks, all manners and compliments, without a double entendre passing his lips never mind a straight proposition. Her hand assesses the cloth of his brown suit jacket, finds it satisfactorily soft. A change from the greasy sheen of the other fabrics she has touched on this August night – their owners drunk, for it's Friday, pay day, and warm enough to provoke a thirst. She has been groped, her feet trodden on, obscenities whispered in her ear as she wriggled in the tight grasp of a succession of arms, insults thrown as the music changed and she extricated herself from their greedy hands. How much nicer to be in the clasp of her current partner. She hopes they will continue to dance, until the end, saving her from the lone walk back across the floor to the table where Teri and Rose from haberdashery lick melting ice cream from cornets bought for them by the laughing, proprietorial gents who now flank their seats. It is not a night to be a woman unspoken for, the clientele of the Ballroom seem to have one thing and one thing alone on their minds.

Agnes wondered if girls today bought these dresses, wore them to the dancing now as Vina and her friends had then. The window displays changed every week, and the shop kept going: it couldn't all be fancy dress parties and Sixties nights. Maybe it was the quality, clothes you'd pay a fortune to get new these days. Agnes found herself thinking that they didn't make things like they used to, just as her mother had told her forty years before, when she'd suggested a look at the younger fashions in the basement at Macdonald's. Reeta's would have been beyond the pale, she reckoned.

Suddenly the door of the shop sprang open with a twinkle of wind chimes, and a girl came out with a large brown paper bag. Glowing with the happiness of a new purchase, she turned to her friend and said,

It'll be perfect, totally perfect, just as soon as I find someone to alter it for me.

We could go into town, try and find the place the woman mentioned, if you want.

The girl paused for a moment, looking at her watch. The friend wasn't carrying any bags, and looked as though this shopping trip had already gone on far too long for her liking. Without thinking Agnes called over,

Excuse me hen, launderette three streets up on the left takes alterations. Cheapest you'll find and they do a good job.

Agnes walked back up the road with a wee spring in her step, though her better judgement was telling her she was a silly old cow sometimes, and didn't she have enough on her plate without starting this kind of nonsense? She'd have to go and buy thread, she realized, a measuring tape and chalk. The toilet would be fine for getting changed in, and the kitchen for the pinning into shape. And as for Jean MacPherson, what she didnae know wouldnae hurt her.

Myrna and Siobhan were surprised to see their boss

humming away to herself as she sat at the desk, busy with coloured card and magic markers.

What the fuck's she doing? Myrna whispered.

I can't see what she's writing. Putting the prices up maybe?

All in good time girls, all in good time. Now one of you with your young legs go and find me that Blu-Tack that's through the back.

Shrugging, disappointed that this should rouse her curiosity to such an extent, Myrna went to get it.

Agnes felt restless throughout the afternoon, smoked more than usual, felt her temper fraying a couple of times with the customers. She continued her list of things she'd need if she was going to do this, planned a trip to Remnant Kings. She couldn't remember the last time she'd opened her sewing box, but she knew for a fact she had needles of all sizes and plenty of pins. The scissors could do with sharpening, she was sure, though they were a good make. She could get Margaret to keep odds and ends aside for her in the charity shop, buttons and the like. Save herself a few pennies here and there.

By half four she'd decided there was no point, and was kicking herself for thinking the girl would actually turn up. Anticipation gave way to disappointment, and she went through the back to get herself a cup of tea without bothering to offer the girls one. It didn't need the three of them in anyhow, it was dead. She'd have to change the rota.

Runner-up

Determined to make the most of it, Myrna inclined her champagne flute for a top-up from the waitress, who looked like someone she'd gone to school with, except she'd introduced herself as Amanda, and Myrna was sure there hadn't been an Amanda at school. It was at times like these – not that she could think of another occasion quite like this – that she really missed Magda, always good for a laugh. None of the other girls she'd asked wanted to waste a Saturday in this place, so Myrna had settled for Will, who appeared at perfect social ease, conversing with authority on great goals of our time, and other such shite.

This is brilliant, he said, all smiles.

Glad you're enjoying yourself, you look quite at home.

He straightened his tie, self-consciously,

Is it a bit dull for you then?

Naw, I'll be fine. Don't look a gift horse in the mouth and all that.

Well, thanks for bringing me. I haven't seen a match in years, not live, well, you know, in person. You'll like that bit, it's dead exciting.

Cannae wait. Cheers.

And here's to being a runner-up.

They chinked glasses, and instantly the waitress was there again with the bottle. As she refilled his glass, the man next to them looked down her top, with little subtlety, but the girl just gave him a smile and continued circulating. Myrna noticed the criss-cross back of her Wonderbra showing through the thin white fabric of her blouse.

After a pie and coffee at half time, Myrna decided not to venture back out into the stand. Even with a blanket on her knees she was Baltic, besides, she didn't have a fucking clue what was happening on the pitch. Amanda invited her to stay inside while she cleared up, then revealed that she was in fact the girl from Myrna's modern studies class after all.

Yeah, well, this is no place for a Bernadette. My first day, the boss told the other girls to call me Mandy, but I argued for Amanda. Hated my name anyhow, always wanted something a bit less pious. I like to wear this though.

She held out her hand, showing off a chunky St Christopher ring and a glossy French manicure.

Now, remember, if anyone comes in I'll leap up and pretend I wasn't smoking in here. It's a sackable offence, unless you're in with the bricks. Thank fuck for the money though, eh?

Is it good? I'm kind of in the market for something. If they ever need anyone, that is.

Amanda smiled,

No, the hourly rate's pish, always is for this kind of work, but the tips are good. I've got regulars. They're away this week, which is why I'm in here with the plebs, no offence. They'll bring me back duty-free though, always do.

All right for some.

Yeah, well, you know the score. Working class made good, or if not good, rich. They always flash the cash. The posh ones just take their freebies and don't leave a fucking penny. These guys though, hundred and fifty every time. Extra if we win.

Myrna whistled,

Wow-eee.

I know, not bad, is it?

God, I'd do anything for that kind of cash. I just need to sort myself out, get a few debts cleared. I had a bar job, but it was crap pay.

Tell me about it. I've got a kid now as well, Cherie. Expensive business, when you're on your own.

Oh, what age is she?

Three next month. Show you a picture.

Amanda got her purse out, but at that moment an almighty cheer went up that set the floor shaking,

Bugger, that's it over already. Here though, if you need some money fast, I do the odd shift for this woman as well. Pays really well. Say Amanda recommended you when you phone.

Thanks.

Myrna took the card just as the others came bounding in, Will arm in arm with another delighted fan. Amanda went over to the table to direct them to their drinks, whispering on the way past,

Don't show your man though, eh?

Myrna, too taken aback to say that he wasn't her man,

glanced at the card. *Promenade*, it said, in gold letters, above an embossed pink flower motif and phone number. She slipped it into her pocket just as Will came up and grabbed her round the waist, giving her a big kiss on the cheek,

You missed yourself there Myrna, that was fantastic. Were you okay in here?

She nodded, a little overwhelmed by the noise, the stadium quaking under her feet and the feeling that the walls were trembling with the movement of thousands of people above and below her. Will's hand, still resting on her waist, kicked off another feeling, one she wasn't sure that she wanted to indulge. She wriggled free and headed off in search of the ladies.

A few drinks later, however, Myrna had overcome her doubts. Fuck it, she thought, you're only young once. Standing too close, brushing against each other, looking up from under her eyelashes, licking her top lip ever so slightly. Myrna revelled in this, her power, and felt vindicated when Will's hand started drifting down her side, round her back, over her hip. And then, after the bar had closed, taking the stairs rather than the lift and leaning back against the wall, wrapping her arms around Will's neck and pulling him towards her, automatically hunching her shoulders so he couldn't help but look down her cleavage. Kissing deeper and deeper, parting her legs so she could feel him against her pubic bone. He stroked his hand up the outside of her thigh, found that she was wearing stockings, caught her eye. She thought it best not to mention that she suspected she might have a touch of thrush, instead leaned in, let her tongue flicker across his neck. His hand moved round, squeezed her buttock, then it was back and edging between her legs, rubbing her through her knickers until she thought she'd go crazy for the need of more. He had to force her gusset to the side to get his hand in, and she felt her pants loosen as the stitching burst, then all her wetness oozing out until he gasped and stuck one, two fingers right up her, slid them in and out, until Myrna had to move her mouth off his to breathe. She took him by the hand and led him back towards the ladies,

In here. Come on.

Will sat on the toilet lid, trying to stretch a condom over his erection.

I never thought I'd actually end up using those whisky flavour things, he said, finally succeeding with a rubbery snap of elastic that made Myrna wince.

Either that or pina colada, she said, looking down at her bare thighs, mottled bluish by the cold of the bathroom, her pants round one ankle.

He stood up and started to kiss her again, pulling her breasts out of her bra, squeezing them. She could feel his penis against her leg, the latex slightly sticky, the hardness curiously unlike flesh. Her heel skited across the tiled floor and she had to clutch his arm to stop herself from falling. Will tried lifting her up, but the cubicle wall rattled loudly and she couldn't quite get her legs in the right position round his body, didn't want him to feel her whole weight.

No, hang on, try it this way, she said, struggling down

again. She turned round and bent over, feet on each side of the toilet, leaning her arms on the cistern, face almost touching the wall behind her.

Okay, take it from the top.

She shut her eyes, made an involuntary, high-pitched noise as he thrust straight in, deeper than she expected, hitting against her cervix. Arching her back so that her nipples pressed against the cold edge of porcelain with each lunge, Myrna opened her eyes to find she was nose up against a jaunty little plaque that advised, NOW WASH YOUR HANDS!

When they left there wasn't a taxi in sight, and the tube was stowed with supporters, happy and rowdy or lurking in corners sour-faced, as their colours dictated. Opposite Myrna, a man took a dog-eared photograph out of the inner pocket of his jerkin, looked at it intently, bleary eyes sharpening as he mouthed words she couldn't begin to lip-read. Nudging the hard-faced girl next to him, he showed her the photo, nodding with an urgency fuelled by alcohol and emotion.

Aye, she's lovely, so she is. Beautiful, the lassie said, the hardness metamorphosing into character as she smiled. A dead wife, a lover who'd left, a partner who was under the floorboards, wrapped in binbags and duct tape. Myrna wanted to know, to see the photo. The man nodded again, with approval this time, patted the knee of the boy on the other side of him.

It's a good photae mate, she's a fine-looking wuman.

Another stranger who knew what to say, another tacit

agreement made. Finally, the man leaned across the carriage to an older woman on Myrna's left. A woman who looked too old to be wearing that tartan skirt, who should have left those casual, less than the minimum wage jobs behind her years ago. She took the photo and scrutinized it, tilting it to the light to see more clearly, before smiling as though something suddenly made sense.

Yes, I see her.

The man replaced the photo in his pocket, satisfied. He got off at the next stop. Home to an empty house, or home for the woman in the photograph to give him a hiding, Myrna didn't know. Didn't know why she felt disappointed that he hadn't shown her the bloody photo, why she should be left out. She'd like to go home as well, maybe even take Will with her. A quiet night in together, get some wine and takeaway, watch the shite telly. Switch their phones off so better offers couldn't break in and expose the sham of domestic bliss. She knew that nothing would come of it, but it might have been nice to pretend, just for one evening.

Sure enough, when they got out into the street Will's mobile bleeped with text messages from friends in bars. Myrna couldn't be bothered checking hers. She'd tag along with him for now, not wanting to drag against the momentum by going home alone to get changed. Everyone would end up in the same club later anyway, she and Will merging into a larger group of friends and acquaintances. She knew she had a duty, to make that switch into life and soul mode, tell funny stories of her day out. To drink and laugh and drink some more, to dance and mingle and talk. After all, it was Saturday night.

For part of the evening, when she was coming up, she had thought she might be in for a repeat performance with Will, but she lost sight of him after his third E. He got caught up with druggie pals she wasn't so fond of, who took him to a party she didn't want to go to, in the flat of a guy she detested. The girlfriends were worse, chock full of the attitude – misplaced in Myrna's opinion – required to work bad hair and seventies anoraks as a look; staying damaged because somehow it lent that extra little edge of desirability. Myrna drew a rather arbitrary line through what she considered hard drug use, and went off to someone else's house with the drinkers and stoners.

By 6 a.m. she was bored shitless and horribly lucid, as though each sip of wine was sobering her up. She walked home alone, wishing the night went on and on, until you woke up in fresh sunshine, rather than being left high and dry in this crapulent half light. Before even kicking off her shoes, Myrna drew her curtains against it, clinging to the darkness. That was one good thing, there must've been a residue of ecky in the soles of her feet, for they didn't hurt a bit. Suddenly and completely, she felt bloody knackered, but still endeavoured to complete the ritual of her three-step skincare regime before she hit the sack, pulling the covers over her head to drown the racket of the birds outside her window.

11.05 a.m. – Darren

Agnes wonders if she should say something to him. Like: stop bothering my customers. Because he's incorrigible, he really is. Students, housewives, women with wedding rings, women without. She's heard it a dozen times, more. He suggests a drink in the pub across the road, while they're waiting on the machine. A perfect first date, when you think on it, because they'd be limited to half an hour in each other's company. He goes for one while his clothes are washing, and another while they're drying, which in Agnes' book is verging on a drink problem. A step on the slippery slope, as her mother used to say. She's noticed that he asks more people out after his first pint, the washing one. And he's never – not that she's seen anyway – had any luck. She's heard the responses:

I've got a boyfriend

I'm a teetotaller

I've found Jesus, have you?

Ich spreche kein Englisch

Fuck off

He's even asked Myrna out once, and if Agnes had been in that day she would have have spoken to him. Definitely. Bothering her customers is bad, bothering her

52

staff verboten. She won't have any rudeness from customers. But Myrna has her head screwed on, she'll say that
for the lassie. She'd settled for a simple, but emphatic, no
thanks. So she said. Not like her to mince her words. The
language Agnes has heard, but that's another story.

Thinking objectively, the problem might be the tattoos.
He's very proud of them, never passes a chance to show
them off. T-shirt in all weathers. Agnes has never figured
out whether Anne and Shirley, the names which decorate
each arm, entwined in blurred hearts and flowers, are ex-
girlfriends, sisters, daughters. Another one who doesn't
believe in casting ne'er a clout till May is oot; today a
string vest makes it apparent that he *really* loves his mum.
An admirable sentiment, which Agnes hopes he expresses
in other, more useful, ways as well. There's the straggly
hair too, mind you. Agnes never can understand why a
man that's receding lets his hair grow into those rat's tails
at the back. Cut it short, you'll look better, she's dying to
whisper.

But he's harmless, really. When he started bringing his
washing in, he took the trouble to introduce himself. I'm
Darren, he said, and held out his hand for her to shake.
That's rare, these days. She feels a bit sorry for him, truth
be told. As she said to Myrna that time, a pleasant enough
chap, but the day he gets a click, the world will shift on its
axis.

Another day another dollar

Things can happen quickly, Myrna thought. Almost without you noticing. One day you're walking along the street. A sunny day, like this, when everyone's looking a bit more cheerful than usual and you can feel the freckles springing out across your bare shoulders. Then it hits you. You can walk alongside all the bright sunny people you like, pretend all you like, but you're walking along a different street. Just as you're telling yourself it's not noticeable from the outside, you pass someone and catch their eye, and there's the merest flicker of recognition before you hurry on. The next time you pause for long enough to think, you realize you've been pulled under, and the city has merged again over your head. You're distanced from those people all around you, caught in eddies and currents that swirl you past them, beneath them. And even if you're lucky, and you manage to touch the surface again, you'll never quite rid yourself of that feeling.

So, Myrna my love, she told herself, you might as well get used to it. She jingled the keys from one hand to the other, feeling for the right shape as she approached the door, blood rushing to her head as she bent over and dropped the heavy padlock by her feet. A moment's pleasure as her eye caught the ankle strap and elegant wooden heel of her new sandals, and she saw them afresh as if they were in a shop window rather than on her feet. To die for, and they were in the sale. Straightening her back, Myrna cranked the shutter up just far enough for her to unlock the door, and slipped underneath into the shop. She turned and pulled the shutter down again behind her, not wanting anyone to come in until she'd had a cup of tea and a fag and held her head in her hands for ten minutes.

Myrna did not work in the launderette because she cared how white Mrs Taylor's boil wash would turn out, or whether or not that expensive viscose dress had shrunk in the dryer. No, it was the fact that there was no real hassle that had attracted her, along with financial desperation and the fortuitous circumstance of walking by just as Agnes had been sticking a notice in the window saying STAFF REQUIRED, ENQUIRE WITHIN. In her mind, Myrna had tossed a coin, heads you win. What the hell. Now she'd been there for almost five months. There was an anonymity to the launderette which suited her very well. In theory, you couldn't be more in view than in a glass-fronted shop on a relatively busy street, but in fact most people didn't notice, didn't care. Most people had washing machines in their own homes.

Brrrr brrrr, brrrr brrrr, Myrna knew exactly who'd be phoning at that hour in the morning, and why.

Hello, launderette, can I help you?

. . .

Yes, Mrs MacPherson, I was in early today actually.

. . .

It's Myrna.

. . .

Okay, I'll ask Agnes to give you a ring back.

Although Jean MacPherson had owned the launderette for many years, she was an infrequent visitor, preferring to phone once a week or thereabouts to check that nobody was opening late or closing early. She had a jaggy hello, Siobhan always said, to match her jaggy nature, and never gave any indication of knowing either girl's name. Myrna was very glad that Jean took a hands-off approach to her business concern – despite only meeting her once, she disliked her even more than she disliked Agnes. Must be getting on a bit now, as far as Myrna could make out she'd had the place since the early seventies.

Studiously ignoring an overflowing bag of dirty Baby-gros, Myrna tuned the radio in to 4 just so that Agnes could get annoyed and change it to 2, and waited until ten past the hour rather than eight on the dot before she got up and switched the lights on. Then she pulled the shutter right up, flipped the sign to OPEN, and stood there, with her arms folded, waiting for the first wash of the day.

11.15 a.m. – Fraser and Yolanda

Oh no, Myrna thinks. No, no, no. Although her break is over, she ducks back into the kitchen. What the hell's he doing here? One thing's for sure, she's not going back out while he's sitting there holding hands with some giggling trollop who, Myrna notes, has hair like a shampoo advert, all glistening in the sunlight which streams through the window. She hasn't washed her own hair for what, three days, and it shows. Edging into the doorway and hunching down so her head is below the level of the row of dryers, she beckons Siobhan, and explains the situation.

Look, would you mind if I stayed in here, until he's gone? I know I'm a pain, but it's just . . . oh, you know what I mean.

It's okay. I can manage.

Thanks. It was a while ago, but I don't really feel up to talking to him. I mean, he was a nice guy and everything, but we didn't have much in common.

Why did you go out with him?

See, that's one of the things I like about you, you're direct. Good question. All we did was go clubbing, take loads of speed and fuck all night. Pissed off half our friends, always leaving early and disappearing at parties.

Couldn't have been all bad.

Well, I did lose tons of weight. But in the end it was just kind of relentless. And dehydrating. Parched skin and thinking back my vadge must've been like sandpaper. We were both always so wired that neither of us ever came.

Euugh, sounds horrible. Why did you keep going?

New habits die hard. Guess we kept thinking we'd hit the high again. C'est la vie. It was quite upsetting, actually, when I finally finished it. But it was getting bad for the health, you know. And now he's got flesh on his bones and a chick who looks ten years younger than him, and somehow I'd rather he didn't see me shovelling stinky sheets and wearing a motherfucking tabard.

Don't worry. You stay here and I'll give you the nod when the coast's clear.

Thanks pal. I owe you one.

No problem. Better get out and put their stuff in the spinner.

God, I mean, what kind of couple does their laundry together? Pukey or what?

Myrna takes advantage of her extended break to light up another cigarette, remembering the tingle of Carmex on chewed lips, feeling an unwelcome leap of excitement as she recalls those first couple of weeks, skinny limbs knocking against each other, that edge of desperation which made it better.

11.47 a.m. – Lillian

The woman is losing patience.

See, when she gets like this, there's not much you can do with her, she confides, before rushing to retrieve Lillian before she heads out the door.

Okay, you give the money to the lady. Give the money to the lady.

Lillian looks at the coins in her palm with little interest, shrugs, and hands them to Siobhan, who says thank you, then wonders why she's enunciated her words so clearly. Lillian is not, after all, deaf.

Good girl. Now take the token.

Lillian accepts the chunky hexagonal token, puts it in her mouth. She has to be coaxed to spit it out. Finally the woman manipulates her jaw, in the way that dog-owners remove unmentionables from the mouths of their pets.

Don't do that Lillian. Dirty.

Not edible, Siobhan adds, and Lillian looks at her with interest, before trying out the new word for herself, hesitantly.

Ed-ib-le.

Not edible means not for eating.

But Lillian's lost interest, and is off wandering again.

The carer herds her towards the washing machine it has taken them half an hour to load, and starts explaining how it works. Her tone suggests that she holds out little hope of Lillian mastering it.

But you can always ask the lady for help.

Juice?

When you've finished this.

I want my juice.

There's a slight kerfuffle, from which Siobhan guesses that Lillian has nipped her carer. But eventually, the machine is switched on, juice and crisps materialize, and Lillian is settled on the bench.

They'll do an assessment, the carer explains later, but the fact is she's not capable of living in unsupported housing. Some things she can manage on her own, not many. There needs to be someone on hand twenty-four seven. And that costs money.

Siobhan doesn't want to ask what's wrong with Lillian, because she knows it isn't a question of wrong, so she says,

Where does she live now?

Hospital. She's been in hospital eight years. It isn't so bad, where she is. Before that she was in the Castle, you know, the old asylum. She'd been there twenty years. Hated it. Family couldn't cope, not when she hit puberty anyway, and they realized she wasn't going to get better. Oh, is that it finished already? Right, spinner next then, is it?

Yes, that's right.

Siobhan is still caught up in the idea of Lillian, held

prisoner in the Castle. (Prisoners are always held, implying a gentleness which, she assumes, is absent in practice.) The rightful princess, in her sensible anorak and Littlewoods slacks. Awaiting rescue, from locked doors and stern auxiliaries, uncomprehending misdemeanours and sharp reprisals, utter isolation and terrible vulnerability.

The spinner is not a great success. The noise sends Lillian running round with her hands over her ears.

Wheeeeeeee, she says. Wheeeeeeee.

The carer looks tired,

Sorry about this. But I might as well let her work off a bit of steam. It'll make life easier later on.

By the time the clothes have been through the dryer, her tiredness looks more like exhaustion,

Right then Lillian, on the bus again and we'll be back in time for lunch.

Lunch?

Yes, that's right.

I want my lunch.

See, she says to Siobhan, a one-track mind, this one. Haven't you my love? She puts her arm around Lillian, squeezes her shoulders. Anyway, thanks for your help. Bye bye. Say bye bye to the lady, Lillian.

Lillian waves as she leaves, shouts gaily,

Fuck off!

Imagining dancing

Kneeling on the lino floor of the launderette's kitchen, Agnes sat back on her heels and surveyed her handiwork. Not bad at all, she thought. Out of practice maybe, but she hadn't lost her eye for an even hemline. She wrenched herself to her feet, using the edge of the table for support, and stood back from the mirror.

Have a look and see what you think of that hen.

A silk shift dress, sleeveless, with a high slash neck. Properly lined too, she'd have to be careful with that. Beautiful fabric, nice bright colours. Aqua, mainly, with greens and pinks and yellows in with it. A pattern like waves crashing, delicate coloured spray sprinkling out. At the time that was in fashion, Agnes would have been two years married and already sick fed up of trying to explain why there was no pitter-patter of tiny feet. (Except for those of Fritzie, the miniature dachshund Donald had given her for their anniversary. Lovely sleek coat he had, and the nicest nature you could wish for, loyal to his mistress above all else, come chocdrops or butcher's bones. If there was an 'other side', it was Fritzie-boy that Agnes hoped would run to greet her first.)

Anyway, this frock was high quality to have lasted so

long in such good nick, although it could hardly have been worn. Too fragile to cope with many of the nights out they had these days. Agnes nodded,

Aye, it's lovely on, that one. Lovely.

The girl twirled round in front of the glass, fair away with herself as she twisted to catch a glimpse of her back. And good luck to her too, Agnes thought, indulgently. The smooth skin, the shiny highlighted hair. That slight, healthy, no make-up tan that modern girls seemed to have. A million miles from the pale faces or pancake of her youth, when only two skin tones seemed possible, alabaster powder or sandy beige sheen. The sleekness of flesh was new too, an indication of sportiness but without any obvious muscle tone. If she was young now, Agnes thought, she'd want to look like that. Ridiculous really, when she'd spent years hoping for the upholstered curves of the fifties or the skinnymalinks of the sixties. She had always fallen in between, never matched the mood of the moment. Whereas Vina had been perfect, the pallor that looked so soft, like she shouldn't be out in daytime, yet so striking with a bit of lipstick and blush. The bust that wasn't all bra, the legs which were actually shapely, like in the advertisements for Pretty Polly. It was no wonder she'd had boyfriends.

This one would be the same, with the lads, and sure enough,

I wonder if you could take it up shorter, please? It's for a Sixties night, and you know how they wore things back then . . .

She trailed off, as though she couldn't imagine Agnes wearing such things, ever. Agnes nodded and started again. It wouldn't do to lose her first customer by asking what exactly she thought she knew about back then, and who precisely wore things that short? Maybe in the pictures, or in so-called Swinging London, but up here it was a different story. Four inches of thigh was daring enough, thank you very much, if you didn't want to look tarty. Agnes pinned the hem up further though, and the girl seemed delighted. Fashions changed, and she was slim enough to get away with it, but when she sat down it would scarcely cover her bum.

I'll replace that wee bit of muslin under the arms, Agnes offered. Freshen it up for you. Deodorant wasn't such a necessity back then.

Thanks. People must've danced as much as they do now, though.

Oh yes. They danced all right.

At home, Agnes set her sewing machine up at the top of the table, directly in line with the television, and wondered what the dancing was like these days. She passed nightclubs, or clubs, as they called them now, in town, but they were seldom more than doorways off the street. Nothing to tempt you inside. Not like the illuminated deco facade she remembered at Dennistoun, a remnant from the thirties that was right back in vogue when she went there. Lit up letters spelling out not dancehall but *Palais de Danse*. The French that bit classier, yet with an edge of the risqué as well. Proper doormen on the entrance. To get out a taxi and walk up those steps, well, you felt you'd arrived. The Barrowland never had quite the same effect, though it certainly had the good bands, and a glamour and excitement all of its own. Her mother had always told her it was rough, and when Agnes finally did go she felt slightly out of her depth. They'd stopped the spot dances by then, that Vina had told her about. Looking back, it felt as if it had been every other night that she'd sat in front of the mirror, secretly, when she was supposed to be in bed, arms aching as she tried to secure her hair in a French roll with dozens of bobby pins.

Vina's mother, solicitous, prepares a hot water bottle, while Vina goes upstairs to untangle the sanitary belt.

No dancing for you tonight, I reckon.

Maybe I should give it a miss, Vina agrees. There's always tomorrow, isn't there?

The pair of them pass a pleasantly companionable evening, broken only when the befuddled rattling of Jack's key in the lock heralds his return from the pub. Maureen shakes her head.

You get off to bed love. Sounds like he's had a skinful.

Night night, says Vina, and retires to the still wonderful newness of her bedroom. Although small, it is cosy and feminine and most of all private in a way that the bed recess never was. A place where she may give vent to her imagination, and think of what else could be.

How Agnes used to love imagining dancing, heels click-clickety-clicking off the sprung floorboards as she whirled and twirled and shimmied, a hazy partner as her foil. Infinite variations on steps learned for the school social tripped off her toes, as she moved with the music she'd heard Vina play on her Dansette. The spotlight flicked over her, once, twice, then came to rest, illuminating her until everyone else stopped dancing and stared. They whistled and clapped, parted to let her through as the MC called her up on stage to open the Mystery Box. The moment of communal anticipation – would it reveal something nasty or nice? Agnes smiled a wide smile (Summer Rose, by Rimmel), untied the ribbon and opened it, oh the suspense, she worked that crowd like a pro, then held aloft her prize to gasps and another round of applause – they hadn't wanted her to get the rotten egg. The MC fastened the clasp around her neck, and a necklace sparkled against the smooth, pale skin of her Chanel-scented décolletage (she no longer had pimples, that went without saying).

Come on now ladies and gentlemen – and the rest of you lot as well – a big hand for Rita!

Then Rita stepped down from the stage to lead the next dance, arm in arm with a member of the band, the saxophonist perhaps, who had the look of James Dean, in his shimmery shadow check suit from Maxie Man.

Agnes sighed. It had never happened, of course. Vina had a diamanté bracelet that she claimed came from the Mystery Box. It used to glitter round her wrist, attracting dirty looks from Agnes' mother, who maintained that there was only one way a girl like Vina got a present like that. Agnes would have liked that bracelet, as a keepsake, but it was long gone, now. The Barrowland itself had survived, thrived even, with its exhilarating starburst of coloured neon. The sign of a good night, it was said, though not infallible, as Agnes knew. The Palais on the other hand was no more. The building had been used as a supermarket, for a while, and Agnes had persuaded Donald to drive her there to get her messages once, for old times' sake. The shiny facade turned grimy by years of traffic, the posters for bands replaced with special offers on bacon and broccoli, the inside gutted. She'd never gone back, and eventually a tiny paragraph in the free paper announced it had been demolished.

A beginning

Negotiating the traffic was the awkward part of Siobhan's way to work. Not that the roads were particularly busy, and she lived barely fifteen minutes away, at a brisk walk. But this morning she was still clumsily tired, after a late film on the television and just enough wine for her to wake early and parched. A lorry decided to use the narrow streets as a cut-through, and the engine noise reverberated between the tenements, leaving her pressed against a hedge, disorientated and nauseous, until the visual disturbance subsided. Like seeing stars, as she'd told Myrna once, unwilling to explain that the stars were in fact rectangles, angry and khaki. They filled her vision, so that she staggered for a few yards, risking broken glass and dog shit underfoot.

Sound was her main trigger, always had been. She would've liked to be able to lose herself in music, notes and melodies surrounding her, living the chromaesthesia of Favre's colour symphonies. But so often music was too much, a bombarding of the senses, instruments vying with each other across her vision. Traditional jazz was sometimes stimulating, modern jazz rarely. Old style country a possibility, nu-metal most certainly not. Debussy in,

Beethoven out. She had tried Scriabin, Messiaen, Rimsky-Korsakov – what synaesthete hadn't? – but at low volume. Had she been at the Paris exhibition the surge of the fountains would have been enough, without Favre's lights or music. A simpler, more accessibly musical, noise.

Despite her haphazard start, Siobhan arrived at the launderette on time. She could still recall the first time she'd walked through the door; the noise of the washing machines, unexpected then, was attractive, a gentle, turquoise amorphy. Siobhan had immediately hoped she would get the job, eager to immerse herself in the mild blue tones and the subtly different smells of the powders, fabric conditioners, fresheners. A warmly hued background to her working day – although Agnes herself had been more challenging, her voice scraping against all the other sounds.

No time for airy-fairyness in this job, she'd said, detecting a propensity for such in Siobhan.

No. I'll work hard. It makes the day go faster. And I need the money.

That for Agnes was the deciding factor in employing anybody. Why else would they keep turning up, day after day?

Okay then. Any questions?

Is there any paperwork? I'm not so great with admin.

No hen, I take care of it all. Accounts, ordering, invoices, wage slips. The full bhoona.

This was a distinct advantage for Siobhan, for whom letters could be rendered dyslexic, sentences surreal, by the colours of the letters and the patterns they formed. No such trouble at the launderette though, and now she'd been there six steady months, slotting in to a comfortably fixed routine.

Which was about to change.

This morning, the first thing Siobhan noticed was the laundry bag. Cheap, thin plastic, with a zip across the top, like most of the others she saw, day in, day out, except that instead of the usual red or blue checks, there were Japanese images set against an azure ground. Big-haired geishas with fans, repeating Mount Fujis, cherry trees in bloom, a tacky-cool Hiroshige print which Siobhan had seen somewhere before . . . oh yes, of course.

The Girl.

She remembered quite clearly now. It seemed silly calling her The Girl, but when Siobhan checked the outside of the bag there was no label, no surname. She tried to get on with her work, but fascination crept up on her, memories of the corduroy skirt The Girl had been wearing, her crocheted tights. Finally, curiosity became necessity and Siobhan made sure this particular wash was hers.

She loaded the machine, taking as much time as she could, though not as much as she would have liked, to examine each item. Sheets which should have seemed boring took on new significance, as Siobhan learned that The Girl slept on heavy white linen, flat not fitted. On closer inspection, she discovered that what at first looked like an ink stain was a deliberate marking. RM9. Siobhan worked her way along the hem, until she found another

mark, this time in smaller, neater letters. OH, carefully
formed in indelible pen. She put it in the machine, looked
at the pillowcases. Inside the flap of each, in the same
script, OH. Finally Siobhan extracted a light seersucker
duvet cover, with ribbon ties along the bottom. On the
inner seam her eye caught the words: Ossington Hotel.
There were plenty of hotels and guest houses nearby, but
she couldn't think of anywhere called the Ossington. Nor
could she imagine that live-in staff – let alone guests –
would be expected to wash their own bedclothes.

Agnes, come and have a look at this.

Well, Agnes said, clipping her reading specs behind her
ears, there's a blast from the past. I haven't heard that
name in years.

I haven't heard it at all. Does it still exist?

No, and you're way too young to mind it, I expect. Are
your family here? They'd remember.

Siobhan shook her head,

They're overseas. My dad works overseas.

Not strictly true, but she liked the word, and it saved
some explaining. She had taken to thinking of her parents
like those in the books she had read as a child. The clever
mother, prone to scattiness, the ever-so-busy father. It
made sense that they should be in Madeira, or Brunei, or
somewhere equally un-visitable. Letters were written, and
Christmas exerted its annual draw, but aside from that
they remained perfectly inaccessible. Before Agnes could
quiz her further, Siobhan asked,

Was it near here, the hotel?

Used to be up on the terrace, you know that one above the shops? I remember it well enough. There was a big fire, with all the rumours about insurance jobs, of course, and then what was left of the building was demolished, oh, twenty years ago, at least. New flats there now.

What was it like?

Well to do, on the outside, but it had its fair share of scandals, the Ossington. Public figures caught with their trousers down, the old Mr and Mrs Jones routine. Always coming up in divorce cases, I was told, in the days when divorce made the papers. And that wasn't the worst of it.

No?

One of the chambermaids was found murdered. Aimee something, it was, I remember thinking it was a pretty name. She'd been strangled. In one of the rooms. Hard to recover from that kind of press.

Yes, I suppose murder's never good for business. Unless it's somebody famous. Poor girl.

It was said she was a prostitute, mind you, at the time. Hinted at anyway.

I wonder how the customer got hold of the linen.

Who's to know? These places sell things off, they end up in charity shops. Good-quality linen lasts a lifetime, near enough. Maybe she worked there.

Siobhan didn't mention that the customer was too young to have worked at the hotel. She returned to the bag, hoping for more clues, but was disappointed as towel after towel emerged. Egyptian cotton, no markings, save a smudge of lipstick here, a trail of mascara there. Siobhan hadn't thought of The Girl wearing make-up, had assumed it was nature that made her lips rosy and her eyes defined. Then, feeling an unexpected texture, she withdrew a pair of trousers. Linen blend, 40 degrees, according to the care label. Utterly unsuitable for a hot wash of whites. Leave them out, not our problem, Agnes would say. Myrna would stick them in and hope for the best. How lucky then, that Siobhan had a bag of her own washing through the back, ready to run through a machine during a quiet spell. Perhaps coincidences did mean something.

She held the trousers up, appreciating the smooth, fine weave of the fabric, imagining how they would skim The Girl's hips, hang loosely down to her sandal-clad feet. Quickly, while no one was looking, Siobhan measured them against her own waist. Yes, they'd fit, though they'd be just a bit too long. Gently she tucked them in with her non-fast coloureds, set the controls to 40 and a slow spin. Water poured into the drum, and Siobhan watched the trousers darken to a deep green as they saturated and began to rotate, tangling amongst her own clothes. A black jumper, a red vest, then a flash of dark green again as they pressed against the window; black, red, green; and again; until the speed increased and everything blurred together.

Once the trousers had been washed, Siobhan realized that tumbling was bound to shrink them. It seemed churlish not to roll them up damp and take them home with her own non-tumbledries, to hang on the pulley overnight. And then to iron them, early the next morning, when they had dried creased. After all, she was doing a couple of things of her own. It was no trouble. More than that, it was a pleasure, a strange, secret pleasure which Siobhan couldn't have anticipated: to push the nose of the iron into the pockets, to press along the seams, to flatten the waistband, to fold them up carefully, ready for wear.

She wouldn't mention it to Myrna or Agnes, of course; would just slip the trousers back on top of the neatly folded towels and sheets when nobody was looking, to be handed back as if nothing had happened.

But when it came down to it she was nervous, even after she'd effected the return of the trousers to the bag. The moment of their collection grew into a momentous event, swollen by the uneasy possibility of discovery, as Siobhan waited, visualizing scenes, reprimands, who knows, even her dismissal. Was it still stealing when you put things back?

In the end she almost missed it, coming out of the kitchen after a lunch she was too tremulous to eat just as The Girl was leaving.

It's a miracle they weren't ruined, Agnes said. Imagine getting them mixed up with your whites like that.

I know. But now I know it's okay, I can put them in with anything.

Siobhan realized she was going to have her work cut out for her. Along with this came a burgeoning sense of responsibility, which more than made up for failing that first interview. It was as if she'd been offered the job after all. When The Girl turned to say goodbye to Agnes, she noticed Siobhan and smiled.

12.30 p.m. – Kenneth

Myrna knows his type, a favourite phrase of Agnes', but true nonetheless. All her suspicions are confirmed as she watches from behind the desk, where she's been whiling away a quiet morning with the *Guardian* crossword. He immediately zeros in on a girl – fresh away from home; unmuddied trainers and shop-stiff pink suede jacket – with an opening line which is straight from the manual. Situation 4a – On spotting an attractive person reading in a public place, approach with confidence, then say with utter conviction:

Angie/Steven (delete as applicable)? Oh god, I'm sorry, I thought you were someone else. Hey, I can't believe you're reading (insert title of choice), that's my favourite book. What do you make of (insert name of most obviously complex character)?

And it works. The wary expression on the face of his target turns to a smile, as he presents her with the long-stemmed blue flower he's been carrying, idly, as though merely appreciating the scent. As though that's the kind of thing the sensitive man about town actually does, in this town.

The girl is a student, probably. He's a drifter, south for

the summer, east for the festival, back as autumn falls, bringing with it the influx of new blood. A little work here, a benefit scam there. A lot of flirting here, even more there. A couple of friends like himself, the better to get the attention of the ladies; besides, there's a pleasure in that slight competitive edge. And they look good together, dressed to impress, with practised struts. He favours a beatnik vibe, while the others have muso, little boy lost and modernist down to a T. They hang around the art school, though none of them can draw. Sit on the steps of the drama school, though they've never auditioned. Go to the student unions, though they don't have matriculation cards. Myrna expects they share a flat, some manky dive, the smell of which she can imagine precisely. Not that it matters as there'll always be a girl with a warm, tidy flat and a cupboard full of food, just dying for a bit of company.

Myrna realizes, with a start, that she's jealous. She hates them. She wants their lifestyle. No more hands chapped by the constant cycle of wet washing. Sitting in a pub all Tuesday afternoon just because you fancy it. Summers that aren't grey and wet. All that easy sex with people younger than yourself. She considers going over to the girl he's been talking to, whispering in her ear . . . but no, she's sitting there with a rosy glow in her cheeks, twiddling that bloody delphinium (or whatever the fuck it is, Myrna's not big on horticulture). Moist-lipped and ready to fall for the first man she'll cry herself to sleep over, because already he can't stop himself thinking forward to

Section 10 – In event of boredom/a better offer, mix and match from the following options: stand up your date, if necessary, say you forgot, or that something came up, DO NOT elaborate, NEVER apologize; be seen walking arm in arm with another person (if challenged, smile wistfully and say they're just a friend); say, hey, don't get heavy on me, we agreed this was just a bit of fun; ensure that you sleep with someone else, for maximum impact a friend of your previous lover is recommended, and if a points system is in operation, extra marks should be awarded for public display and a bonus may be earned if the previous lover is a witness.

Yes, Myrna would like to intervene, she's kind-hearted that way, but she knows that the only way you learn this particular lesson is through the practical. Besides, what would she say? He nicked that flower from someone's garden, you know?

Curiosity killed the cat

Agnes felt ill at ease. It was too late for her to be going home and having her tea, too early for bed. Everything looked grey, twilit, in between. The streets the bus passed through were quiet, shops shut and a few stragglers heading home from the office. Bars open, naturally, and some people trickling out of them, top buttons undone, inebriation highlighted by their smart work clothes. She felt a little tipsy herself, after those couple of drinks with the girls. It had been a while. She hadn't been going out much, round to people's houses maybe, out for lunch or coffee, but not to pubs. Mind you, it wasn't as if she and Donald had been party animals, not in recent years any-way. Sometimes, since he'd passed away, she slipped one of those mini bottles of wine into her basket at the super-market, or perhaps a can of ready-mixed G&T, but even then she heard her mother's voice, extolling the evils of drinking alone. Vina's father, Uncle Jack, had been a drinker. Held down a good job, well paid, but a drinker nonetheless. Her mother would nod knowingly if Auntie Maureen mentioned that Jack was Tired. Or a Little Under the Weather. These conditions arose after he'd been

Working Late or had Just Popped Out for a Breath of Fresh Air.

Tonight, after three in a row and one left unfinished, she had known she was likely to start talking. Too much and too personally. She wouldn't have been able to hold it in, had already felt herself succumbing, and so she'd had to leave. She'd always been a blab when she had a drink in her, and there was nothing worse than a drunk woman, according to Donald. Except perhaps a drunk man, she used to reply, but under her breath. And if she got the chance now, she'd have a few more words to say to him on the subject of women relaxing and letting their hair down.

She worried suddenly about Myrna and Siobhan, whether they actually liked her or had merely felt obliged to have her tag along. Perhaps sometimes, at work, she was a little hard on them. You needed some discipline, some respect for your boss, it didn't work otherwise. Either way they'd have wanted her gone, so that they could get on with their night. Out until all hours, she supposed, going to these places she saw advertised on the posters which covered every bit of hoarding, every empty shopfront. Women with Afros wearing hotpants, school uniforms, bikinis. DJs and hard house and deep funk and God only knew what it all meant. There would be a couple of sore heads in the morning, she predicted. And why not, they were young. Footloose and fancy-free. As Agnes gathered herself together and dinged the bell to stop the bus, she realized that she couldn't quite remember the last time she'd had fun.

She changed out of her glad rags as soon as she got in, if a new top and cardi set from the Cat Protection constituted glad rags. Margaret always phoned to alert her when anything good in a size sixteen came in. Lilac, which set off her gold jewellery nicely, she thought, looking in the mirror before she peeled off the top. Standing there in her bra and slip (flesh-coloured, goes under everything), Agnes wondered where the time went. She tried to see past the creased and sagging skin to the girl she had once been.

The MacIntyres have moved into their new house, at last, and Vina is over the moon. Semi-detached, a room of her own, it's onwards and upwards from now on. She's ditched Mack, to celebrate. No more of that kind of thing now. All mod cons, Maureen says proudly, displaying her built-in kitchen to her sister and niece. Their own bathroom! Jack's promotion has come through as promised, along with payment for all those homers he's been doing. He hosts a drinks party – how modern! – to entertain those who've lent a helping hand. It's the guys from the Lodge, mainly, so Maureen spends all day preparing then leaves them to it, after dragging Vina in for a guest appearance before she heads out to the Plaza.

Maureen mistrusts the secret gatherings of men – The Pub, The Football, The Masons – but the benefits are undeniable. They're on her back in that new winter coat, under her feet in the shiny new linoleum, on her plate in the vol-au-vents she has assembled for this evening. She would like Willy to be different, to go it alone, but he needs the best start, does he not? There's talk of getting him into Allan Glen's, and although they couldn't manage the fees themselves, strings may be pulled. Jack's been on the shipyards for twenty-three years, after all, and a Mason for seventeen of those. Yes, Maureen knows where she has come from very well, and would prefer that her son and daughter never go back there.

Agnes remembered her first twinset, as clearly as if it had been yesterday. Her mother had bought it in Treron's sale, an uncharacteristic black number in a soft lambswool mohair blend. Agnes had stroked the material, rubbed it against her cheek, and imagined that at a distance it might be taken for cashmere. It had hung in the wardrobe, unworn, for two weeks, waiting for an occasion. Then, out of the blue (or so it seemed), she was told to get changed out of her bright summer gingham and into something more respectful. The twinset and her grey pleated school skirt would have to do.

Agnes put it on happily, swirled in front of the mirror, unthinking. It was not until she came back through that her mother told her Vina was dead.

That afternoon, Agnes couldn't show that she was furious at being sent through to Maureen's kitchen with the children. She was fifteen, for heaven's sake, even if she didn't look it. Old enough for grown-up business. She sulked as she brewed the endless pots of tea which were deemed necessary under the circumstances, itched for information as she arranged doilies on the good plates, seethed as she stacked biscuits and sandwiches on top. (Untouched by Auntie Maureen herself, these weren't wasted on her companions, whose sensitivity did not affect their stomachs in quite the same way.) Agnes, back-and forward from the kitchen, collecting ashtrays for emptying, heard only snatches. Enough to figure out that this was no accident or illness, no falling under a tram or contracting meningitis. Noticing her daughter lingering, Frances hissed,

What did curiosity do?

Sorry, Agnes said, retreating, whereupon Maureen, who had been quivering in quiet agitation, suddenly jumped from her seat and grabbed her, hugged her close, started telling her to look after herself, not to go out at night, not to end up like her little girl. Frances gently loosened Maureen's grip, releasing a startled Agnes, who backed away until she was surprised to find herself sitting down in a vacant chair. Then her mother and another woman took Maureen by an arm each and, together, propelled her towards the bedroom.

All she needs is a wee lie-down, that's all.

Stopping, Maureen turned to Agnes' mother, and said in a hoarse, too-loud voice,

All I need is my little girl back Frances, that's all I need.

As they left the room Agnes heard her add, quietly now,

Why did he have to kill her? He'd got what he wanted. Why couldn't he have just left her?

Agnes thought of Vina's jewellery, imagined, ludicrously, her cousin draped in diamonds, notes spilling from her purse. When Maureen was safely out the way in the bedroom, sandwich-eating reached a crescendo as events were analysed. Agnes brought in fresh tea, and talk inexorably circled round Vina's having been interfered with, and it being her time of the month. These weren't concepts which were altogether familiar to Agnes, but she knew enough – mainly from Vina herself – to piece things together in her own, still childish way. She heard something else too, something familiar from the school playground, where the bogeyman was now simply the bad man, and the bad man was real.

In a lull in conversation – and here Agnes wondered if her memory was playing tricks on her because it couldn't have been the same day, surely, not so soon after the news came . . . people were jealous, of the new house and the linoleum on the floor, the three-piece suite and the fitted gas fire, but they weren't callous, were they? – a woman she did not know had said,

Of course, the lassie had been running around a bit.

The lull became a dense silence, gorged with anticipation. Agnes saw her mother look towards the door of the room, as if weighing up whether the tablets left by the doctor really had rendered Maureen out for the count, as promised. Finally, with a slight waiver in her voice, she asked,

Did she have a boyfriend then?

The neighbour from across the way leaned forward,

Well that's what the polis'll want tae ken, isn't it?

She waited a beat, as if, like Agnes' mum, she couldn't decide whether to go on or not. Fastidiously wiping a smear of lipstick from the edge of her teacup, she said,

And I could let them in on a thing or two, I tell you.

Frances turned sharply to her daughter and said,

Agnes, get back through there and see they weans are behaving themselves.

Naturally, Agnes tried to listen from behind the door, but with little success. The neighbour was saying something about coming home at all hours, then her voice dropped lower as she hinted at goings-on out the back. Agnes could guess what she meant; Vina's insinuations were beginning to make sense. She always had trouble, she said. She stayed so far from the places she went dancing that walking her home was what they called a passport job. Whoever got her up the road would need to be pretty keen on her, and they might expect more than just a kiss and a cuddle when they reached her house. If you know what I mean, Vina had said. Agnes had nodded, as she usually did when Vina asked this question – then later on she'd think about it again, try to figure out exactly what her cousin was talking about.

That night, lying in her bed, Agnes had tried to solder together this connection between how far Vina went, and her being killed. She wasn't sure why the time of the month was particularly significant, but accepted without question that it would be. She was still waiting for hers to come. When she plucked up the courage to ask her mother about it, she was told not to worry, she'd learn soon enough to be glad that she was a late starter. They didn't call it the curse for nothing. But Agnes wasn't comforted. Her class at school had organized itself into two cliques, based on those who had started and those who hadn't. The Hads would compare underwear as they got ready for gym, make no secret of their contempt for the flat-chested girls in their white cotton semmits. On rare occasions, they'd even get out of games altogether if they pleaded cramp (but only if it was Miss Thomson, Mrs Johnstone had no time for skivers). They wore training bras and smoked; Agnes wondered if the smoking had anything to do with the capacity to fill a bra, and decided that as soon as she got a job she too would smoke. Hopefully it wouldn't be too late to increase her bust size.

Sitting on the wooden cloakroom bench, worn smooth by generations of eager and not-so-eager bahookies, Agnes listened as the Hads talked, tentatively, about who had done it yet. Once she realized what *it* was, she was all ears. She was convinced that Ina May must have, with her woman's figure crammed with apparent difficulty into her school uniform, and her boyfriend Bobby who was in his twenties. Years later, she could still remember her friend Marion blowing her nose in excitement as she whispered the gossip about Ina May. That Bobby had been fingering her, and after, he put his fingers in his mouth.

It was funny how small things stayed with you, even when people were more open and they'd ceased to be shocking. Her own mother, then past seventy and a crossword devotee, had once, after finding an unfamiliar word in the dictionary, told Agnes that she would never guess what they'd invented now. Not just the C-word, oh no, but the very long C-word.

Donald had certainly never performed this on Agnes, and she had always felt that asking him to attempt it would be like suggesting he tried deep-sea diving, with him unable to swim a length at the baths. He had, eventually, learned to touch her, and would do so sometimes before they had sex, with the same precision and concentration which he applied to wiring a plug, or any of the other manly tasks she was now learning for herself. Donald always used to wipe his fingers on the sheet afterwards though, and it was a long while before she stopped feeling slighted. If only he had exhibited such restraint elsewhere.

That day she'd worn the black twinset had been Agnes' first experience of death. It took her some time to truly realize that Vina would not be coming back and even longer for her to understand that Vina hadn't just upped and left of her own accord, or disappeared. She had been taken away.

The Randan

A corner bar, originally for working men, the Randan now catered largely for those who did not work, or who had retired from doing so quite some time ago. A slightly uneasy mix of old and young, as during term-time students were attracted by the low prices. However, it was clean, close to the launderette, and you'd almost always get a seat. The Randan's one distinction was an impressive collection of beermats from around the world stuck to the wall above the picture rail, too high up for anyone to nick. Siobhan wondered who had been to these far-flung places, to carry such trophies back.

Agnes had just left, apparently in something of a hurry. Myrna raised her eyebrows,

Was it something I said?

Just not her scene, I guess.

I wouldn't be too sure. Probably gone home to hit the gin.

You're terrible, Siobhan smiled.

That's my job. Mind you, it isn't that long, is it, since Donald-where's-yer-troosers passed away?

Passed away was the term Agnes preferred when she had to tell customers who asked after his illness. That or lost, as in she'd lost her husband. As though she might be hoovering behind the couch one day, and find him, curled up in a ball next to two pounds fifty in change and her granny's engagement ring.

No, not really, only a few months.

Poor soul, must be hard for her going home to an empty house. Still, it was good we persuaded her to come out for a wee while.

I thought you couldn't stand her.

Oh, it's obligatory to hate the boss. You know how it always makes life easier if you demonize someone. But she's okay really, when you see her out of work mode. And I do feel sorry for her. I mean, can you even imagine being with someone for thirty years?

Was that how long they were married? Siobhan could scarcely imagine being with someone for one year, never mind thirty.

Myrna nodded, looking straight ahead as though trying to catch a glimpse of something through one of the high, etched windows which kept the clientele anonymous and free from external distractions.

You see, the problem with me is that I'm into the thrill-of-the-chase, she said.

Uhuh?

Well, it's like it doesn't matter if you follow through or not, just as long as you know you could.

You mean you want affirmation, to feel attractive?

To feel in charge, more like. I mean, you get to the hand up the skirt stage, and half the time I'm just like see ya, flag down a cab behind his back and I'm away. Sometimes it's as if anything else is just going through the motions.

Siobhan imagined little rowan leaves of arousal prickling out in front of her eyes, and thought of times when anything else wasn't just going through the motions. She didn't want to work out how long it had been.

I find it hard to meet people, she admitted.

Only one answer to that.

What?

Get out more.

Siobhan nodded. Months had passed – more than that – of not biting the bullet, not getting out more. She'd never even managed to take herself down to the women's library. It made her feel queasy, the calculation involved (weren't these things meant to be spontaneous?) and yet, hearing Myrna speak, she wondered if it might just be worth it.

It's the voice that swings it for me, she said, thinking of that inflection as red as the walls of her living room, as red as her tongue.

Yes but you're weird.

It's important, though. I think it must be to everyone with synaesthesia. I couldn't sleep with someone if they had a horrible voice.

You don't need to talk, Myrna suggested.

I'd still know it was in there, somewhere. Waiting to get out.

Siobhan slid into quietness as the evening progressed, letting her eyes drift over 130 Jahre Zittauer, Cobra gold medal lager and Pedavena birre as she listened to Myrna telling her stories, growing more and more animated as she did so.

Aye, so this guy right, he hands me a pill, and he's all like, oh are you sure, it's dead strong, just relax, I'll look after you. All that crap. So I'm lowering my eyelashes and going oh, I don't know, okay, thanks. Acting all innocent. I mean if he couldnae tell I'd already had one . . . but I'd been drinking, so it's not so obvious I s'pose. Totally thought he was educating me, opening my mind.

Your mind? Siobhan winked, and knew that each and every one of her five gin and tonics were dancing round her bloodstream, twiddling and poking and loosening.

Yeah I know, by that point he'd have shagged anything that moved. But he was on a hiding to nothing, though I played along. Never one to turn down a free lunch, me.

Myrna paused for breath, continued,

Mind you, there is a wee kick in there somewhere. There was this girl there who was totally like, oh I want to try E, I want to know what it's all about. She was a right wee chooky pie too, all silky hair and big eyes. So I popped a pill on her tongue and gave her a drink of water. She was trembling. Watched her coming up, an hour later she was all over me, loved me, I was her best pal ever. Honestly, I could've fucked her myself, she was such a wee doll.

Siobhan smiled. Myrna talked like that sometimes, it meant nothing. She used to be able to tell these things instantly, but she was out of practice. She didn't feel like sharing, though she knew the stories she would tell if she did. The weeks of never seeing daylight, never getting up until teatime. The bed unchanged, the dishes unwashed. Unrivalled, before or since. An unfortunate analogy, but she hoped it was like riding a bike. She looked back at Myrna,

Maybe she'll never be the same again.

No danger, that one'll be an assistant in an art gallery by now, or selling pillowcases made out of fucking antique saris. And good luck to her.

Lorna. Siobhan had almost forgotten her name, lost it in memories of tangled sheets and sweat-damp skin. The colour of milk, like her voice. The colour of her boy-friend's jeans, when he came back from university. The colour of the silver embossed wedding invitation – for her alone, rather than & partner – which Siobhan had care-fully set fire to over the sink, wishing the couple every happiness as she ran the taps and watched the charred remains swirl down the plughole.

What was her name, your chooky pie?

Vanessa.

Insipid. Like the colour of pistachio ice cream.

You're nuts. Ever taken acid, what happens then?

Oh, the usual teenage phase, you know, Huxley and De Quincey, patchouli and tie dye, listening to the Cramps and giggling at your own hands. Soon got fed up.

But what was it like?

More of the same. Sometimes less, which was discon-certing. I suppose I didn't really need it.

Mad. Saves cash though I guess, if you're tuned into your own internal psychedelia all the time.

It certainly makes the world more . . . I don't know. Vivid.

Siobhan wanted to go home. She felt like a clockwork toy, about to wind down. The noise and bustle of the bar were beginning to throw up irksome colours and textures in front of her eyes, and now, alarmingly, there was activity over by the karaoke machine. Besides, although it had been delayed by the night out, she had an assignation to keep, of sorts. Suddenly she glimpsed her escape in Myrna's eyes, as she followed her friend's gaze to a fresh face on the other side of the bar.

Handsome man at six o'clock.

Siobhan edged round in her chair to look at him,

Not bad.

Hmm, I've always been a sucker for that pseudo-intellectual sex in specs look. Probably thick as mince, but betcha he's got one good line about how not going to bed with him would be a damning example of *mauvaise foi*. And you know what? I fall for it every fucking time.

Within fifteen minutes, Siobhan was walking home. Her senses had been blurred by drink, so that the light traffic noise registered only as a subtle orange miasma, which subsided as soon as she turned off the main road, and the night grew darker around her. Nearing home, she could feel a distinct pulse of excitement moving across her chest. In her bag was something she was longing to take out and run through her fingers, a cap-sleeved Victorian style top, tiny sprigs of violet printed on a taupe ground, hook and eye fastenings leading down from a high collar.

Definitely hand wash only; it would crinkle, even in a wool cycle. Still you'd spend ages ironing it, easing the fabric smooth, stretching it to fit again. Siobhan quickened her pace.

Slippery slope

Like Agnes, Myrna had found herself fighting back an urge to confide. To lean over to Siobhan and say, I don't know what's happening, I think I've got in too deep, what should I do? But it would be the drink talking, surely. They'd been having a nice time, she didn't want to spoil it. So she had swallowed her words, stuck to safer topics. She should've known that Siobhan wasn't going to help her kick the arse out the evening, that she'd have to find another way of filling the long, lonely night ahead. And there he was, up at the bar for last orders. Better make it a double, she'd said, wondering as he got up whether she really fancied him. With late-night resolve, she decided to make some changes. Just not quite yet. Tonight she'd relax, go with the flow. Enjoy herself, have a bit of fun. Tomorrow was another day, a fresh start. Smiling, Myrna accepted her drink, raised it to her lips straight away.

A taxi, another bar, another taxi, and as if no time at all had passed, Myrna found herself precipitated unceremoniously into a hallway as the door she'd been leaning on sprang open and banged loudly against the wall. Fuck's sake, she thought, why do these things always happen when you're trying to impress someone? Attempting to recover her poise, she turned to her companion and whispered,

Who put that door there?

He looked at her oddly,

S'all right, don't worry about the noise, they're probably still up.

She could anticipate the smirks of his spotty student flatmates. They probably had a score sheet pinned on the kitchen wall, or else there'd be some sneering female, full of unrequited passion for Doug, or was it Dave? There was no way she was going in there to see them. And this was the last time she went home with a student, even a nice-looking one who kept the drinks coming. With an elaborate yawn, she said,

I'm really tired.

Doug/Dave looked a bit pissed off. Was he slow, or what? All the education money could buy and she'd still have to spell it out,

Maybe I could have a wee lie-down for a minute and you could bring the coffee through to us?

They went into his room. For a minute it looked like she wasn't going to get her coffee, but she prised him off her face and said,

Milk and two sugars, thanks.

Okay. Put on some music if you like.

Myrna searched for something laid back and gentle in the morass of hard house anthems. Anything apart from alcohol in his bloodstream and he'd try and match the b.p.m. with his strokes, and she'd probably wake up with cystitis. Which reminded her of Peter, all of a sudden. She wondered what had happened to him. Like name like nature, he'd petered out, disappeared from the scene for one reason or another. Finally she found a Love album and put it on the turntable, smiling at the irony as she lay down on the bed and stretched out. Doug/Dave had been quite a good kisser, she thought, anticipation spreading pleasantly through her body.

And so Myrna twisted and writhed and found herself shouting out harder! because it was not, ever, enough. Her late discovery of the clitoris (she'd been twenty, something she now found flabbergasting) had made her rather competitive about such things, so when Doug/Dave failed to live up to his initial promise, she masturbated, letting him put his fingers inside her to feel her as she came. Which made him hard again, just when she was ready to go to sleep. With her encouragement (it seemed the least strenuous option) he straddled her, and she squeezed his penis between her breasts. Tell me when you're going to come, she said, but of course he didn't. At least it was meant to be good for the skin, not to mention the hair, though that might be a nefarious myth perpetuated by men, she thought, wiping herself clean on the cover as he rolled over and started snoring.

Still horizontal, Myrna slid out from under the duvet, tucking it back round the slumbering body next to her – not out of tenderness, merely to prevent him from waking up. The overhead light was still on, bright and bleak. She hunched over, holding her stomach for a second, feeling bloated, then started plucking her clothes from the purple-carpeted floor. It seemed like a good idea at the time, could be her epitaph, for she could never shake the belief that something was always better than nothing. Myrna squeezed her toes into her shoes, and snapped the sling-back strap against the part of her ankle it had rubbed tender earlier. More than she could afford, they'd been, but worth every penny. The silky lining of her jacket felt cold against her bare arms, goosebumps prickling in protest that she wasn't in her own bed, asleep.

Myrna's heel caught in his discarded jeans as she crept towards the door, and as she stooped to free it she noticed his wallet, lying open where it'd fallen out of his pocket. After a swift glance to ascertain that he was still out for the count, she took a sneaky peek and saw that he had over forty quid left, in fives and change mainly, but with a tenner as well. Obviously he really was loaded, she should have figured that straight away from the way he talked. In fact, he probably wouldn't notice if she liberated a few quid, he'd think he'd spent it. Just to keep her going until pay day, she thought, sliding out a couple of the fives. She deserved it, after all that. She glanced at Doug/Dave. He was still sound. Myrna nabbed the tenner as well.

Just as she reached the door, she heard a moan, then the springs of the mattress groaning. She froze, turned to see Doug/Dave reaching his arm across the side of the bed she had occupied, flashed the light off.

Myrna?

His voice was groggy, muffled by the duvet. Her heart

pitter-pattered in her chest, feeling like it could jump into her throat. Easy does it, she told herself.

Uhuh?

Where're you going?

Toilet. Back in a sec.

She held her breath for what felt like ages, until finally he said,

Okay doke.

Once in the hallway Myrna felt the nervous pressure in her bladder, ripe for a pee. He had sounded half asleep, but she couldn't risk it. Thank the lord she kept up with her pelvic floor exercises. Music issued faintly from one of the rooms, but no voices. Stay calm, she told herself, and crept towards the door, turned the Yale. Nothing happened. She tried the other way, and felt the lock release. Edging the door open slowly, quietly, she felt the cool, musty air of the close. The lock didn't catch when she eased the door closed behind her, but she didn't dare slam it, even though it would've given her pleasure to do so. This scorn for her conquest was nothing new. Under her breath she murmured,

And she's off . . .

But she wasn't off quite as quickly as she'd have liked, not having bargained for the steepness of the stairs, worn and uneven under her wobbly kitten heels. Myrna had to cling to the banister all the way, taking care with every step. By the time she got down the three flights, she was pretty certain she'd made it undiscovered. Back on even footing, she jigged from side to side, she was so bursting.

What was that Oasis song? I need to pee myself . . . ah, the old ones were the best. She and Jonny used to sing that, after a dozen gin and tonics. The college romance that didn't survive his move to W5. She was sure he'd have edged his way into Zone 2 by now, according to his master plan. Once they'd sat propped up in bed, reading names from the tube map in the back of his diary, a magical mystery tour of places they'd never seen. Notting Hill and Holborn, Limehouse and Whitechapel. The desperate seedy glamour of anywhere mentioned in a song. Mile End and New Cross, Ladbroke Grove and Dagenham. They'd get off at every stop, eventually. Like the clockwork orange pub crawl, every weekend for a year, however long it took. For an instant, their breathless arrival at Victoria seemed as real as the burn marks in the bedclothes. She should've known better. In the future, she would know better.

Still no noise from upstairs. She must have made it. Moving swiftly to the side of the stairwell, Myrna hunkered down and pulled the waistband of her tights over her knees. Watching as the stream circled then swept away a discarded crisp poke, she smiled to herself, then shook her head.

Outside, she got her bearings, realized there was a taxi rank on the next street along, and started hobbling towards it, her shoes really hurting her now. She had the too-late-at-night-too-far-from-home shivers, pulled her jacket tighter round her body. The taxi driver was extremely friendly, making her wonder how come he was so awake at this hour. Not that it bothered her, as long as he got her home in one piece. He kept asking about her night, if she'd had a good time, what she'd been up to. Party, OK, she answered in monosyllables. She gave him a tip though, an extra few quid, wanting to pass on her luck, if that's what it was. As she walked towards her own door, he called after her,

Cheers hen, take care of yourself.

It wasn't until she got up the stairs and into her own house that she realized that her bra was trailing out of her coat pocket.

1.42 p.m. – Sally

Adrift on life's highway. That's how Agnes thinks of Sally. It's hard to tell her age. Although her skin is a little rough and her hair slightly thin, she could be early thirties, worn down by life. Despite this, Agnes never refers to her as a woman, only as a girl. (Mind you, she still suspects that lurking at her own core is the teenage Rita, stuck there from years ago. Years before Sally was born, probably.) Agnes watches her loading the machine, humming tunelessly to herself as she stuffs in a mish-mash of her own brightly coloured bits and pieces, then larger, heavier, sweatshirts and sports socks. The same man, or a new one? Agnes has never seen Sally's boyfriend, but she's noticed marks on her face, badly covered by foundation and powder, orange lipstick not quite managing to draw the eye away.

Sally likes clothes, obviously, and has a strange style of her own. Coloured underskirts, layer upon layer of purple and red net, stick out above polkadot popsocks and gold sandals. Even in the middle of winter, her bony knees protrude, blue-tinged with cold. Although Agnes has seen similar outfits on the pages of the fashion magazines which Myrna reads, she knows that this isn't where Sally gets her inspiration. Margaret once told her of the giro day when Sally came in to the charity shop and tried on a blancmange bridesmaid's dress in peach satin. Then swirled in front of the mirror like a film star, handed over the money and waltzed out the shop still wearing it, her old clothes left in a tangled heap on the changing room floor. A magpie for anything fancy. She loves evening gloves, so Margaret puts them aside for her, knowing she'll always buy them. Doesn't like her arms, she says, though they all know why she keeps them covered.

She's been around for years, Agnes can't remember the first time she saw her. She fully expects that Sally'll still be around long after she herself has retired. There's something eternal about her. Weeks, even months, pass, without any sign. Now and then, without really thinking about it, Agnes stops and wonders if she's all right. Wonders, but not very seriously, if there's anything she could do to help. Not that they've ever really talked, beyond passing the time of day, exchanging details of their various ailments. Sally suffers from what she terms kidney trouble, a euphemism if ever Agnes has heard one, though she always goes along with it. When she sees Margaret she sometimes works Sally into the conversation, to learn if the health problems or the boyfriend have finally become too much for her. But then out of the blue she reappears, same old Sally, thin hair backcombed up behind a new Alice band, yellow remnants of a bruise on her face, skinny legs still standing.

Third time lucky

Siobhan saw the bag at Myrna's feet, frowned at the design, then looked back at the pair of full black briefs her colleague was waving in the air.

Hey hey, check these out! Hardly seasonal are they? Must come up to the waist.

Who do they belong to?

Myrna checked the name tag she'd stuck on the bag,

Auerbach. In a wee while ago. Too young for granny pants. Tall, dark hair?

Yes, Siobhan thought, about five foot eight, a little taller than she or Myrna, with deep brown hair, like polished wood. And a name, now, a surname that had not been there before.

These sticky labels are useless, they keep falling off, Myrna muttered to herself, scrunching up the tag and throwing it in the bin.

Auerbach.

Siobhan tasted it, realized she had spoken out loud, quickly added,

Unusual name.

Like the painter.

Yes, I suppose so, Siobhan said, feeling guilty at her

surprise. She wondered why she had never tried talking to Myrna about art, about her own little obsessions, when they spent so much time together.

She's really familiar. I'm sure I've seen her somewhere before. On TV, maybe.

Nah, don't think so. Not lah-di-dah enough. Unless she's on *River City*. I don't watch it.

Must be imagining things.

Siobhan was unable to tell if the pants were supersoft cotton or that kind of yielding, synthetic microfibre. How would Myrna react, if she reached out and took them, rubbed them between her fingers? Surely it was possible to act with such assurance that nobody would question you. She looked again at Myrna, decided not to risk it.

I don't think they're so bad. In this kind of climate a girl needs a larger pant, even in summer. You don't see many thongs in here, do you?

True enough. And the ones you do see are usually men's.

Siobhan laughed:

Oh dear, my girlfriend's stuff must have got mixed up with this.

Who do they think they're kidding? I prefer the full trannies that come in. You know they're not women, and they know that you know, but you just play along with it. And ignore them when they make a meal of loading their machine, one stocking at a time. Typical man underneath though, doesn't know you're meant to handwash them.

You don't suppose they get a bit of a kick out of it? I

mean, especially the ones who put all their fancy pants in for a service wash, mixed up with their shirts for work.

Myrna pursed her lips, as though toting up all the manky lingerie she had handled in her time at the launderette,

You mean like a sexual kick?

What else?

Yeeuch! That's not fair, we should charge them extra.

Myrna dropped the pants in disgust, as though they were themselves to blame.

Go and stick the kettle on, Siobhan said, I'll finish that for you.

Gratefully, Myrna headed through to the back shop, grumbling something about having thought it was only so that their wives wouldn't find out. While loading the machine, Siobhan ascertained that The Girl, no, *Auerbach's* undergarments were made of a polyamide elastane blend with a cotton gusset. Comfortable, but she also imagined they would look quite good on. There was something fifties about them, as if they should go under wide circular skirts, the kind that swirled up and around when the wearer danced. Siobhan decided she might venture into town and get a pair for herself. This thought was chased into her mind by another, unbidden one. A terrier of an idea, small, niggling, and impossible to ignore. If she had the same pants, in the same size, she could swap them over. Just the once, just for fun. Siobhan shook her head to rid it of this notion. She wouldn't do that, of course she wouldn't. It would be weird, not funny. Weird. The previous two occasions, the trousers and the top, had been okay. But now she had to get a handle on this quirk, nip it in the bud before it went any further. Siobhan finished loading the machine, banged the heel of her hand against the button to switch it on.

And then she found them. At the bottom of the laundry bag. Mephistophelean in their irresistibility. She looked at the machine, at the water which was pouring down the perspex door. It was too late to hit stop. Only one thing for it. Siobhan balled the pair of knickers into her hand and tucked them up her sleeve, then scooted through the back under the pretence of asking Myrna for coffee instead of tea, and slipped them into her own bag. She'd overlooked them by mistake (these things happened), and so she was doing The Girl a favour. There was nothing weird in that, nothing at all.

Anxiety was close on her heels. What if she didn't manage to replace them in time? She'd got away with it before, yes, but underwear was more emotive, quite literally closer to the bone. And she didn't start work until eleven tomorrow, what if it was the one day The Girl came in early? Maybe she wouldn't notice, maybe she'd think that she'd left the pants elsewhere, not that Siobhan wanted to dwell on that possibility. Should Auerbach come into the shop to complain, Myrna would make a show of looking through the back, whilst knowing that if something was missing, it was almost certainly lost for good. Agnes, on the other hand, would probably tell her where to go; she wasn't yet one of the regulars, that small elite indulged with a marginally higher level of customer service, such as a smile, or other indication that they weren't part of some persistent, irksome infestation. (Better ring environmental health, we've got customers again.) No, it couldn't be traced back to Siobhan. She was safe.

Myrna soon discovered another garment for examination and comment. She was in that fidgety, flighty kind of mood which made her grasp at any distraction.

Jesus Christ Siobhan, would you look at this.

She held up a t-shirt, pink like cheap strawberry flavouring, almost child-sized. Something was written in small, baby blue letters across the chest. Siobhan moved closer to read it: Porn Star.

Just as well Agnes isn't here, she said. Don't think she'd approve.

Well, for once I'm on her side. I'm so over these stupid slogans.

Yeah, they do my head in too.

They're meant to be empowering though, Myrna said. Reclaiming our bodies and all that.

Siobhan laughed,

Would you wear it?

No. I might not be renowned for my subtlety, but this kind of thing is the preserve of the sad and desperate.

Only one thing for it then.

What are you suggesting?

Emboldened by her success with the pants, Siobhan rushed through to the kitchen and grabbed the squeezy ketchup bottle, tucked it into the waistband of her trousers and adopted a cowboy pose in front of Myrna, who was still holding up the t-shirt.

Aha, Myrna said, catching her drift and starting to hum a Morricone score:

Ti di di di di.

Hwa hwa hwa, Siobhan echoed, as they circled each other.

Tii dii dii dii dii.

Hwa hwaaaaa . . . Siobhan flipped open the top of the bottle and fired three generous spurts at Myrna, who juddered at each hit, then sank to her knees, scrunching the t-shirt up and rubbing the ketchup well into the fabric. Siobhan blew imaginary smoke off the top of the bottle, just as Agnes returned from doing the banking.

Everything okay, girls?

Myrna struggled to her feet and Siobhan hid the ketchup behind her back.

Fine Agnes, they replied, in unison.

Short-term gain

Myrna felt like she was temping again.

Before the launderette, she'd worked in a succession of offices and call centres, trying to pack each job in before she got sacked for too many sickies. Temporary respite, a couple of days of sleeping late, drinking in the afternoon, which turned into evening, and back to morning again. Then the old problem, money. Back up and at 'em. Clothes ironed, new pair of tights, CV enhanced, and hawked round the agencies again. She got a kick out of interviews, liked waiting in the flash foyers which artfully concealed floors graveolent with sick building syndrome. Sipping double expresso in gallery cafes between appointments, having it all in a non-specific fantasy career – one which didn't involve any of that work nonsense. Then, a day or two later, the phone call, and back to the headset and computer screen, filing papers and franking mail.

Until her tuna sandwich epiphany. Sitting on a bench in George Square, eating her lunch. She raised it to her mouth to take another bite, but the stink of onion, suddenly sent bile-soaked mush back up into her throat. Another ringing phone, more data entry, was untenable. Myrna chucked the sandwich in the bin, along with her security pass, cut her losses and left her trainers in that week's office. Her work shoes chafed her toes, but it seemed to Myrna that she'd never felt so good as when she walked the long road home that day, her suit jacket flapping behind her in the breeze. She hadn't eaten tuna since.

The launderette was better, undoubtedly. Not good, but better. But money was still the problem, debts which seemed to appear out of nowhere and the hangover from all the nights out and comfort shopping trips which had saved her sanity. The rent overdue, the days when she had to return Irn Bru bottles for enough cash for a loaf of bread and a tin of soup, the candlelit nights without a powercard. Myrna didn't know how the fuck she ended up this way, at her age. Other people managed. In some cases they managed cars or even mortgages. But money was there for the making, and quickly. Fate had put Bernadette in her path, and now her luck was in.

The office was difficult to find, the main doorway obscured by scaffolding. Up the stairs, covered with heavily patterned, pub quality carpet, non-flammable and stain-resistant. Past walls papered in textured fleur-de-lis, gold plastic charms and bells dangling prettily, if incongruously, from the ceiling. After the first floor, and the New Cantonese Garden, the stairs changed to marbled lino, the walls to greying whitewash. Myrna passed a jeweller, who bought and sold for cash (Best Prices Paid!), a hatch onto the landing with a sales assistant leaning on the counter, bouncer's neck straining against collar and tie.

He looked up quickly, caught her eye then returned to his paper. The next floor had financial services at one side (Payday advances! Why wait?), and a partnership which didn't specify the nature of its business at the other. Then a narrower stair to the attic floor, at first glance deserted, as if used for registered addresses and mail drops only. Myrna stood for a moment, recovering her breath and letting her calves recover from the hike. A door with two glass panels led onto a dingy corridor, guarded by a telephone entry system. She scanned the names, then straightened her skirt and pressed the buzzer marked PROMENADE.

After an anxious delay, a woman's voice crackled through.

Hello?

Hi, I've got an appointment to see Belinda.

What's your name?

Celia.

Myrna was rather proud of her assumed name. She thought it conveyed the right impression.

Yes. Second door on the right.

This was the moment Myrna had anticipated, the swithering between going ahead, and forgetting the whole thing. She pushed open the door and walked straight through, letting it ease shut behind her.

Belinda was in her early forties, smartly dressed and heavily made up, with expensive copper lowlights. Myrna shifted in her chair, cradling her instant coffee and trying to ignore the reek of floral air freshener as it battled in vain to obscure the inherent staleness of the room. A small bright square of sky shone through the roof window, and Myrna caught a glimpse of a large city seagull soaring overhead.

So you see, Celia, that's why I chose the name Promenade. Stepping out. Businessmen and the like are away from home, they want to see the sights, check out the theatre, go for a meal. But not on their own. Who doesn't like a bit of company, someone to have an intelligent conversation with, over a few drinks in a nice restaurant?

Myrna nodded her best enthusiastic nod.

And the beauty of it, if it suits you, is that you're going along for free. Meeting new people, having a nice time, and not paying a penny. I mean, they're never going to be your best friends, let's not kid ourselves, but some of the girls develop nice little working relationships with their clients. They request them again and again. Nothing romantic of course, just because they get along nicely. And that's when the tips become extremely generous.

Myrna wondered how often the woman could say nice. Perhaps it was some kind of hypnotic technique. She leaned forward, feeling very gauche,

I was wondering, em, what exactly do these clients expect when they go out for an evening?

Belinda remained unfazed.

Well, as I was saying, company, conversation, a night out with a girl who's dressed up, put a bit of effort into her appearance.

I see, said Myrna, although she didn't, as yet.

And I'd hope you'd be available at least two or three evenings a week, including weekends. Is that a problem?

No, not at all.

It would be okay to miss the odd night out. She didn't want all her new wages disappearing before she had a chance to make some serious money.

Belinda seemed to be warming to her subject,

Always wear heels, always. Be properly made up, hair looking nice, that sort of thing. Don't smoke, incidentally, not even if you're offered a cigarette. Never wear anything too short or revealing. Hotels will turn you away when you go to meet your client. Do you have a nice selection of clothes you can wear?

I think so, Myrna said, then noticed Belinda was wearing court shoes and had a bag that matched, slouching with the softness of the real thing, rather than the market stall rip-off. This could end up more hassle than it was worth, if she had to invest in lots of appalling shiny girl clothes just for work. But her wardrobe wasn't Myrna's main worry. She'd have to be blunter.

What about the, em, physical side of things?

Belinda sat back and sighed, looking rather intent all of a sudden, as though gauging the likelihood of a hidden tape recorder.

I'm not in the business of selling sex.

That was emphatic enough, Myrna thought, wondering for a split second if there could possibly be such a thing as easy money. Belinda met her eye, held her gaze for a moment before continuing,

However, what the girls who work for me do is their own business. Any personal arrangements they make are just that, personal. It's entirely up to them what they feel comfortable doing.

Down to the nitty gritty then, thought Myrna, and sure enough,

Let's talk money. The client pays the girl a flat fee, the agency rate. She passes this on to me, preferably the next day. At the moment it's £80. Tips are yours to keep. As I said, the tips can be very impressive. Anything else is entirely up to you. I won't ask and I don't want to know. Unless, of course, there's any problem with a client, any inappropriate behaviour.

Does that happen often? Inappropriate behaviour, I mean.

To my knowledge, never. Most clients come to us every time they're in town. If anything did happen, I wouldn't deal with them again. And you know, it's not the case that they're all old, or ugly. Young men don't want to sit in their hotel room on their own all night. After a glass or two of champagne you may well find you want to take things further.

Myrna wasn't sure if she trusted Belinda, but perhaps that was irrelevant. After all, Promenade was in the phone book, it had an office (albeit one which could be packed up without trace in under two minutes. Not a computer nor filing cabinet in sight, no scrap of paper apart from Belinda's diary. Only a phone, and the answering machine which gave her mobile number). She seemed reasonable, even – if Myrna dared say it – nice.

Belinda carefully placed a hand on Myrna's arm as she showed her out of the office.

Think it over, in your own time. Give me a ring when you've decided. No pressure, no strings.

She flashed a huge, warm smile, so convincing that it made Myrna wonder if Belinda had graduated from doing the job to running the business.

The work is certainly available, if you choose to go ahead. It's a busy time, coming up for conference season. A lot of money in town.

Shrewd, this last comment. After all, why else would Myrna be considering it? As she made her way towards the tube Myrna passed a recruitment agency. Through the glare reflecting off the plate-glass window she could see two girls sitting waiting for their typing tests. Belinda knew full well that Myrna would call. It had been written all over her face.

Never found

There was nothing to beat a mouthful of strong coffee, ever so slightly too hot to drink. That, a cigarette, and a new magazine. The service washes were all on, Siobhan was at the desk, and Agnes sincerely hoped she'd get half an hour to herself for once so she could enjoy it. She looked at the cover headline: The Face of Evil! Complete with suitably menacing-looking photo of Britain's Worst Serial Killer Ever! She was a bit bored with that one, much preferring scandalous new information, or descriptions of how the police had run the culprit to ground, especially if it involved profiling or a psychic. She'd never cared for the supernatural, but recently, on passing the Spiritualist Church, she'd caught herself checking the times of the services. Piece of nonsense, con artists the lot of them, she'd chided herself, and walked on so fast her sciatic nerve started grumbling. Nevertheless, it gave her pleasure when something ancient and inexplicable got results where all the new-fangled databases and DNA failed. Of course this particular case was still dreadful. She scowled at a highlighted quote about his wife standing by him, stupid bitch, then flicked through the rest of the magazine.

And then she saw her. Page 31, the No Mean City

feature. Agnes' coffee went down the wrong way and it was only after a fit of coughing that she could read the article. Lavinia 'Vina' MacIntyre. Complete with photo, one which Agnes had never seen before. Different from the school portraits that Maureen and Jack had given to the police. This was Vina at the dancing, smiling straight into the camera, eyelids closing as though caught mid-flutter, cigarette in hand. A copy of a film star pose, Agnes suspected, and it suited her. Must have been a boyfriend that took that one. Lips slightly parted, full of promise. No Lolita, the set of her hair and the powder on her face made Vina look older than her eighteen years. But everyone had looked older then, the teenager having not yet been invented, except, perhaps, in the American pictures that showed at the Alhambra.

In death Vina had made new friends. The bridesmaids to her bride, their photos, smaller, flanked her own. On her left, poor Aimee Gallagher, the trial run. Stiff and unsmiling in a hat that was years out of fashion even then, as she posed for her first studio shot, hands clasped around her little daughter who, balanced on her mother's knee, smiled as she pointed a chubby finger towards the camera. To the right, Vina's successor, dark-haired and smart in her nurse's uniform, new fob watch glinting in the flash. Neither of them a patch on Vina, oh no.

The Glasgow serial killer has never been found.

As such, the editor had deemed him worthy of a double-page spread rather than the usual meagre column awarded to No Mean City criminals; gangsters for the most part, and a smattering of real-life Sanny-shoe Sams, stalking children in the blackout nights. The Box Man of Partick, the St George's Cross Chisel Man. Nightmarish figures, but caught, brought to justice. Agnes looked at the article once more. An old story, learned by heart. Words she had seen so many times before leapt from the page.

Eighteen-year-old blonde . . . dancing . . . assaulted . . . strangled . . . stockings . . . strong sexual motive . . . to this day his identity remains a mystery.

Mack fastens the clasp of the bracelet so that it fits tight around Vina's wrist. She turns her hand to make the rows of diamanté sparkle in the light from the candle in their corner booth.

They're not real, he says, smiling.

Vina tuts, assumes a look of disdain, then gives up, It's beautiful.

Like you.

And she knows she can't put it off any longer, and besides, truth be told, she doesn't want to. Wine-warm and eager, she feels herself open to the touch of his leg against hers under the table. So they, or rather he, gets the bill, and despite the martini, and the white Bordeaux, and the scotch, he drives them to a hotel not so very far away from where Vina lives. It is set discreetly on a terrace above the main road, with bay trees in pots on either side of the bright doorway, and a shiny brass plaque which announces, THE OSSINGTON. Vina pretends she is imagining things when the desk clerk calls him Mr Smith before Mack has even signed the register.

There, in a cheap room on the third floor, Vina removes the lace-trimmed French knickers she has saved for weeks to buy, and Mack exacts his payment with gusto. She arches her neck, then her back, and thinks that her little death is worth it.

Oh, Agnes said, her hands shaking in a sickeningly familiar way as she laid the magazine down. This was different, of course, but it brought with it the same jolting feeling of shock she'd experienced that day at home.

Oh Vina.

What did you say?

Come and look at this Siobhan. See this photo?

The blonde girl? Yes.

That's my cousin. That's Vina.

Siobhan took the flimsy magazine carefully, as though she was handling the most precious of artefacts rather than thin, cheap paper. She looked intently at the photo, then at Agnes.

You never said anything.

What's to say? It's a long time ago, now.

The Glasgow serial killer has never been found, Siobhan read, in that trademark tone of celebratory condemnation. Of act and victim.

You can see the family resemblance. The nose and mouth are really similar.

Agnes looked at the picture again.

Do you think so? That's odd. We were never alike, me and her. Never. She was the pretty one, as you can see. But opposites attract, don't they, and we were great pals. So close.

I'm sorry. It must be upsetting to see her again, like this. Unexpectedly, I mean. Why don't I make you a cup of tea?

Well, there's a lot of water under the bridge since then. A wee cuppa would be nice though, thanks doll.

Agnes had never agreed with counselling. The best anyone could hope for was solace in the passing of time, and each year brought a covering like snow on a pavement, until the kerb became a slight irregularity, which you knew to avoid, instinctively. For a while she'd forgotten where her own uneven edge was, but now it had reappeared, perilous. Talking might sprinkle salt on it, make it less of a hazard.

Here you are.

Siobhan put two cups of tea on the desk, and perched on the small stool by Agnes. They both looked towards the bright window and the panels of light it cast on the floor of the launderette, beyond which the world looked too sunny a place for girls to be murdered and their killers to stay free. Eventually Siobhan asked,

What age were you when it happened?

Fifteen. A young fifteen, mind, not like some of the teenagers you see these days, though when you think on it there's always some who're old for their years. A while ago now, but you don't forget a thing like that in a hurry. Vina was, I don't know, different. Glamorous. You can see that from the photo.

Yes. She's beautiful.

Like something out of the *Photoplay*, I used to think, all done up to the nines. When she was old enough, she worked in Forsyth's, the department store. Gone now, of course. I was still at school. My mother always tutted at her false eyelashes, but I thought it looked good. I wanted to be like her, I suppose, but I was a real plain Jane. I could have dyed my hair or worn make-up, but at the time it didn't seem worth the hiding I'd have got for it.

It must have been hard, when they didn't catch him.

Maureen and Jack, that was her parents, went through hell waiting for news. Days, weeks passed, and nothing. They put the photofit in all the papers, see – Agnes held out the magazine again – but it looks like anybody. It got huge publicity, and people cared, they were even trying to make citizens' arrests. One poor guy had to get a signed declaration from the chief constable that it wasn't him. They must've questioned hundreds of folk. Went under-cover at the dancing, but they never got anywhere.

Seems strange, doesn't it? I thought most murderers did get caught eventually.

Well, he covered his tracks. Must've gone away, I suppose, abroad maybe.

It's awful. Unimaginable. I don't know how families cope.

They don't, not really. Jack drank himself to death, though he was always that way inclined. And Maureen babied William, my cousin, he never had the life he should have because she would hardly let him out of her sight. He married a woman as bossy as her, who made him up sticks and go to Australia. Maureen didn't last long after that, with both her children gone. Oh yes, it broke that family, in the end.

I'm sorry.

So am I. But it doesn't do to dwell on things. Life goes on, doesn't it?

Agnes could hear the appeal in her own voice.

Break a leg

Myrna looked at the display on her phone: Belinda calling. Answer? She hit the button, took the details. Mr Walker, a regular, handpicked for her. The hotel was just up the road, not that she told Belinda this. 7.30 in the lounge bar. Okay, Myrna said. Okay. Belinda told her to have a great time, but the way she said it made it sound like she was wishing Myrna good luck. After she hung up, Myrna felt there were lots of questions she should have asked, but hadn't.

There was no time now to get something new to wear, and she didn't want to go in her normal clothes, it didn't seem right. She planned to keep things separate, controlled. Looking round the launderette at the bags of untapped service washes, an idea marched into her mind. Thursday afternoon, when people put their good clothes in to get washed ready for Saturday. It was a shame they didn't take dry cleaning, but with any luck, there'd be something half decent. Agnes was off, thankfully, but Myrna confided her idea in Siobhan, pretending she was going to a friend's dad's 60th.

Quite staid really, but I have to go along for moral support. For my friend that is, her dad'll have to cope.

Would madam prefer a dress, or a skirt and top combo?

Something kind of smart. Not too short, not too dowdy. A dress would be ideal, to go with my good black jacket.

They rooted and rummaged, with little success.

Balaclava? Siobhan asked, holding it up, quizzically.

So last season, darling. Besides, I'd never get past the CCTV. What else is in that bag?

Dread to think. Socks, mainly, by the looks of things.

Zip it up, quick, I can smell them from here.

What about this one then? Siobhan held up a promising-looking plain black shift.

Myrna looked it up and down,

Uhuh, quite low cut but long enough not to be tarty. What size is it?

Twelve.

Might be too wee. That kind of shape can be dodgy over the old hip and thigh region.

It's got a bit of give in it, and things always get bigger after someone's worn them in for you.

Chuck it over then, I'll try it on.

Myrna checked the dress for stains, then sniffed the armpits tentatively,

Not too honking. A wee skoosh of Febreze and it'll be fine. I've never done this before, honest.

After a second she laughed,

God, you'd think I was some knicker-pinching perv.

Siobhan went rigid, couldn't even get a word out, but Myrna didn't seem to notice, kept talking,

But that's what they do for the Oscars, isn't it? Borrow, I mean. Always thought it was minging, myself. Can't tell me models don't sweat on the catwalk.

They get their armpits injected, Siobhan stuttered.

Aye, with heroin probably.

Well I think it's fine. Absolutely. I mean, she'll never know, the customer, and it'll be clean anyway, when she gets it back. Not that you'll dirty it, of course.

Well, I'm not going to lose any sleep over it, but thanks.

Myrna went and tried on the dress, came out and did a twirl.

What d'you think?

Needs an iron. Badly. But it'll be fine with tights and shoes.

Myrna grinned. Fate was smiling on her. And her horoscope had said that Aries should expect a much-needed financial boost. If only she'd been able to finish early. It was not as she imagined it, this rushing home to get ready. It bore no resemblance to her teen fantasies, when Nana was her heroine and Myrna was secure in the knowledge that she would've quit while she was ahead, when she'd got the chateau. None of this not making old bones nonsense for her.

While she was waiting for her ceramic straighteners to heat, a new worry arrived. What if someone saw her? Not that she knew anyone who worked at the hotel, and it was unlikely, no, preposterous, that any of her friends would end up drinking in the bar there. But still. She didn't know what people would think if they saw her wandering about in that get-up, never mind having a drink with Mr Walker, whatever he was like. She looked at herself in the mirror. Any of her friends would twig straight away that something wasn't kosher, and this would not make an entertaining Saturday night story.

In the end, Myrna decided to get a taxi, even though the hotel was a mere fifteen minutes' walk from her flat. She could phone a private hire, to save a couple of pounds, but maybe that would give the wrong impression. Not that she knew exactly what the right impression was, but a black cab seemed more like it. She'd get one quickly, surely, without giving anyone the chance to see her.

Although she had careful plans for being fashionably, but safely (ten minutes max) late, Myrna ended up arriving early, and had to buy her own drink. The impression of the black cab was wasted, and she'd just spent six quid on one gin and tonic. Fan-bloody-tastic, she thought, crunching angrily on a complimentary Japanese cracker.

Expense account, love, have whatever takes your fancy, Mr Walker – call me Jim – said. Presumably *she* wasn't covered by expenses, but Myrna felt obliged to make the most of it. Grilled langoustine to start, then the duck. A nice change from 3 a.m. chips and curry sauce, that was for sure. And the more she ate, the more she drank, with Jim seeming to take pleasure in topping up her glass. He wasn't so bad, really, tried his best to put her at her ease. It was quite relaxing, in an odd kind of way. No need to have opinions, or think of things to say, just listen, smile and sympathize about the Beacon, Brown and Gilbert account. Only when Myrna was cramming her last roast potato into her mouth did she realise how hungry she'd been. The food lay heavily in her stomach, and she wondered if she shouldn't have been more prudent, chosen lighter dishes. Oh well, if she ended up farting all night, that was just tough. Besides, Belinda probably knew a man who paid good money for that kind of thing.

Glad of a moment or two alone while Jim was in the toilet, Myrna drained yet another glass of wine, flipped open her compact and applied more lipstick. Pinker than her usual shade, it matched her flushed cheeks. The waiter swooped over to refill her glass, with an embarrassing flourish. He was younger than her, with the remnants of acne on his face, and a uniform of polyester shirt and tie that matched the decor.

Thanks, Myrna said, stuffing her make-up back in her bag.

You're welcome, madam, the boy smiled – no, smirked – in response. Myrna knew a smirk when she saw one, and this was a prime specimen. He'd probably seen Jim before, with a different girl each time. She felt like a chancer, all of a sudden. The waiter might as well have leaned over and said, I know your game. She wasn't high class, and Jim wasn't a high roller. He was just a man who paid for companionship when he was away from home. Maybe more, as the personal ads said. No strings. That casual arrangement. And it wasn't as uncommon as Myrna had thought. Belinda had twenty-five girls on her books at the moment, she'd said, all kept in work, and Promenade wasn't the only agency in town. Myrna saw Jim crossing the floor towards her, got her smile ready.

Liqueur with your coffee Celia?

Oh yes, definitely. I'll have whatever you're having.

That's my girl, Jim smiled.

She tried desperately to see what kind of tip he left the waitress, but couldn't read the credit card slip. He should have left cash, then the girl would have got it all. Never trust that dotted line on a receipt, she'd learned, an unscrupulous manager will whip the lot and the ones doing the hard work won't get a look-in. If only she could work out in advance how much money he'd give her. Or was she supposed to ask? She'd read the articles in the broadsheets, seen documentaries, so-called serious journalism, but salacious nonetheless. High-class escorts claimed to make hundreds of pounds, but they all looked like models. All Myrna could do was play it by ear. After all, he wasn't repulsive, not her type certainly, but not actually offensive. And it wasn't as if she hadn't had some lapses of judgement in her day, through drunkenness or bloody-mindedness. At least she could be sure of getting something out of it this time.

Shall we go upstairs for a nightcap then?

For a second Myrna thought there was another bar upstairs somewhere, but then she realized what he meant.

I'd like that, she said, feeling mildly queasy. That last petit four had been a mistake.

When she thought about it, Myrna realized that she'd always assumed she was pretty good in bed. So tonight could be like a kind of exam, after which she'd find out how proficient she really was. After all, Jim wasn't any stranger to this kind of thing. Belinda had said he was a regular. A good one to get her started. Maybe he wouldn't even expect that much. A hand job might do him, and that wouldn't be such a huge trauma for her. She'd condoms in her bag though, just in case. You couldn't be too careful these days.

The doors closed and the lift lurched upwards.

Whoops, Myrna mumbled, bouncing off the mirrored wall. Jim took her arm to steady her. She yawned so widely that she thought she could fit her whole fist in her mouth.

Don't worry dear, I won't take long. You'll be home to bed in no time.

S'okay, I'm fine. Can we have more champagne?

Whatever makes you happy Celia. If you're happy, I'll be happy too.

2.15 p.m. – Francesca

Excuse me, Agnes says loudly, although she doesn't really need to get past. They irritate her, that type. And this girl is certainly that type. Yammering away in Italian, nineteen to the dozen into one of those little tiny mobile phones. Agnes has a mobile phone, that Donald gave her last Christmas. She'd been hoping for perfume and a bathrobe, but never mind it was the thought that counted. And she does feel safer, marginally, on her way home in the evening. If nothing else, she can beat any potential assailant over the head, so large is it compared to the one this girl is using.

She's washing less than half a load, which is wasteful, and the same price as a full one. Mind you, her clothes are that skimpy that she probably couldn't fill a whole machine. Those trousers. That top. Maybe she doesn't have anyone to tell her to be careful, or else she'll get a chill round her kidneys. Though even if they did warn her, she wouldn't listen. And the shoes. Agnes thought they'd gone out in the seventies. Donald's niece, she'd done her ankle in wearing platform shoes, and it was never the same again. Nasty big clumpy things, not elegant at all. And this girl could be elegant if she chose, she has the looks all right. Long hair, dark curls everywhere, and natural, not a perm.

When suddenly she breaks into English all Agnes' suspicions are confirmed:

Oh come on why don't you just trust me, huh?

She'd like to snatch the phone and tell whoever's on the line a few home truths. Like never trust someone who says trust me. If it's a man she's speaking to, well he deserves all he gets for going for that sort. And if it's a woman, she should run a mile because this one's a boyfriend stealer, as sure as sugar. Agnes' lack of faith in girls of this type is exceeded only by her mistrust of men generally. Her observations have led to the hypothesis that most of them will dip their wick anywhere, if they think they can get away with it. Even those you think you know are wont to surprise you, and not with flowers and chocolates.

Electrical impulses

Siobhan eavesdropped, hiding her blushes as she crouched down to empty a machine. Agnes was getting on at Myrna.

What do you have to remember?

Name and contact number, Myrna recited.

We've had enough crap left here and not collected. Agnes turned to The Girl, Auerbach, and added, no offence.

Nip nip nip nip nip, Myrna mimicked Agnes' voice once she'd gone through to the kitchen. Honestly, you'd think I was completely incompetent.

Oh, I'm sure you're not. So what happens when people don't collect their stuff?

That voice. It swooped round Siobhan's ears, like red silk streamers in a gust of wind. With a voice like that she must be a singer. And now she was talking to Myrna, smiling at her. Myrna, the straightest girl in the world. Perhaps Siobhan had got it all wrong.

We keep it for a month or two, depending on how much room there is through the back, then take it to the charity shop. Or chuck it, depending. Happens all the time, you wouldn't believe it.

I guess things happen, people forget. Go away. Die.

God, don't be morbid. Mind you, could be worse. Round the corner, in the Cat Protection, they know when someone's died because at the top of the bag of clothes there's a pair of glasses or a hearing aid.

False teeth too?

I'm sure it's happened. Best one we had here was a guy who'd got out of jail and came to ask where his clothes were. He'd put them in for a service wash two years before.

Well, I'd better leave my number with you. In case a life of crime beckons.

Auerbach reeled off the digits. Pink three, blue four, purple nine, grey one, white zero, orange five, green seven. Siobhan knew she would remember this number, that she couldn't forget it even if she wanted to. She also knew she would never dial it. It was inconceivable, like suggesting she went bungee jumping or abseiling. Her mind was on other, more achievable, goals.

Oh, and can you put a name tag on your bag for next time, as well? Myrna said.

Sure. Anything else?

Just your passport. Once we've cleared you with the intelligence services, we'll be able to do your laundry.

It was easier, now she'd done it before. Siobhan waited for Myrna to go outside for a cigarette, and slowly loaded the clothes into the machine, checking no customers were watching. A man, young, engrossed in a game on his mobile; a woman, older, reading a textbook. Siobhan only had to decide which item to choose, from a wash disappointingly dominated by t-shirts and towels. Not even a vest. She riffled through the bag more quickly, in the hope that something had fallen to the bottom. The launderette didn't sort items into whites and coloureds. Shrinkages, a sign above the counter announced, were the Responsibility of the Patron. A service wash did what it said, washed. Wools and delicates could take their chances, and only the most highly favoured customers could expect them to be saved from the tumble dryer. And there, suddenly, between Siobhan's searching fingertips, the feel of pure silk. Without looking, she reeled her prize in through the towels, up her sleeve.

Siobhan was impatient for the afternoon to pass, but the eight o'clock close didn't come any faster. All her nerve-endings seemed awake, anticipating. Everything she touched, she felt more intensely: damp from wet cloth soaking into her fingertips, cold metal change shrinking her skin, hot tea filling her mouth and seeping down her throat, warming her blood. She could imagine a bright silvery aura, a millimetre in diameter, encircling her entire body. If somebody touched her, she thought they might get a shock of static electricity. Walking past a basket waiting for the spinner, she tripped over a bag and spilt two scoops of powder all over the wet clothes. Agnes snapped,

That'll all need done again. Man's coming in for it at five, and there's no machines free now.

Myrna stood behind Agnes, hands on hips, sticking out her tongue as Agnes pronounced,

More haste less speed.

Siobhan felt how easily her pleasant agitation could turn to anger, imagined it flooding out of her, darkening the concrete floor of the launderette. But all she said was,

Don't worry. I'll get it done.

Aye well, you can deal with him if it's no ready in time.

Here's one finished here, Myrna called, hastily unloading the sodden clothes into a plastic basket, and whispering to Siobhan,

Never mind her, she's been Mrs Grumpy Drawers all day.

But it wasn't just today that Agnes seemed a bit frayed about the edges, and Siobhan couldn't help thinking that it had something to do with the porn-mag-behind-newspaper, frigid-old-bitch incident. That and seeing her cousin in that other magazine.

She experimented with guilt, and the feeling seemed to fit. Nothing would have happened had she not pointed out the man, had she not been looking over his shoulder in the first place. Nothing would have happened and Agnes would not have been upset. Besides, it wasn't as if Siobhan's own viewpoint was pellucid. Not a few times had she been lying in bed reading one of her rare literary novels, or even catching up with an obligatory classic, and found her hand slipping downward. Words rather than pictures, yes, but their effect was not always as Siobhan might have expected. She remembered a growing-up book she'd been given at puberty, which had told her a great deal she didn't want to know – largely through lurid diagrams of bisected male genitalia – and little she did, except that she shouldn't worry if her fantasies took disturbing twists and turns. She had comforted herself with that thought for a few years, and again more recently, after the acquisition of a bashed-up paperback de Sade in the 50p bin at Oxfam. At least it had the comfort of a somewhat arid de Beauvoir essay to salve the conscience, on instances of surprising arousal. (Siobhan hadn't travelled further with the Marquis though, finding something unpleasantly appropriate in the distinctive brown-ness generated by his prose.)

Guilt, however, and Agnes, passed from Siobhan's mind the very instant she let the launderette door slam behind her at 7.59 p.m. and rushed home. She edged into her living room in the dark, felt for the switch of the lamp nearest the door, the repro Venetian glass one with the truly old red silk shade, faded and burnt in patches, its fringes dangling in long handkerchief points. Even though the anticipation was nearly unbearable, she delayed gratification, placing her bag on the table, washing her hands, changing into her Chinese quilted dressing gown, sliding her bare feet into little beaded slippers, brushing her teeth. All the while, her bag sat there, waiting. Until she could stand it no longer – and she slid out the scrap of silk, passed it from hand to hand, admired the exquisite softness, the almost velvety creaminess of the texture. Not underwear, too frivolous. Dessous. Negligee, as if to provoke negligent behaviour, and oh, it would work. Cafe au lait with a narrow ivory trim, little triangular inserts of lace at the hip. Old-fashioned. Not just old-fashioned but actually old, Siobhan discovered as she looked more closely for a label. Totally unsuitable for machine-washing. From a secondhand shop, perhaps. Siobhan had seen wooden drawers stuffed with such undies, the finer pieces on hangers with gently padded grips, so as not to mark the nap. She always assumed that they were bought for television and theatre props, not for actual wearing. Perhaps these had belonged to Auerbach's mother, or grandmother more like, the age they must be. Twenties or thirties Siobhan guessed, but perhaps just because she could envisage them under a flapper silhouette. Auerbach might have found them at the back of a wardrobe one day, unworn for years, taken them and slipped them into her own drawer, hidden away. A change from those sensible, sporty little shorts. They couldn't belong to someone else – Siobhan felt sick at the thought – and no, it was the same scent, the same gorgeous musky aroma she felt she had known all her life.

Siobhan lay back on the bed, untied her robe and pulled it open across her chest, closed her eyes and began to imagine. Pushing that strip of silk aside, exposing, dipping then delving, with her fingers, her tongue. Tracing the curves, tickling the delicate flesh, breathing the warm seashell smell. Siobhan pressed the silk to her face. Teasing until hips moved and wetness flowed in response. She stretched the soft elastic at the waist, thought of tugging them down to reveal the pale skin and triangle of soft hair . . . and she got no further, except to think of holding the person close, as tight as she clutched the physical fabric of her fantasy to her own bare breasts, as it reached its climax.

Siobhan yawned, and stretched her legs out, trying to get her toes off the end of the bed. What a pity that she couldn't risk keeping her little souvenir. She wanted to roll the knickers up carefully and tuck them under her pillow, to be taken out and looked at whenever she liked. Instead, her alarm was set early, very early, to give her time to steep them in non-biological handwash, and treat them with a touch of extra-gentle hair conditioner. They would have time to dry, laid flat on a towel by a unseasonable radiator, before she went to work, waited until Agnes and Myrna weren't looking then slipped them back in among the vests and pillowcases, in the bag marked Auerbach.

Did The Girl notice these touches, that certain items came back lightly fragranced, pressed smooth instead of rumpled by the dryer? Swiftly, before the uneasiness set in, Siobhan rolled over and flicked the light switch. Pulling the covers up round her neck, she nestled down in the darkness, ready to sleep.

Bits of paper

On the label of the large cigar box, men in turbans shel-
tered from a bright sun under palm trees, topped by a
fancy gold seal. Agnes straightened the thick elastic band
which held it closed, and put it to one side, well aware
of its contents. Last opened to receive Donald's death
certificate, his driving licence, laid carefully on top of their
marriage, her mother's death, her own birth, signed and
stamped. Underneath that, tiny sepia clippings, announce-
ments in the BDM's for aunts and neighbours, colleagues
and friends. Condolences for her father's death, her grandmother's, those were old ones right enough, thin black-
bordered telegrams. Silly maybe, but things to be kept
nonetheless. Agnes wasn't sure when she'd become a
librarian of the paperwork of the dead, when she'd
accepted the responsibility. Little bits of paper that wrote
you into the past, delineated your history in black and
white. Bits of paper which, if she opened the box now,
might flurry and flap like a cloud of moths in her face,
trying to grab her attention, her remembrance, dissatisfied
with their fate. Agnes had seen her share of corpses – her
nan, her mother, Donald; but it was the one she had not

seen which had prompted her to create her very own book of remembrance.

Under sundry wedding menus and orders of service, receipts for desirables and bright, kitsch picture postcards from cruises to Copenhagen and Rome, right down against the lavender drawer liner which had long since lost its scent, Agnes located a pretty cover of thick paper. Familiar, faded flowers outlined in gold, like that gigantic, covetable chocolate box in the window of the Coronation Cafe, which was – she now realized – probably empty, for display only. In the centre of the cover, a raised, be-ribboned scroll on which a younger Agnes had written, in her best attempt at copperplate, *Vina*. The diminutive, her chosen moniker, had always seemed bigger than her given name, the shorter collection of letters holding the more meaning.

Vina's got a boyfriend, Vina's got a boyfriend, chants Willy, incessantly. Until, that is, his sister cuffs him across the ear, not viciously, but firm enough to quiet him. There is silence for a few steps, in which she holds his hand as if to prevent him from running off any-where to spill the beans, and rues the ill-chance that let her kid brother witness her exiting Mack's car, and the not quite peck on the cheek which went before. Asking to be dropped round the corner is not enough, it seems, though it is a measure born as much from Vina's shame at their blackened tenement as the need for discretion: although the MacIntyres are upwardly mobile, they haven't moved far from the area where Jack and Maureen were born (now known as a slum, and a scandal) and they still hang on for word of Jack's promotion, which will take them out of their soon to be condemned block.

I'm telling, Willy begins, and Vina puts her arm around his shoulders and changes tactic.

Oh come on, don't be a daftie, I was only getting a lift off of one of the guys from work.

He's got a nice car.

Has he? I never noticed. Anyway, come on and we'll go to Jaconelli's, will we? I could murder an ice cream.

Mum says I'm not allowed to eat before tea.

Mum doesn't need to know, Vina says, and over knickerbocker glories she outlines the concept of secrets, and how once established, you never, ever, let on. No matter what.

It had been a very private thing, the scrapbook. Although her mother had scanned every newspaper for mentions of Vina, Agnes knew that her own interest would be frowned upon, considered morbid. So, she had sneaked the papers from the bin, cut out the articles and pictures, pasted them carefully in her book, making sure she noted the name of the publication and the date. She kept it far under her bed, well hidden by the valance, so that she had to lie flat on her tummy and reach her arm under to retrieve it. Always with the childhood fear of grasping something nasty, yielding, flaky in the dark.

After she married, she showed it to Donald, extracting it from a new safe place at the bottom of her underwear drawer (uncharted territory, she thought, for her husband). They'd looked through it together, shared it, and she had been warmed by his acceptance, his interest. He remembered Vina, of course. Men did, and women too.

The scrapbook was unfinished, empty space stretching towards the stiff back cover. Pastel pages of pink and yellow and blue and green, each one greyed by time. Plenty of room for the *True Detective* article. And for all the articles that had never been written. Killer caught. New evidence. Another body, God forbid. Anything. Agnes went back to the beginning, flipped slowly through and watched the cuttings leap from Missing to Found.

Oh, she remembered the posters outside the paper shops that day. She hadn't noticed them on the way over to Auntie Maureen's, distracted by her mother, the unfamiliar black cab ride, on a school day as well. On the way back, every newsagent they passed had been out with the marker pens, writing up the headlines. Body of girl discovered at Barras! 18-year-old found dead! And there, before her eyes, under her fingertips, the screaming headline from the *Evening News*: VINA MURDERED!

The body of missing teenager Vina MacIntyre was last night discovered near the Barrowland Ballroom in the east end of the city. The pretty 18-year-old had been sexually assaulted, before being brutally strangled using one of her own stockings, in what a police spokesman described as, 'A particularly unpleasant case.'

A source close to police HQ said that there were certain unusual similarities with the unsolved murder last year of Aimee Gallagher, 23, an unmarried mother from the Temple area of the city, whose body was found in the Ossington Hotel, where she worked as a chambermaid. She was also strangled after being interfered with sexually. However, no firm link between the two cases has yet been established.

Vina's body was located early this morning by Michael Tannahill, a stallholder from the nearby Barras market, who had gone to look for his dog down a lane, not far from the Saracen Head public house. Tannahill, 43, said, 'I thought it was a shop dummy at first, with the blonde hair. Then I got closer and saw it was the body of a girl. It was obvious right away that foul play had been committed.'

DI John Lang assured reporters that no effort would be spared to bring the perpetrator to justice, and urged anyone with any information to come forward. 'We are especially interested in hearing from anyone who attended the dancing at the Barrowland Ballroom on the evening of Saturday 5 August, and who may have noticed Vina leaving, some time after midnight. We would also request that anyone who conversed or danced with Vina over the course of the evening come forward, so that they can be eliminated from our enquiries. Even the most trivial-seeming detail may afford us a valuable lead.'

Police were alerted to Vina's disappearance by her parents, Maureen and Jack MacIntyre, after she failed to return home last Saturday night. Today relatives and friends arrived to comfort Mrs MacIntyre at the new home the family moved into only a few months ago. Vina, who was unmarried, worked in Forsyth's department store in the town centre, where colleagues are today said to be grieving. Floral tributes have been left at the scene.

The next page, primrose yellow. Agnes flicked past the photofit released to the press, Is This the Face of a Killer?

Somebody in the city knows this man, has seen him behave suspiciously, DI Lang said, still confident of a swift result. Over the page again, and the police were no further forward in their investigations. Who killed Vina? the headline asked, its very font size giving up hope in a way that the police and Vina's family couldn't yet admit.

Mrs MacIntyre sat in her lounge yesterday, dabbing her eyes with a handkerchief, as she made her heartfelt plea to the public, 'I thought it was high jinks at first, when she didn't come home. You know how young girls can be. I never expected that this could happen, not to my Vina. If anyone out there knows anything which might help the police track down the person that took my daughter from me, please tell them, or phone them in confidence. This terrible tragedy has broken our hearts.'

After this, the search for a boyfriend, an older man, probably married, possibly a Mason. Don't be f-ing stupid, Uncle Jack said, and he should've known. A red herring, the papers agreed, after a few days. The Lodge had been a tower of strength, Frances said, loudly, for the benefit of Agnes' father, who would have nothing to do with them. Paid for the funeral, virtually, in sympathy donations from members. A Family Mourns, the paper said, above a blurred photo of Maureen and Jack ushering William into the church. Agnes had a new coat and skirt for that, and a wee hat. They weren't going to look like poor relations, not with photographers there, Frances pronounced, straightening her husband's new tie. Even if that's what they were. As for Jack, he began to go to pieces, quietly and desperately. He never said his daughter's name out loud again.

Agnes turned the next page (pale blue this time), and the headlines screamed out at her afresh. Killer strikes again! Third girl murdered! Infirmary angel died after night out, police say. Then, inexorably, each tabloid in turn picked up the refrain that would echo round the city for such a long time to come: Dancing with Death!

The new article was even brasher, with its bright colours and shiny paper. But it had its place. Agnes pasted it onto the next blank page. She thought of what Siobhan had said, and took her wedding photo down from the sideboard, rested the images alongside each other, her and Vina. Different expressions, but the same nose, the same mouth. If Vina had been allowed to age, they might not have looked so dissimilar. Agnes wondered why she'd never noticed it before. Too used to Vina being the beautiful one, by a million miles. And so she remained, an exotic, extinct insect trapped in resin, a trinket for the connoisseur of such things. Agnes wouldn't be buying *True Detective* again, she decided. Not any more.

All part of the service

Siobhan wasn't wearing a Monday morning face, Myrna noticed. She was washing the floor with something approaching enthusiasm, for one thing, and had brought in cakes for tea time. A break from value custard creams usually meant a birthday or Bank Holiday.

Can I have an early fondant fancy? I'm starving.

Sure.

A pink one?

Yep.

Thanks.

Myrna started nibbling the icing off the outside of the cake,

So, what's all this in aid of? Spectacular weekend?

Oh, no, well, okay. Quiet. Pleased to be back, really.

Fuck that. I wish I was still in bed.

Anyway, how was your big night? Saturday wasn't it?

Myrna sighed,

Okay. Nothing to write home about.

Were you out last night too? You look tired.

Christ, I hate it when people say oh you look tired, you look peaky. I'm fine, all right?

Myrna regretted this straight away. Siobhan was one of

146

those sensitive types whose faces crumpled at the slightest hint of snappiness. Only child, probably. She sighed,

Okay, I'm sorry, you're right, I'm fucking knackered. Always makes me a bit nippy. And Saturday was pish. My own fault for building it up.

That's a shame. You were really looking forward to it.

Yeah well.

Myrna shrugged. That's what she got for showing off. On Thursday, she'd come in for the back shift, flashing her department store carrier bag, proudly displaying her new pair of shoes, nestling in tissue in a chic matt brown box. She'd tried on nearly every pair in the shop, loved the expression on the assistant's face as for once she said, I'll take these, and counted cash out her wallet. She knew that Siobhan had overheard the end of a furtive phone conversation, an arrangement to collect a message before Saturday. Thought she was being impressive. Arsehole. She'd really overspent, now she'd need an extra couple of nights – who was she kidding, it could take weeks – to cover the Kurt Geiger and the coke, that treat for her friends. *Mi casa es su casa*, and all that. They'd hoovered it up fast enough. Fantastic music, good crowd, she'd not been able to stop smiling all night. Until she went to the toilet, that is, overheard Hannah and Jess in the queue.

Who does she think she is, all of a sudden?

I know. Pablo fucking Escobar or what? Must've had a lucky break somewhere.

Probably sucked the dealer off.

Aye, that'd be more like the thing.

Yeah, did you know she shagged Will?

No! Did she?

Ye-es.

Who told you that?

Martin. Will told him.

What did he say?

That they were just friends.

Yeah, because he's like, in love with Ingrid.

Is that still going on?

Yeah, totally, and don't say anything to anyone yet, but apparently she's finally going to ditch Chris and go for it.

About bloody time, I mean . . .

A cistern growled, and another voice said, there's no bog roll in that one, by the way, then Myrna heard Jess again, saying I'll come in with you, I've got hankies.

Swiftly she stuffed the last of her own private stash up her nose, licked the wrap and chucked it in the sanny bin, then hurried out without even washing her hands or checking her hair. Okay, they weren't her best friends or anything, and admittedly she might have seemed pretty full of herself, but her intentions had been good, hadn't they? She'd only wanted to reconnect with what, who was important. If only Magda had been there, she'd have shown them.

Come and visit me, Myrna my darling, she'd said, on her leaving night. You'd love it. Teach you how to surf.

Me? Surf?

Why the fuck not?

They'd spat on their palms and shaken on it, Myrna

making a promise she knew she wouldn't keep. And now Magda was back on the other side of the world, and Myrna hadn't even got herself an email address yet.

She tried to salvage the evening, but her confidence disappeared with the high. She didn't want to dance any more, and couldn't seem to break into any of the conversations that were going on around her. The prospect of queuing in bright light for her jacket was hideous, with that pair of cows scrutinizing her shiny nose and sweat-smeared eyeshadow. So she made a quick getaway, claimed she had cramp and uttered a couple of hasty goodbyes. Hannah stretched out her arms for a hug, but Myrna turned and walked away. The least she could do was add kindle to their inevitable bitching session. All part of the service.

Temporarily caught up in unpleasant reverie, it was not until after Siobhan had gone home that Myrna told Agnes what she'd seen earlier. As they were folding bedclothes, stretching the sheets out between them while the cotton was still warm from the dryer, she detected a hint of companionship, and out it came, something she needed to pass on, like in a playground game. Tig and you're it.

Saw a funeral this morning.

Agnes walked towards her, made the final fold in a double duvet and placed it in a stripy plastic laundry bag.

Did you hold your collar until you saw a black dog?

What?

Och, it was just something we used to say. Where was it then, this funeral?

Just along the road there, that house at the end of the terrace. Bedsits, I think it is. Crumbly looking.

Agnes took a Superking from the packet on the counter and lit it, inhaling so deeply it looked like half the cigarette was disappearing in one go.

That'd be old Mrs Caven. Margaret said she'd passed away at the weekend. Son's coming up from London for the funeral, I heard. Did you see him?

No. Just the undertakers carrying the coffin out.

Expensive?

Myrna thought back, shrugged,

I'm no expert. Lilies in the hearse though, loads of them.

The word hearse lingered in her mouth, as if she'd been eating nuts and got a rancid one. She didn't say that she could smell the lilies from across the road. That even now particles of pollen seemed to be stuck up her nose.

Ay the way, isn't it? Agnes said. Leave her to rot while she's alive, splash out on the trappings when she's gone.

She stubbed out her cigarette and reached into the back of the dryer to retrieve a rogue pillowcase.

Myrna felt curiously unsatisfied; she'd hoped to shake the scene from her mind. She'd been walking along, munching on a cheese and onion pasty she'd bought for breakfast. A middle-aged woman was sweeping the steps of the house, chasing small flurries of stour to and fro. Such vigorous activity in the morning, especially in pursuit of cleanliness, was unusual, and Myrna noticed it before she spotted the hearse parked across the street. Just as she got close enough to read the multiple occupancy notice posted on the railing outside, the woman scampered down the steps and stood in front of her, stopping Myrna in her tracks.

She didn't know what to do as they carried the coffin down, so she put her hands behind her back, scrunching up her pasty in its greasy paper bag, so the filling squished warmly into her palm. Taking her cue from the woman, Myrna stayed still and inclined her head slightly, not moving until the hearse door was closed and it had slowly pulled out from the kerb. She had expected the woman to say something, but she merely returned Myrna's gaze for a moment with steady eyes, nodded, then picked up her brush and went back up the steps into the house, closing the door behind her.

Direct action

Revenge wasn't sweet, Agnes decided. It was savoury and nourishing, even if it was packed with calories and cholesterol. As for best served cold, well, she thought it would reheat very nicely indeed. The only problem was, she needed an accomplice. Someone who wouldn't lose their head, which ruled Margaret out. A man would be ideal, but Agnes did not know many men, and where would she find one that was in accord with her? Someone discreet, so not Myrna. Siobhan seemed like a good choice, if only she'd agree to it. And Agnes strongly suspected she might. Sure enough, the next morning, they met early.

So, you understand what you've to do? Agnes asked.

Think so. What are you going to use?

Soapy water.

Siobhan frowned,

Doesn't seem quite right.

I thought it'd be symbolic.

Oh, I see. But what if it isn't messy enough?

Aye, you're right hen. What's the worst kind of stains we get in here?

Blood.

Something we can get though. Bugger, I should've thought of that before.

Okay, how about ketchup then? There's a bottle in the fridge.

Too thick for my skoosher.

It spurts really well from the bottle. Or you could mix it with water.

Agnes smiled, and with a gesture which surprised herself almost as much as it did Siobhan, gave her a high five.

But when she walked through the doors of the shop, she was less cocky. She smiled at the shopkeeper, went over to the magazines.

BUY BEFORE YOU READ!!!!!!!!!!!

The sign was on every shelf. Damn and blast, she was never going to get away with it now, she couldn't just stand there staring like a lemon until Siobhan came in. Buy something, leave, that was all there was for it. Agnes scanned the shelves, seeing only motoring and computing titles. Then *Knitting Monthly*, yes, that would do the trick. But then as she went to the counter the door swung open, and Siobhan almost walked straight into her, but still made a good job of saying sorry as if she'd never seen Agnes before in her life. Siobhan headed towards the back of the shop, where the gift wrap and cards were, and Agnes knew that she had to get over her fear.

Emm . . . I was wondering if I could have a wee flip through this?

She held out *Knitting Monthly*,

It's just that I saw your signs over there, but if you don't check before you buy all you get's matinee jackets and booties, and it's cable knits I'm after.

Go ahead. The signs are for the school kids, otherwise they'll spend all lunchtime in here, sticky fingers all over everything.

Thanks.

Agnes retreated, tried to leaf through the pages at a steady pace, tank tops and mittens blurring into scarves and bunnets. Maybe she shouldn't do it after all, the man had been nice enough, and he was only trying to make a living for himself. She glanced upwards, saw the cover of *Asian Babes*, changed her mind. She was going to stick to the plan. Sure enough, she heard Siobhan's voice rising in a question behind her – I can't reach the confetti, could you get it down for me please? – the scrape of the man's stool as he got up . . . Agnes whipped out her plant sprayer and went for it. Swelling silicone breasts first; then air-brushed, permatanned buttocks; super-depilated thighs and calves; red nylon crotchless panties; anything that said slut, or slag, or whore. Plastic wrap didn't deter her, it was satisfying to see the red liquid running down it regardless.

A sudden crash made her jump. Siobhan creating a diversion – sorry, sorry, I'm so clumsy, here and I'll help you pick them up – giving her time to drop her skoosher back into her bag. She called out cheerfully as she left,

Like I said, all matinee jackets and booties. Thanks anyway!

Back in the launderette, her hands shook as she lit a cigarette and waited for Siobhan.

I shouldn't have asked you to help dear. You could've got into real trouble.

Well, I didn't, so it's okay. Kind of fun, really, though I guess we won't be going back there in a hurry. Did you get what you wanted?

I don't know, to be honest, but I'm glad I did it. Thanks.

Agnes was on tenterhooks the rest of the morning, expecting that at any moment a furious shopkeeper would burst through the doors, or worse still, she'd hear the slow, measured step of the police. By lunchtime she had relaxed, indeed she felt good. There was something to be said for that kind of thing as an alternative to her herbal Kalms. She flicked through Myrna's new magazine, which also had perfect breasts and buttocks but of a different kind – how to fake it on the beach this summer. Real-life stories too, but rubbish ones, all backpacking disasters and cosmetic surgery mishaps. Agnes preferred her Schadenfreude closer to home: jealous husbands and incestuous affairs, psycho stalkers and headmasters who went out with their pupils. Excessive weight loss and weird diseases. That girl who was so allergic to her nail polish that her head swelled right up like a balloon. As long as it wasn't too crass (the woman who found her husband having it off with a frozen chicken, an image Agnes had never wanted to entertain, but which had moved into her mind and refused to leave. Imagine going public with something like that. Sheer humiliation). You had to draw the line somewhere. The stories were told from the point of view of the aggrieved party, she decided, that was the key. The dead should be allowed to rest in peace, not paraded about and exploited.

Vina stretches the fine kid glove over her hands, with their surreptitious shell pink nails, and spreads her fingers to show, open-palmed, the detail of the stitching, the closeness of the fit. He touches her right hand lightly, feeling the fabric below her thumb.

Yes, I see.

Pure chevrette, Vina explains, without moving her hand away. Also available in noir, tan, olive and port.

And this is?

Oyster.

Ah, he says, and still his hand touches hers, though he is no longer looking at the gloves she models.

Not the most practical, perhaps, Vina says, knowing it is up to her to break the contact but not doing so.

I'll take them, he says, as though this is the clincher.

In a six and a half, like this?

Yes.

Very well.

Vina withdraws her hands, swiftly removes and straightens the gloves, replaces them in their tissue-lined box.

Would you like them wrapped?

Yes. For my wife, he adds, again catching her eye.

Lucky lady, Vina says, fixing brown grosgrain

ribbon in a deft little bow over the cream monogrammed paper used by the store.

Thank you very much, he says, holding out a ten pound note but not releasing it until he has read the name badge pinned to her chest, Lavinia.

You're welcome, <u>sir</u>, she says, trying to hide her smile at the unintended insolence of her tone.

Vina finishes work an hour later, and he is waiting by the side door of the store, leaning against his car and smoking a cigarette. When he offers her a lift, she doesn't even hesitate.

I've changed my mind about the gloves, he says, pulling out into the traffic.

Too late now, Vina replies, catching sight of the bus queue where the other shop girls are waiting. You'll have to bring them back tomorrow for a refund.

I thought they looked rather well on you.

And I'm sure they'd look fine on your wife.

No, I mean it.

He reaches over and releases the catch on the glove compartment, where the package sits, waiting.

I'd like you to have them. Please.

Thanks, Vina says, with a shrug, though inside she's thinking that at £3.10.11, the gloves cost more than her best frock.

Oh for goodness sake, would you look at that? Agnes murmured, half to herself, as she turned to the beauty pages. Siobhan keeked over her shoulder, and Myrna, feeling that something was going on and not wanting to miss out, stopped what she was doing and moved closer as well. The model had a distinctive face, very pale eyes and brows, wide white cheeks, rendered even more distinctive by deep midnight blue lipstick and bright red eyeshadow.

She looks lovely, Siobhan said, quietly.

You must be crazy! Who'd do that to themselves? She's probably a pretty girl underneath.

Myrna pointed to the article,

He's famous, that make-up artist.

Gay, I expect. Not that I've got anything against them myself, live and let live, but you know what they can be like about women. Making a mockery, so it is.

Agnes stopped herself. She was getting awful bitter, she realized. It wasn't healthy.

2.57 p.m. – Malcolm

Talk about twitchy. Myrna doesn't know when she last saw someone so jumpy. He's a head scratcher and an ear tugger, a leg jiggler and a knuckle cracker. And he's called her love about twelve times already, between fidgets. Yes, very twitchy. Like this. And this. And this. Myrna's getting twitchy herself, looking at him. Her scalp prickles in sympathy, but she isn't going to give in and scratch for fear of the dandruff that's started plaguing her. She's spent a fucking fortune on salon-recommended product (hairdressers only ever use product, singular, never products). He's up again, looking out the window, swapping seats, rustling an abandoned newspaper without even reading a headline. Maybe he's got a drug problem. Or he could be one of the ones from the mental hospital. Myrna attempts a brief, experimental scratch behind her ear, checks her shoulders for snowflakes. Maybe she needs a trichologist, that might help. Oh bugger, now that bloody twitcher has gone and knocked over his fabric conditioner. Pink gunk all over the floor.

Sorry love, I'm sorry love. Sorry.

Myrna mumbles not to worry and goes for the mop.

I'll get that love, you sit down and I'll do that.

He reaches for the mop, but no, instead he kicks over the pail, and Myrna's so irritated by this point that she snaps,

Just leave it, would you?

He says he's sorry again, almost cowering, and now she feels guilty, and all because he's so cack-handed. So she succumbs, hands over the mop. He made the mess, after all, he can clear it up.

What happens to someone to make them that nervous? Unusual in a man. Plenty of women are like that, you see them every day, but men, that's rarer. She takes the mop from him, hands over a roll of industrial kitchen paper to finish the job. He kneels on the concrete in his shabby jeans and rubs and rubs until the kitchen roll starts to disintegrate and the floor will need sweeping before Agnes sees it tomorrow.

That's fine, Myrna says, repeating it so he stops.

Uncertain, he looks to her for approval, and when she smiles, he smiles.

Look, I'm having a cup of tea. Would you like one?

He looks at her as though it's a trick question, so she helps him out,

Milk and sugar?

He nods, and she turns and goes into the kitchen before he can call her love again. That's a turn-up for the books. She's never made a cup of tea for a customer before. Agnes would not be pleased if she found out. Myrna can imagine what she'd say: this is a launderette, not a soup kitchen,

I've got a business to run here. But there's a first time for everything as well. Agnes has told her to remember that often enough.

Closer

Guilty, guilty Siobhan, jumping at every noise behind her, clutching her bag to her side as though her life depended upon it. This was the worst yet, worse even than the cafe au lait silk. Because this time her intentions were worse. She was toying with the idea of keeping her prize. Even so, she told herself, a squad car was hardly going to squeal up behind her, spill the contents of her bag across the bonnet, expose her for what she had become. Not *just* a thief, no, something more than that. But there were no close-circuit cameras in the launderette, no pictures existed as evidence of her crime. Under her breath she muttered,

Be calm, be calm.

Because nobody could know, not yet, not ever. Such an inexplicable act, not just once or twice, not even three times now, but four. How could she have done such a thing? A tiny thing as well, that could fall from a grasp, slip from a bag, be kicked under a chair. And she didn't really mean to keep it, did she? No. Well, maybe, for would it really be missed? A little thing, sheer and black and flimsy. A band of lace at the top, a scallop around the hem. Narrow satin ribbons, two at each side, one pair still tied together in a bow, the others released. A vee at the back, a mere inch across of fabric on the strip that connected it to the soft cotton lining of the gusset.

As soon as she arrived home Siobhan shed her warm shoes and sticky clothes, pulled a nightie over her head, and skipped fridgewards to get herself a drink. A kir royale, made with icy cold fizz (not the real thing, her launderette wages didn't stretch that far). She was, she knew, drinking more. It went with this whole, what was it, infatuation? But in the safety of her own home, she could drink with impunity. Siobhan lingered by the window, taking in the dregs of a peach and pink sunset, one of those gaudy displays, exotic but out of place, as though it should be over a beach in Honolulu, rather than a city of sandstone and concrete. Yes, very nice, she thought, as she pulled down her blind, clicked on the switch of her silk-shaded lamp, and put Satie on the stereo. She fixed herself another drink, trembling in her eagerness, went to where her bag sat, on the chair by the door, and withdrew the little sliver of an undergarment, fragile and perfect and worn. With that, she threw her leg over the back of the couch, slid down until she was lying there, flushed with wine and excitement, ready.

Siobhan had identified different scents, the acrid sweat of a long day, the lemony tang of mid-cycle, the rusty richness at the end of a period. And her favourite, and she was lucky again this time, the ineffable sweetness of arousal. She turned onto her side, clutched her prize to her chest, wriggled onto her tummy. She imagined holding Auerbach to her, their breasts squeezing together, pushing dark hair from her face so as to kiss her, feeling the gentle tip of her tongue. Siobhan bit her own lip, envisaged The Girl inviting her to run her hands over her body, to touch her anywhere, everywhere. On her back again, Siobhan stroked the fabric across her nipples, brought it back to her face, inhaled it, stretched out her tongue and tried to capture the taste. And then downwards, her hips rising to meet it, the feel of it between her legs and finally she could delay no longer.

It really was quite something, as underwear went, Siobhan thought, untangling it and feeling her wetness grow cold on the fabric. She had never worn anything like that, had no idea how it would look. Intrigued, she went to the mirror on the bedroom door, raised her robe and held the g-string against herself. There was only one thing for it, she decided, and standing awkwardly, her gown hunched under her arms, stepped into the left leg, where the ribbons were tied. No use, she ditched the gown completely, tied and tightened the bows on her hips, wiggled to see that they were secure. The gusset pressed against her newly sated body in a way that was surprisingly intimate and pleasant. Siobhan turned to the mirror, stood and looked at herself naked but for this borrowed garment, so unlike her usual attire. She turned again, stretched, entranced suddenly by her own new, powerful sensuality. More than that. She had touched her essence, brushed against something that had been long dormant.

As ever, Siobhan chickened out of keeping her trophy, and with the washing came the shame. At midnight she found herself scrunching and scrubbing in a sink full of bubbles. Not even handwash, she'd run out of that, but shampoo, which she decided must be kinder to the skin than washing-up liquid, the alternative.

Tomorrow, with impressive sleight of hand, she knew she would get the panties from bag to sleeve, from sleeve deep into the midst of clean washing, as though they had never been away. She'd resolve never to risk it again, but wouldn't be able to contain the lovely welling sensation of having got away with it.

Safe home

Myrna, meanwhile, was picking her way across the worst foyer. The one with the shiniest, slidiest floor and the longest walk to the door. She could imagine the humiliation of falling so vividly that it sometimes jerked her eyes open just as she was easing into sleep at night. Nobody appeared at the flinty echo of her heels on those spotless, treacherous tiles, but she knew the place was not deserted. The concierge and the night receptionist were lurking somewhere behind that vast, polished wood counter, just waiting for her to crash to the ground. She looked over, checked the time in New York, Paris, Hong Kong, Sydney. In London, and here, it was nearly four in the morning. Even the grand piano that played itself, the keys moving as if by magic, was switched off. But the lateness had been worth it, she thought, in the way that she now judged such things. She'd made her money.

The doorman sprang into action, whistled for the solitary cab which was idling at the rank,

All right Walter? Myrna said, slipping a fiver into his pocket on her way past, a subtle little manoeuvre she was getting better at every time. It was worth keeping on his good side, mainly because he could, and as far as his employers were concerned, should, bar her from the premises, but also because she had a notion that he kept an eye out for her, clocked who she arrived with, when she left. Wishful thinking maybe, but still.

Goodnight madam, he said, closing the taxi door behind her with perfect deference, Safe home.

She waved as the cab pulled away, settled back, fingers itching to get her cigarettes out her bag, but unable to disobey the NO SMOKING signs pasted on the glass partition between her and the driver. Finally, in desperation, she asked,

Do you mind if I smoke?

Not my cab love, do what you want. But open the window, will you? The owner'll go mental if he smells it.

Okay. Cheers.

Myrna yanked the window down an inch, lit up and inhaled. The fastest way home was through the business area, dead but for the cold lights of a few 24-hour call centres. The perfect red light district. Flashing past, Myrna saw a young girl in a bleached denim miniskirt, pale legs absurdly spindly above high plastic sandals. She was walking briskly, for a junkie, which she almost certainly was if she was down here, but not too briskly to be looking for business. There was a world of difference between herself and this poor soul, Myrna thought, full of pity and never, not even in her mind, using the P word to describe what she did. She was an escort, that was all, her level of education and accent afforded her that way of earning a living rather than another; *a chacun son métièr*.

Myrna wouldn't have contemplated streetwalking, not in a zillion years. The idea was ludicrous. She looked down at the adverts on the back of the flip seats for the Cheapest Flights Ever!

On they went, down to the side of the river, where the reflected lights of the executive flats skimmed the dark water, and the biggest of the old shipbuilding cranes was floodlit steely blue, down past the derelict granary, jaggedly half-demolished but still monumental. Myrna turned away. It scared her, that building. The scale of it.

Riddled with rats they say, the driver commented, but she ignored him, didn't look out the window again until a flash of neon heralded their arrival on a street whose many bars were closed, but where one unconscionably drunk man was still pinballing between lampposts, bins and the metal grilles on the shop windows. Catching sight of the taxi, he straightened, gawped in, and raised a clumsy hand in salute. Nearly there, and she decided it would be a good sign, somehow, if she hadn't finished her cigarette by the time they reached her door, if she could get out and crush the dout under one elegant shoe. But the traffic lights flicked to red as they approached, the cigarette burned down to the filter, and she had to feed it through the open window, with still a full three minutes to go before she turned the key in her front door.

The shoes off first of all, and Myrna put them back in their box, carefully. Then she ran a bath, deep and scorching and softened with unguents. She could have all the hot water she wanted now she'd been able to convince (via a swift injection of cash) the electricity company to dispense with the power card. While it cooled she went and poured herself a drink, not vodka, she preferred to come home to something smoother and more welcoming, yet equally intoxicating. Armagnac usually, sometimes Benedictine, neither of which she ever drank on the job. Separation, you see, control.

She took her glass through to the living room, switched on one lamp, to warm the dimness, and hit play on the tape deck of her stereo. Her chill-out tape, that she'd compiled one lone late-night drinking session, when she'd come in from work and not wanted to go to bed, not yet. End of the evening songs, of yearning, largely, though for what exactly it didn't much matter.

Sitting cross-legged on the floor, Myrna lit another cigarette, then opened her purse and shook out the contents. Money was one of the dirtiest things around, she'd read, but then she didn't trust crisp new notes. Agnes had taught her that, with her eye for a forgery. Myrna stroked each note flat, laid them in front of her like tarot cards, looked to them for meaning. But Burns and Walter Scott had nothing to say, the queen and Mary Slessor weren't talking. No signs in the distillery, the map, the oil rig, the mouse. Nothing save her own *auri sacra fames*, accursed hunger for gold.

Myrna counted out Belinda's cut, rolled it up and stuffed it back in her wallet. Having proved her worth, she was now permitted to drop off her agency fees once a week rather than the next day.

The tape crackled to an end, and Myrna hit the rewind button, then switched off the light and left the room. It was one of her little superstitions, that she had to be in the bath before the clunk of the tape stopping. Back to the beginning, ready for next time, the time after that. She stripped off her clothes, left them on the floor to sort in the morning, turned the bedroom radio onto the World Service and, naked, padded through to the bathroom to sink into deep, luxurious bubbles of the kind you have to go to a department store to buy. The steam blurred the cracks in the ceiling, but they were still visible. One day . . . but Myrna didn't have the energy for any one-day fantasies. As long as it came, that was all, as long as that good day was coming. She smeared cream cleanser over her face, wiped it off and threw the cotton pads at the toilet bowl, missed, didn't bother to pick them up.

The way things are

Yes, well, she supposed it was only fair that the girl had a fag while she was getting herself ready. Agnes found it hard not to entertain the suspicion that Myrna was pushing it, skiving, taking advantage. It was silly, after all, the door was locked, the CLOSED sign flipped, and Agnes herself had already smoked three cigarettes to ward off the chill that crept around the premises when they were working late and the evening light faded.

You've got to make sure you've got something to show for it first, explains Vina's colleague Teresa. They work together at Forsyth's, in handkerchiefs and gloves, though they both dream of the glittering perfumery hall. Alas there's a strict hierarchy through hosiery, millinery and perhaps even costume jewellery. Teri is sanguine, despite the two years it has taken her to get down to the ground floor from napery, but it's a crying shame for Vina, she says, after all doll, you've got the looks for it.

Vina's mother is relieved. There's something fast about perfumery, and she'd rather Vina was kept away from it. Her only concern revolves around her daughter's fellow-worker, Teresa being 'that kind of name' and not knowing whether her surname is Patton with two T's or Paton with one. Not that she's a bigot, Maureen'll say (though bigotry is scarcely yet acknowledged) but she knows from experience that Catholics are not always to be trusted. It comes of there being too much God in their religion.

Oh? Vina enquires of Teresa, who is as it happens Catholic, and therefore unlikely ever to proceed to perfumery, this being a Protestant-owned store.

Aye, make sure you get a ring on your finger first.

I'm too young for all that.

Well, you don't look it. Age isn't the barrier you'd think, and there's girls younger than you ruined, and not even old enough to tie the knot. Besides, at least if you've got a ring you can sell it.

That's true, Vina says. She has no intention of tying the knot. She wants to get out into the world, to meet people, to have fun. Being ruined is a nonsense, a Victorian leftover which has no relevance to her, in this, the age of rock 'n' roll and American movies. The age of dancehalls. She is not her mother.

Myrna clattered through in her gloss tights and high shoes, all the better to topple off. Agnes thought she saw a tiny spark at her feet, from the scrape of stiletto heel on concrete.

You won't be doing much dancing in those.

Nope. Taxi restaurant taxi.

Very smart.

Thanks.

Myrna turned her ankle to show off the shape, flashed the *Made in Italy* stamped on the leather of the sole.

You should score that sole, save you sliding on shiny floors.

Yeah, maybe.

Agnes knew she was wasting her breath. She'd felt the very same way about her first pair of good sandals, scalloped edge and buckle in taupe suede. And she'd paid the price when she went flying at the Girl Guides mixed social, right in front of Frank Keenan. Not that she'd mentioned that later, when she got home and her mother inspected them for scuffs, whispered how much they'd cost and what a lucky girl she was.

Quick as quick could be, there was poor Vina, lying in the alleyway, and Mickey Tannahill (Agnes wouldn't forget his name in a hurry) chasing after his mongrel dog, as it ran off with the dead girl's shoe. They didn't say that in the papers. The other lost, though whether kept by the killer – he hadn't yet earned his nickname – or filched by Tannahill himself, they never discovered. Certainly he drank for free on tales of his find for a few weeks in the Sarry Heid, if rumours were to be believed. Beautiful Ferragamo court shoes, they had been, soft-as-butter. Vina had let Agnes touch them, to feel the quality. She'd stroked the fine leather sole, unworn, and said it felt furry, looked up at the hint of down on Vina's cheek and wondered if that felt the same. Sheer avarice, cogent and consuming. It was not until years later that she wondered how the hell an unmarried girl of Vina's age could afford a pair of shoes like that.

Myrna sat at the desk and started varnishing her nails light beige.

Shouldn't do that while you're smoking. Nail polish's flammable.

Whatever.

Myrna stubbed out her cigarette, coated her pinky nail in one smooth stroke. It used to be any excuse to get away early when she had some pressing social engagement. Not that Agnes was complaining. She wasn't so keen on locking up alone, on late nights, though she wouldn't admit it. Myrna stretched out her completed left hand, blew on the enamel.

What happened to the blues and greens and sparkles?

Guess I'm just growing up.

Oh aye. Who is he then?

Who's who?

Your hot date. Show me a girl who's changed the way she dresses and I'll show you a girl who's met a new man.

It's not that. I just fancied a change.

I'll believe you, thousands wouldn't. Well, you look very smart anyway.

Thank you.

Agnes tipped the coins from the cash box onto the desk, and tentatively, using only the pads of her fingers so as not to chip her nails, Myrna started helping count them into plastic bags.

What goes around comes around. You'll not believe me when I say I used to have a skirt like that when I was your age.

Uhuh?

Pencil skirts were in then as well. Tight, so they were, tighter than you've got on the now. Had to stand sideyways and kind of hop, to get on the tram. Ridiculous to think of it. Of course, it looks a lot nicer with proper nylons on.

Liquid stockings was it?

You may laugh. Whiffed a bit, but it worked. Eyebrow pencil down the back, a vee at the heel. You had to get a pal you trusted to do it. Lots of lassies would be walking about with wobbly seams, because their friend was getting them back for something.

But what happened when you took your clothes off, did it not look weird?

We didn't take our clothes off then.

Some people must have.

Oh well, there's always a few. But they did it with the lights out.

So how did you manage to dance in your tight skirts?

With difficulty. But we did. God, I used to work with lassies that went to the dancing seven nights a week.

Agnes didn't say that she'd wanted to, more than anything, go to the dancing seven nights a week. That when she was eighteen she still had to jump through hoops convincing her mother to allow her to stay out late on a Saturday night.

I don't know how they did it, Myrna said. Two nights out in a row and I'm done in.

What you've got to remember is that one in the morning was late opening, and most places didn't serve drink. Folk danced all night on lemonade and ice cream.

Sounds like a big kids' party.

Oh no, it was anything but that, believe you me.

I can't believe there was no alcohol at all.

Well, folk were crafty, they always are where drink's concerned. I had an uncle that would hide bottles in the cistern, he was so worried about being without a drop of whisky. Anyway, women would take hipflasks in their handbags, because they were never searched, only the men. And depending where they were, they'd sneak out to the pub for a half between dances.

Have you got another bag there for pounds?

There you go. They're like proper money, the coins, aren't they?

Yes. Doubloons or something.

Agnes turned a new coin in her hand, let it catch the light,

What does it say? *Nemo me impune lacessit.* What's that mean?

Search me. My school classics never went that far. Something about impunity?

Ach well, it sounds good, doesn't it? Any more twenties?

Nup. So what was the music like then, when you went dancing?

Oh, the bands were wonderful, real dancing tunes. I don't know how you manage when you go out and it's just someone playing records. The atmosphere they created, Billy McGregor and his Gaybirds, Dean Ford and the Gaylords.

Myrna sniggered.

Things weren't the way they are now.

Oh come on Agnes, things were always like they are now, it's just people didn't mention it.

Maybe so. Anyway, we can't sit here all night blethering. You go and put this in the safe, and I'll start pulling the shutters down. Don't want you to be late for your date.

It's not a date. Not really. Nothing serious anyway.

Well, never say never. Nice to see you enjoying yourself again.

Myrna smiled, and turned away. If only Agnes knew.

Vertigo

Escaped crumbs of dark chocolate melted into Siobhan's nightshirt as she lounged on the couch, watching television and munching her way through a tray of violet creams. A sudden blast of angry noise hit her right between the eyes, and startled, she sat bolt upright. Nobody visited her unannounced, not these days. Her first impulse was to ignore the bell – it couldn't be for her – but it sounded again, with an urgency that made her stand up. A third buzz and she lunged for the door entry handset.

Hello?

The reply was indistinct, as though it had been caught in the wind and blown past the intercom. She wondered for a second if she'd imagined it.

Siobhan?

Yes?

It's me, Myrna. Can I come up, please?

Siobhan dashed around the flat, quickly turned the television off, slid the violet creams under the couch. She caught herself in the mirror, the unflattering hang of her loose cotton nightshirt between her breasts, dived through to the bedroom, flung the shirt off and struggled into her dressing gown as she ran back to unlock the door. Why it should be unacceptable to be caught eating chocolate while watching television and looking a state she didn't know, but she was sure it was. Especially by someone like Myrna. Drawing her gown tighter round her body, Siobhan peeked out into the dim hallway, checking it was empty before she went to perch on the small occasional table on the landing, and wait for Myrna to ascend.

She waited, and waited some more, rubbing her bare feet to warm them up and looking back towards the cosy chink of light at the edge of her door. Then she remembered the stairs, and sure enough, when Siobhan peered over the balustrade into the gloom she saw Myrna. Hunched against the wall, halfway up the final flight, palms outstretched against the painted and repainted wallpaper, trying to hold on to the flat surface. The last curving sweep of a once grand staircase got narrower and steeper as it approached the upper storey. Each tread sloped downwards away from the wall, so that even Siobhan never used the banister, for fear her footfalls would be enough to tip the balance. She called out softly,

Are you okay?

Myrna, trembling slightly, swayed on her heels for a second as she looked up, saw Siobhan in her dressing gown.

I'm sorry Siobhan, you were in your bed, I'll go. Didn't know it was so late, silly of me.

No, no, it's fine, I always stay up late. Come on up.

Myrna wavered,

Vertigo. Stupid, as always.

It's okay, it's safe.

Is it?

Myrna gathered herself, scuttled up the last dozen steps. Though it had been a warm evening, she looked cold, so Siobhan quickly ushered her into the flat, switched on the gas fire and indicated the chair beside it. Myrna was wearing a long black dress with a neat jacket, sheer tights and a pair of expensive-looking pointy toed high heels with thick straps round each ankle. Siobhan had never seen her dressed up like this before. She looked good, if not like herself, though the effect was somewhat spoiled by streaky make-up around her eyes and puffy lips. Siobhan hovered for a second, wondering if she should perhaps hug Myrna, realized that her hesitation had lost her the necessary spontaneity, and instead blurted,

I'll go and make some tea.

Thinking she might have sounded a little harsh, she added,

Make yourself at home. I'll only be a minute.

Siobhan laid out a tray with milk and sugar, brewed the tea in a teapot, deliberately slowly. She should have at least patted Myrna consolingly, or got her a tissue. As if to compensate, she shook out some Happy Faces onto a plate, hoped their little grins looked cheerful but not flippant. She tried to exude a calm normalcy, as she dropped down and sat on the rug by Myrna's feet, now minus the heels, which were bundled to the side. Myrna wiggled her toes,

Hope you don't mind. They were hurting a bit.

No, it's fine. Best to be comfy.

Bit of an obstacle course to get here, what with those stairs and that pair on the doorstep.

What?

You know, the Egyptian chicks. The spooky belly dancers out the front.

Caryatids.

Yep, I couldn't get the word there.

I've got used to them now. Funny, they were one of the things that attracted me to the place. Always meant to look up the architect.

An entrance to entrance, she'd thought at the time. Eerie in the dark though, Myrna was right. Siobhan would never have confessed to it, but she used a password, whispered it every time she stepped across the marble doorstep. *Pace tua.* By your leave. It had worked so far.

Myrna raised her cup to her lips, felt the heat and put it back down again.

I don't suppose you've got anything to drink in the house, do you? I could do with a straightener.

Would you like a cocktail?

What kind of cocktail?

Oh, I've got a couple of things, Siobhan said, non-committally. She felt rather embarrassed suddenly, nodding towards the corner of the room, and a small fifties' bar in the shape of a ship's prow. The first hint of a smile showed on Myrna's face, as she raised her hand in a naval salute,

Anchors a-weigh then bo'sun, ready to set sail.

Siobhan hurried through to the kitchen, found an almost past-it lime in the fruit bowl and pared off a couple of twists of peel. Bit clumsy, but never mind. Over at the bar, she reached for the vodka and triple sec. As she didn't entertain, there was little point in stocking up on gallons of booze, but she tended to have the makings of a Cosmopolitan at least. She hoped that she looked assured, cool even, as she shook the ingredients together, but it changed things, having someone from outside suddenly within. Made her struggle to avoid looking at her house, her life, from another angle. She was surprised Myrna had even remembered where she lived, it had been weeks ago that they'd talked about it. Siobhan returned to her spot on the rug, and poured the drinks.

Do you mind if I smoke? Myrna asked. Whatever it was, Siobhan thought, it was coming now. Rows with boyfriends, pregnancy, money trouble; all had flitted through her mind. But what Myrna did confide was altogether unexpected, and rather unpleasant. Siobhan had no moral objection to Myrna's new line of work; indeed she found it hard to dismiss from her mind the dirty glamour of Bijou the whore, and all the other ladies of the *maisons close* introduced to her though the art book and the French novel. Ladies with whom Siobhan had spent many languid evenings, reclining on red velvet divans, indulging in philosophical discussion and comforting kisses. Tarnished images perhaps, but if confined to the realm of the imagination, they could polish up as bright as you liked. Clients, however, had little or no place in the tableaux. And certainly not businessmen called Matthew, who didn't pay for their pleasure.

What did you do? Siobhan asked.

What could I do? It's not like I can go and see my union rep.

But he might have become dangerous. Violent.

No, I mean, we're in fancy hotels, not up some alley in a Mondeo. Besides, the clients, well, they might be sad fucks but they're not psychos.

How do you know?

Well, that's why they do it this way. Properly. With an agency and everything. And you get paid more, except for this guy, fucking tight bastard that he was. Do you know how much he tipped me?

No.

A tenner. A measly ten fucking quid for a night of smiling 'til my face ached and drinking the cheapest wine on the list, then an extended guilt trip about not letting him carry on up the Khyber. It's an outrage, I tell you. The waitress that served us probably took home more than that, and at least she could kick the chef in the 'nads if he tried it on.

Maybe he made a mistake, did you mention it?

Siobhan felt very naive asking this. As soon as it was out she realized it was a silly thing to say.

No, I just wanted to get out of there.

Do you want another drink?

Yes please.

Siobhan got up and topped up their glasses. Myrna

gulped hers down in one, sighed and wiped her mouth on the back of her hand, then said,

It wasn't quite like that.

No.

I didn't leave, he put me out. I said I wouldn't do it, you know, so he shoved me out the door before I'd even got my jacket on.

Did he . . . hurt you?

Myrna shook her head.

I suppose I should be thankful. He threw the money at me, a handful of change, so that I had to scrabble about the corridor floor for it, in front of him. I should have left it.

Myrna hardened, visibly. Siobhan hesitated then said, It's natural that you would want to get the money. I mean, that's why you do it. Not for the good of your health.

He said it was more than I was worth.

That's stupid. And not true.

Well, I should still have left it. Shown some pride. But I didn't, I picked it up. I should have spat on him.

Has anything like this happened before?

No. It's been okay. Is there any drink left?

Yes, here you go.

What about you?

I'm okay, I'll make another batch in a minute.

Are you sure you don't mind me being here?

It's fine. Don't worry.

I just didn't know where else to go. Nobody knows, about the job. I don't want anybody to know.

Siobhan nodded. She wouldn't tell anyone, that was true. Myrna reached for a Happy Face, smiled at Siobhan as she scattered crumbs down the front of her dress.

Mmm, these are good. Haven't had them in years. Oh God, why am I so stupid? I can still smell his stinking bloody aftershave, some cheap shite.

Would you like to have a shower? Or the water might be warm enough for a bath?

Thanks, but I suppose I should get home.

Look, why don't you stay over? I'll make up a bed on the couch. It's no problem.

Really?

Really.

Siobhan smiled.

There are good bits, you know, Myrna said.

Uhuh?

The money, usually. Going to the bank. You saw what I used to be like when I had to go to the bank at lunchtime. I'd come back in a right strop, ranting about whatever it was they'd done or said this time.

Yes.

And have you seen me do that lately?

No.

Exactly. Now, I'm handing over bundles of notes to the very same snotty-nosed cows who used to tell me, we're very sorry Miss Prior but given your record the bank can't really see it's way to another overdraft extension.

I can see that would be satisfying.

You're damn right it is. There's this one in particular, told her I was a Ms about twenty times, thinking she might as well call me by the right name when she was telling me where to go . . . anyhow, the other day I told her less than the amount I was paying in, so when she counted it she had to say, actually that's three hundred and fifty Ms Prior. I'm a Ms now all right, and she's still stuck there sweating in her cheap nylon uniform. That sounds terrible, doesn't it? Makes me sound like a real bitch.

No.

I'd left there in tears, more than once, after talking to her. Not any longer.

That's good.

Yes, it is, isn't it? My credit rating's still crap, can't even get a fucking contract for my mobile, but things've changed. And it's not forever. Just for a little while.

Myrna yawned.

Sorry. Would it be okay if I have that shower after all?

Siobhan made up the bed while Myrna was in the bathroom. When she came back through with wet hair and no make-up, in her borrowed nightshirt, she looked both younger and older at the same time. All the try hard sophistication of her outfit had vanished, but the faint smoker's lines had reappeared on her face.

Siobhan?

Uhuh?

Thanks.

Siobhan succumbed to Myrna's hug, patted her awkwardly on the shoulders,

Goodnight.

Sleep tight, Myrna called after her, as she left the room.

Siobhan lay in bed, quiet and still. She hoped Myrna was asleep, felt mildly unsettled by the presence of another person in her house. When was the last time someone had stayed overnight? Two years ago, maybe more. Not something she wanted to remember, the next day awkwardness, the accepting of a phone number she knew she'd never call.

This sensation, an inability to settle, to relax, she'd had it a few times now, and wasn't sure how to trace it back. The night out, helping Agnes, meeting Auerbach? (Even thinking her name felt like being held.) Something had crept into Siobhan's consciousness, and lodged there, ready to lay eggs and breed. For the first time in ages, she felt like talking to someone, not about anything in particular, just talking for the sake of communicating. She'd seen these adverts for phone lines you could ring up to chat to people, assumed to do so would be silly, and sad. But maybe not; there were different ones, for talking to particular kinds of people. Men talking to women, men talking to men. Women talking to women. Maybe it would be interesting. Siobhan sighed. She knew she wouldn't try the phone lines.

There was another option though, one she'd thought of before, vaguely. If she could get a computer, she would be able to visit chatrooms on the internet. Silent communication:

no unpleasant voices, no need to reveal yourself. She could even, should she feel the urge, have virtual sex.

When she went to the library she sometimes paid for time online. Once, not so long ago, she'd looked up the history to try and get back to the site she'd started at. One of the URLs visited by a previous user caught her eye, and after a quick glance over each shoulder to check she wasn't observed, Siobhan clicked on it, apprehensive but curious. The site itself didn't look tacky, as she had feared, nor was it overtly pornographic; she certainly didn't want to be caught viewing anything of that nature, after once seeing an elderly man reprimanded by the librarians. A harmless fellow of the sort that might be referred to as gentlemanly, he'd been extremely apologetic to the woman who asked him to leave, saying he didn't mean any offence by it.

You see dear, it's the closest I get these days, he'd confided, as he picked up his hat and walking stick and prepared to go.

But Siobhan was only reading text, there was, surely, a difference. No one was close enough to see what it said, which turned out to be just as well, as what it said was quite an eye-opener. Siobhan wondered who had been on the computer before, who had known about this site. Had even, possibly, contributed to it. She scanned the names of the people who had been engaged in conversation, the times they had posted their messages, the last only a few minutes beforehand. Siobhan furtively glanced round the library, trying to spot likely candidates, wondering if a young mum in a floral skirt, pushing a toddler in a buggy, might have an alter ego as a dominant butch. Or might an Afro-ed chap with a stack of Len Deightons like nothing more than a spot of gentle vanilla? Suddenly a floating window appeared, a tough-looking girl with parted, wet-look lips invited Siobhan to another site, where all major credit cards were accepted. A banner ran along the bottom of the screen, flashing letters screaming GIRLS! GIRLS! GIRLS! Some were Explicit! Others Naked! All were Dirty! Not to mention Sexy! Especially when they wore Leather! Siobhan manoeuvred the mouse, frantically clicking, but the windows remained even after she'd shut down the browser. As soon as she got rid of the GIRLS!, they were replaced by MEN! In desperation she hit the off button, and breathed a sigh of relief, before grabbing her books and scurrying out of the library as fast as she could.

Still, the words she had read stayed with her, and she sometimes revisited them, making up pictures of her own.

A temporary aberration

Myrna was subdued. Agnes saw her pausing in the middle of tasks, and Siobhan noticed that at break-time her tea would get cold or her cigarette burn down in the ashtray. When Myrna became aware of this, she'd leap up and empty the cup, or catch the last draw of the fag, as though in doing so she'd succeeded in making a tricky decision, and was going to stick to her guns no matter what anybody said. Twice in the past week Siobhan had asked if she was feeling okay, and even Agnes had said that she didn't seem her usual self, whatever that was supposed to mean.

And now today, a day off, the kind of empty day she used to adore, and Myrna felt at a loose end. Before she might have spent time with friends. Having coffees with the girls, setting the world to rights. Shopping for that tight top, those low-slung trousers, and most of all, the shoes. Something patent, something with heels, a t-bar or peep toe, a bright colour or fancy detail. Getting the dip dye, the lowlights, the asymmetric fringe. Rifling through vinyl alongside the boys with the record bags, making sure she had the right tunes to put on when people came back to hers in the wee small hours. Taking half an hour to decide which pair of trainers and oh-this-old-thing to put on to go scruffy to the pub for that afternoon beer or six. Proving to nobody in particular that she was one of them, whilst acting like she had nothing to prove. In with the in-crowd. She remembered that it had been fun, enough to feel the lack of it, but she couldn't quite recall what had made it so.

It was Saturday, that was the problem. Myrna dreaded having Saturday off most of all. Hated avoiding the obligation to do something with her day. Of course, she didn't entertain the notion that she might miss the launderette, that disliking the nature of the work or having a run-in with Aggie were part of a constant. Reassuring and reliable, like Siobhan, the only person she'd told about her other job. Siobhan, who was a safety net of sorts, but one Myrna was afraid would dissolve were she not to see her at work. It had been weak of her to turn up at Siobhan's door that time, in the middle of the night. Lurking underneath this thought was the awareness that she only did so because she didn't know where else to go, because she was too embarrassed to go to one of her friends. Myrna couldn't predict the reactions of people she thought she'd been close to, if she was to tell them just how far from them she'd grown. This was meant to have been a temporary aberration; a month or two and then she was supposed to be able to slot back into her social niche. And everything would be back to normal again.

If she did venture out, Myrna avoided all her old haunts, ducked into shops if she spotted a familiar figure in the distance, hid behind greetings card racks and deodorant displays until the coast was clear. Today though, she'd spent all day at home. Sleeping until two, soaking in the bath, watching TV in her dressing gown, pondering whether it was too early to open a bottle of wine, settling back into melancholia as if it were a squashy old chair, moulded over the years to fit the shape of her body.

Until Belinda phoned.

Myrna realized that this was what she'd been hoping for all day. The dead zone, those hellish hours between five and seven thirty, suddenly transformed into time to get ready. She livened up, started practising her smile as she painted on her face. A nip of vodka, that didn't smell or make her cheeks flush too red (Stoly now, none of your supermarket own brand shite), and she contemplated her wardrobe. Proper clothes, grown-up clothes that you did-n't have to cut the label out of in case anyone saw. She'd let it get about that the wolf was licking at her door, that she'd had to take a job in a 24-hour call centre. Shift work, telephone banking. She encouraged the rhyming slang, thinking that joking about sex lines would build her cover, ease her excuses.

A quick toot before she went out the door, that was the boy, just the ticket. Tickety boo. And one song, a dancing one. Stevie Wonder. Superstition. Her song. Four minutes twenty-six seconds to enjoy the high, and she walked out to her minicab feeling like a million dollars, hoping against hope to clear a ton. Belinda had recommended a car firm that was discreet. Run by the right people. The driver didn't make small talk, which Myrna appreciated, listening instead to the Islamic radio station. It was playing music, a good sign, she thought. Praying made her jumpy. Regardless, she always tipped.

When she got up the next morning – and it was only her shift at the launderette that made her leave her bed – Myrna felt heavy and tired. As if her flesh and skin were hanging off her bones, her face slumping, no blood flow or muscle tone to animate her. It would be better if it all sloughed off, dropped into a slobbery mess at her feet, exposing the shiny, clean skeleton at her core. But she had to go to work, couldn't let Agnes down. Sunday shifts were okay, the late start made it a nice length of day, and at least she could be rude to the customers or slink off for a cup of tea and a fag every now and then. She imagined trying this with Belinda's clients,

Okay, that's me off for my tea break. See you in fifteen minutes.

As she was dabbing concealer around her nose, she heard her mobile bleep with a text:

fuckin rtn my calls for once ya bitch x x x mags

Her finger hovered over reply. She didn't know whether to imagine Magda just in from a night out, or lying on the beach, so instead she deleted the message and went back to her make-up, leaving her eyes naked but adding a smear of lipstick. She caked it on so much at night that she couldn't be bothered during the day any more. Just as she was tying the laces on her trainers her phone started ringing. Magda probably, she thought, guilty, but not to the extent that she was going to answer it. The last thing Myrna wanted to hear about was someone else's happiness. When she looked at the display though, it was Belinda's name it announced. She wasn't in the mood for working again tonight, but she picked up anyway.

She remembered that she'd thought that the job would be a breeze, because men would be too embarrassed to ask for sex. If she didn't bring up the subject, then they'd have their nice night out, and she'd still be raking in the tips. How wrong could you be? She should have known that the same would apply as in any other service industry. Give someone an inkling of power, and they'll run with it. It hadn't occurred to Myrna before how perfectly suited to hatred the sex act was.

That's my girl, Belinda was purring down the phone. See, you're like me, you can't resist a challenge.

No Belinda, I'm not like you, and if I thought I was, I'd top myself right now. Shove the job up your arse, or better still, you go out and work for a change.

Myrna didn't say this out loud. Instead she wrote down the details and said she'd be fine. She knew the ropes now, knew what got the money out the wallets. It was only after she'd hung up that she thought to wonder what exactly Belinda meant by a challenge.

Green eyes

The girl rushed into the launderette, wet top in hand, adamant that she must be allowed to use the dryers even though two large signs stated unequivocally that there would be NO DRYING UNLESS MACHINES ARE USED FIRST. It was the same in every launderette, a strict rule, but the girl had been so bloody persistent that Myrna called upon Agnes for back-up. Then wished she hadn't as Agnes, unusually, was sympathetic,

Well dear, when the shop's quiet there's no reason why the dryers can't be used without the machines . . . no, wait a minute before you get too excited . . . it'd be no use anyhow hen. Just sticks to the side if there's only the one thing. No matter how much money you put in it, it won't dry.

But I want to wear this top tonight, I need it to be dry in time.

Myrna rolled her eyes at Siobhan, finding herself deeply irritated by the girl. She was wearing a vest, for one thing, which exposed her midriff. And it wasn't exactly a scorcher outside. That wasn't sufficient reason to dislike her of course, but add on the annoying voice . . . Myrna had discovered that as she got older her awareness of those who were younger had become keener, as had her intolerance.

It went along with finding lines on her own face, subtly etching their way in around her mouth, under her eyes, exploiting the barely perceptible loss of elasticity in her skin. She wasn't quite thirty, for fuck's sake, and she used moisturizer. Expensive stuff as well. If only she could get away with nicking it, like she and her pals used to nick roll-on lip gloss from Boots, but those women at the cosmetics counters were like Rhodesian ridgebacks in blusher, guarding their rows of cellophane-wrapped, gold-embossed beauty.

Well, maybe just this once we could stick it in to dry with one of the service washes.

How long will that take?

Agnes reached out and rubbed the fabric between her fingers,

No time. Ten minutes, maximum.

The girl got out her purse, pulled out a note as though she seriously thought it could cost a fiver to get a top dried,

Thanks, thanks so much, you've saved my life! How much will that be?

No, dear, don't worry about it this time. Dryer's on anyway.

She took the girl's top and went to tug open the door of the tumble dryer. Siobhan watched dismayed, then before she could stop herself screeched,

Not that one!

Agnes turned and looked at her, astonished,

How not?

Myrna had no idea what was up with Siobhan, though she had viciously dark circles under her eyes and had been clumsy all day. Myrna knew that feeling herself – if not the reason for Siobhan's outburst – so she decided to come to her rescue,

Dye was running like crazy, and it'll still be wet. It'd get stained to buggery in there. Give me it, I've got another load on over here.

As she passed Siobhan she whispered,

Dogs' blankets. I practically boiled them but they're still hairy. And you should have smelt them when they came out the bag. Vile.

Thanks, Siobhan said, hovering by Myrna's side, as if standing up in class, waiting to be asked what nine sevens were.

Don't mention it.

Myrna walked away, didn't ask. She had enough on her plate without Siobhan going weird on her, and if she didn't want to explain herself, that was fine. Maybe it was her own clothes in the machine. Perhaps she had one of those obsessive compulsive things; someone else's top might have contaminated her washing. Her house had been pretty neat and tidy. Myrna hated housework, thought it a waste of time and effort, especially in a rented flat, already irrevocably imbued with the dirt of previous tenants. The best solution would be to move, and one day she would, somewhere clean and fresh that she could furnish from Ikea.

By tea break time she'd completely forgotten about the girl and her top, and although Siobhan hadn't, she was too tired to worry what Myrna might be thinking.

You look shagged out. Late night?

You wouldn't believe it, Siobhan sighed.

Oh aye? Try me.

One of my neighbours died.

What? I thought you were going to say you'd pulled.

No.

Sorry. It must've been upsetting.

Well, I didn't know her that well, but I am sorry she's dead, of course.

Myrna was amazed Siobhan could be so matter of fact about it. She wasn't sure what to say.

So what happened?

Well, there I was, reading my book, quite happy, when there was this knock at the door, and it was one of the downstairs neighbours, Miss Samuel, all in black with a hat on. I thought she was about to tell me something nuts about UFOs or elves or something. But the other neighbours were having what they called the sitting-up, and she asked if I'd go.

All night?

Yes. Drinking tea and eating cakes.

What, with the body there as well?

Yes.

God that's weird.

Siobhan smiled,

Yes. You're right. It is weird.

I'd never have done it. Yek. I'd have made any excuse. I'm allergic to death.

I didn't see how I could've got out of it. At six they took pity on me and said I could go to bed. So I did get to sleep for an hour or so.

Siobhan yawned, then added,

The cakes were good, mind you.

Myrna looked askance,

Tell me you're joking.

No, they were home-made.

I've told you before, you should get out more.

I know. Something's not right when the latest night you've had in ages is spent in the company of two elderly spinsters, a widow and a corpse.

Oh, stop talking about the corpse, please. Didn't they ask your other neighbours?

No, just me, because I've been there for a while. And it used to be a rooming house for women, apparently, so they didn't want to ask any men. Miss Samuel's lived there for decades. Bit of a wake-up call for me, the whole thing.

Metanoia time.

Eh?

Greek. A change of mind or heart.

Oh.

Mine of useless information, me. On the subject of which, did you hold your collar until you saw a black dog?

Didn't have to. That's just for funerals, or hearses. Can't remember.

But you've heard of it?

Yes, of course.

Damn.

Myrna wished that she hadn't asked. It soured the rest of the day for her, all this talk of death.

These little inexplicables

Siobhan lay in bed, squirming in anticipation of a day inundant with possibility. Wide awake, despite an erratic sleep, she forced herself to wait for the alarm, altisonant triangles in sharp grey, bleep bleep bleep, then swung her legs round and stretched as she got out of bed, as though she was trying to touch the ceiling. Being up early suited her, she decided, singing wordlessly to herself in the shower. She'd already laid out her clothes, spoils of a shopping expedition on Tuesday morning, when, Myrna had assured her, the shops were quietest. Aware that some stores played loud music, Siobhan had wedged her earplugs in firmly. The assistants, deciding her tardy responses to their offers of help were due to a hearing impairment, were extra pleasant. Siobhan returned with new tops, trousers, a shortish skirt and a pair of patterned tights to go with it (she wasn't quite ready for bare legs yet).

But for today, jeans, in the softest, darkest distressed denim she could find, and a fitted cowgirl shirt with mother of pearl studs. Her new bra, plain black and sheer, hung over the arm of her chair. And there, on top, a perfect match, the *pièce de résistance*. She picked them up, raised them to her nose, inhaled the warm, light blue scent of washing powder. She'd been tempted not to wash them, very, but it made sense that they should come to her fresh, as they did to their owner.

Breakfast first, a crucial ten minutes before the act. Siobhan made toast, spread it thickly with lemon curd, hoping to calm her butterflying stomach, and sat at the little folding table in her kitchen to eat it. She always bought Hovis bread, because she liked to walk past the factory and look up through dirty windows at the huge mixing vats. It wasn't often she got to see such intense movement, with the volume turned off. If she was actually in the building, the noise, she was sure, would be blinding. She imagined being lowered gently into the warm, light dough, and shoogled in one of these vats. Lovely on the skin, it would be, oozing between toes, sucking on the softer flesh like quicksand. Better still, what if Auerbach were to do it, if she could eat bread made from dough which had wrapped itself round every inch of her abstracted lover's body, feel it sinking down into her tummy. If that was her breakfast every day, anything might become possible. Siobhan allowed herself to imagine a link stretching between herself and Auerbach, an unconscious pathway along which nerve impulses could travel . . . then she jumped up, and went to get dressed.

She descended the slanting stairs, slowly for once, feeling as if for the first time how a foot could slip, a heel catch on a threadbare tread. Halfway down she heard a crackle, then a bright lingering ting like a fingernail testing the quality of glassware. A flashing downwards in the corner of her eye, and she skipped to the outside of the staircase, her palm outstretched in perfect time to grasp one pendant of dusty crystal. Wiped against her sleeve it looked as fresh as if just removed from a bowl of vinegar by an industrious housemaid. Siobhan paused, watched the newly free strand of the chandelier swing slowly to and fro, but no more crystals were forthcoming. She moved on, tucking the pendant away, a good luck charm snug in the pocket of her virgin denims.

On the walk to work she was unfazed by a street sweeper, merely crossed the road to avoid it, where, looking down, she saw a ten-pound note at her feet, slightly the worse for wear but serviceable nonetheless. She made an impulsive detour to visit the flower stall on the main road, blew it on freesia and gerbera in the gaudiest colours she could find. The woman threw in an extra bunch for luck, saying it wasn't often she saw such a nice smile so early in the morning. It had been years since anyone had mentioned Siobhan's smile, although it had been lurking around her face all along, like the shy animal at the zoo that frustrates children and parents alike.

Oh hen, you shouldn't have, Agnes tutted when she saw the flowers. Waste of good money. But I'm glad that you did. Really brightens the place up, and the smell of them's lovely. Takes me back. I had freesia in my bouquet when I got married.

They're pretty, aren't they?

Well, I always thought I'd have orchids, but then, I

always thought I'd marry a man who was well off. One minute you're dreaming of a white wedding, the next you're traipsing down the aisle in a dark suit from Lewis's. The mink collar was detachable, mind, so I got the use out of it.

Siobhan launched herself into her work, channelling her simmering energy into loading and unloading the machines, until she was flushed and moist with sweat. As if her body was demanding to be used, to exert itself, to dance. It was a long time since she'd been dancing, anywhere apart from round her living room, late at night.

When Myrna arrived for her shift at eleven, she did a double take as she passed, noticed that Siobhan wasn't wearing her tabard for once.

Someone got out of bed on the right side this morning. Or was there someone else in it with you?

Do you have to be so crude? Agnes asked.

Just feeling happy, that's all, Siobhan said.

Ah, new outfit high, I see. Very nice. And is that lipstick I see on your face, young lady?

I was just . . . experimenting.

Shameless.

Oh stop teasing her, Agnes said. It's about time we saw her out of those saggy old cords and jumpers. And look at the flowers she brought in.

Myrna looked, shivered slightly,

I'm not a big fan of cut flowers, they give me the heebie-jeebies. I'd rather a proper living plant anyday.

I'll get one next time, Siobhan said.

Deal. And I wasn't teasing, by the way. You are looking good. Keep it up.

Thanks.

Oh bugger, not again, Myrna said, suddenly, and ducked behind the big washers. She whispered over to Siobhan,

I'm not here.

What?

Guy that's about to come in. Tell him I've left, anything, I don't care.

With that, Myrna skulked through the back, looking, Siobhan thought, like nothing so much as a fussy cat who'd been presented with tinned food instead of sardines. She fastened a stud which had popped on her new shirt, and started rummaging through the desk drawer, searching industriously for nothing in particular.

Excuse me.

Siobhan looked up.

Does Myrna still work here?

Yes, she does – maybe best to hedge her bets – well, she did.

He smiled,

Either she does or she doesn't. Don't worry, I'm a friend of hers. Will.

Oh, hello. The thing is, I'm not sure if she still works here.

Oh.

Oh my God, Siobhan thought, why's he looking at me like that? There was definitely something awry in the way he was trying to hold her gaze. Was it possible that he was flirting with her? She adopted a sterner tone, felt her voice deepen.

She had to take some time off. We're not sure when, or if, she's coming back.

Is there anything wrong?

I think she said there were family problems. She's been running about all over the place, Siobhan added, with a vague gesture of her hand that could have meant Myrna had been running to the end of the road or to the other side of the world.

I see. I was just passing by, thought she might fancy grabbing a quick coffee. Haven't seen her in ages, as it happens.

Have you tried phoning her?

No. I'll maybe give her a ring then. She's not been out and about for a while. You think she's okay though?

Maybe she should tell him that she didn't think Myrna was okay, that she thought she needed help. Myrna would be furious, but it might be the right thing to do. But Siobhan hadn't entirely taken to Will, and she had no idea how well he knew Myrna, what good he could possibly do. Instead, she smiled, tried to make it more convincing when she said,

She seemed fine, last time I saw her.

That's good. Well, if she does come back, could you tell her I was in looking for her? Hannah, you know Hannah? – Siobhan shook her head – Well, it's her birthday on Saturday and we're all going out, if she wanted to come.

Not like Myrna to miss a party. Or she could give me a call, when she gets a chance. I think she's got my number.

Sure.

Okay, thanks. See you . . . sorry, I didn't catch your name?

I didn't tell you my name.

Will you tell me it now?

Siobhan.

Well, Siobhan, if you fancy going out on Saturday, it'd be nice to see you again.

Thanks, but I'm busy.

Maybe next week then?

Saturdays aren't good for me.

It doesn't have to be a Saturday.

Thanks, but actually, men aren't good for me.

He held up his hands in exaggerated apology, then looked more closely at her, as though she was a specimen hitherto lacking in his collection,

Hey, no problem. You will tell Myrna that I was asking for her, won't you?

Yes. If I see her. You should phone.

Yeah. See you later.

Siobhan turned back to her open drawer, continued rummaging until he was out of sight. She couldn't believe it – she had been asked out, and she had said she was a lesbian, well, almost (it was just the word she didn't like, it seemed so . . . slithery). All on the first day she had worn Auerbach's clothes. Maybe it wasn't out of the question that she should speak to her. Myrna had blethered away with her quite the thing, what was to say Siobhan couldn't? As long as she was dressed for it. Something old, something new, and of course, something borrowed, to give her the confidence to see it through. No, it wouldn't work, it couldn't, could it? Siobhan hurried through the back to fill Myrna in on Will's visit, but decided to leave out the last part of their conversation. Even with that omission, Myrna didn't seem impressed.

He's got my number, and he knows where I live. But I guess he's allergic to phones. And doorbells. A condition associated with the Y chromosome.

He did seem concerned. Genuinely.

Siobhan realized that things billed as genuine were usually anything but, and felt she was being a bit unfair on Will. He had invited her out, and she was flattered, in a theoretical way, even if such a night was utterly beyond her comprehension.

Maybe you should get in touch.

Yeah well, I'll see. He had that look about him, as if his on–off with bloody Ingrid has gone off again, and he's looking for a bit of comfort and joy. Well, he came to the wrong place.

Yes.

Thanks Siobhan. I owe you one. Another one. Just put it on my tab.

Hey, it's not a problem.

Siobhan volunteered to wipe down the machines, eager to keep occupied, and pondered further whether she might be considered attractive. She felt as though she was putting one foot, lightly, on a tight rope. Once she started tiptoeing across, there would be no turning back, and a very real danger of losing her balance, falling down, head over heels. She remembered, suddenly, the day she went eastwards to see the exhibition of Breitenbach photos. One image in particular caught her imagination: two actresses with ravaged, beautiful faces and marcelled hair. She could well imagine them sinking absinthes in the cafes, before moving on to the dirty opulence of some secret hashish den. Turkish coffee and a Pernod for breakfast, make-up over the dark shadows under their eyes and off to an audition. Theatre rather than film, red and gold rococo grandeur with dusty curtains and torn velour, scuffs on the walls as you climbed the twisting stairs to the cheap seats. Actresses with no starring roles, but plenty of gentlemen callers bribing their way to the shared dressing room after the show. Siobhan had stood in front of that picture for longer than all the others.

And then, on the train back, a man had tried to impress her. On his way home from work, racing through reams of Very Important Papers before he reached his stop, shredding anything he didn't need. From his case he'd taken out something small, silver and electronic, and a little pointer thing with which he made quick, definite pokes at the screen. Then, as the train approached one of the wife/kids/two-car garage commuter towns, he got out his keys with a flourish, the keyring logo showing. Completely wasted on Siobhan, who had no interest in cars. But the thing that got her, the final thing, was that just before he got up he whisked a hanky out his pocket and put it in the bin. A proper cloth handkerchief. Blue cotton. As if to say, look, I can afford to treat this as disposable. Siobhan always used cloth hankies, and she knew they lasted a lifetime, more. She had ones that must've been fifty years old, and still perfectly serviceable for nose-blowing. It was an appealing idea that lots of other people might have laughed and cried into the same piece of cloth, though she took care to wash them thoroughly. When the man was gone, she looked behind her to see if there was anyone else sitting nearby. It came as a strange realization that he had been showing off to her; Siobhan had never envisaged herself as that kind of woman.

And then, that same day, in the bleaker landscape, she'd seen another man, this one standing on top of an old bing, stretching in the spring sunshine. He was wearing a black and white tracksuit top and jeans, and she wondered why he had chosen to climb the bing rather than a hill. In the second before the train whizzed past, she had time to think that maybe he was about to commit suicide, to topple and tumble and roll down the scree. Of course, she never found out, and he had probably just been enjoying the view. These little inexplicables stayed with her, and she couldn't help wondering.

Night time

Agnes didn't look forward to going to bed these days. She procrastinated. Already tonight she'd decided to clean the oven (though it was only three days since she'd done it last), and watch the late news bulletin on the television (though how much had the world changed since teatime?). Now she was thinking that maybe she should start on those trousers that needed hemming for that man, although he wasn't collecting them until Thursday. Don't be stupid, she told herself, you're tired, you'll botch it. A hot drink, that might help. Hot milk, she hadn't had that in years. When she reached for the honey to sweeten it, tucked behind the jar was a framed photo of her and Donald, which had been on top of the fridge until she became sick of looking at it and hid it away in the cupboard.

They'd had it taken at the Palais, the photo. Agnes wet her finger with spit, rubbed at a blob of honey stuck to the glass, obscuring her hair. A few men covered the dancehalls between them, approaching the courting couples, offering them a souvenir of their special evening. You knew how serious someone was about you when they paid their money, copied down your address so the picture could get sent out when it was ready. Donald stood there, upright in his suit, single-breasted with three buttons. Always smart, clothes made to measure by Norrie Fraser, cheaper than the big stores but still the good Italian fabrics. Hair brushed to the right, just a hint of brilliant on it. Agnes shut her eyes, and yes, she could conjure up the smell of it, though Donald had stopped using it many years before. One arm resting lightly around her shoulders, the other held outwards, perhaps in an attempt to keep his Embassy tipped out of shot. He never smiled in photos, because he had a squint tooth, though Agnes had thought it charming, and perfect teeth were a rarity then. Funny seeing herself, twenty-two years old, and Donald clearly a good bit older. She remembered getting ready for that night, for once her mother had told her she looked nice, without any qualifications. Maybe she had suspected what was going to happen. Not even a mention of Agnes' liberal application of Miners mascara, her pearly nails. And there in the photo Agnes had her left hand spread wide, prominent against the dark of her dress, the ring just noticeable. Later it came out that he'd got it at a pawn shop. Agnes hadn't cared, but by Christ her mother had gone mental then: start as you mean to go on, throwing yourself away. When Frances had cried at the wedding, Agnes suspected it wasn't from happiness.

And though the last time she'd seen it, Agnes had almost chucked the picture in the bin along with the other, less savoury mementoes of Donald, something had stayed her hand. The same thing that now made her cry, until her body was racked with sobbing and she could hardly see to stir the honey into her drink. Agnes had, she realized, been surprised when Donald died. Not at the fact of his death, which had been on the cards for months, but at her own placid response to it. She had been sad, yes, she had cried, of course. But she had done the necessary, even catered the funeral herself. Maybe making all those bloody sand-wiches had kept her mind off things, or else it was just her reaction to Donald's sister. Phemie had insisted on staying, and more hindrance than help she'd been, greeting in the sponge mix and burning the sausage rolls. Mind you, it had hit her hard. Not the natural order of things when the younger sibling goes first. Agnes would put money on Phemie not being long for this world. The old saying came back to her, death always comes in threes.

Vina is, rather awkwardly, wedged against the door of the toilet, in the narrow inset on the ground floor of the close. Her legs, stretched out, allow her feet to just touch the green wooden door of the cupboard opposite. She looks at the toes of her silver dancing shoes with approval, and concern. They won't last forever, already they're showing a scuff, and she certainly hasn't the wherewithal to procure another pair, not with her wages going straight to her mother for housekeeping.

She wonders how long this is meant to take (possibly she's doing something wrong?), clings tighter to the neck of Roddy Campbell, as he industriously continues his humping. She feels his breath on her cheek, smells the hops on it, and remembers the stories she has heard other women tell. The Palais is not licensed (indeed this is a reason she is allowed to go there), and where the girls make do with a hip flask of brandy, if that, there are men who tank up in the bars beforehand. By ten they're plastered, by the time they get home, incapable. Regardless, it is not as much fun as she expected. The nice feeling departed some time ago, and she is now uncomfortable, and cold. With a last, rasping grunt, he shudders and stills, and Vina feels something inside, warm and trickling. The water will be icy, in the top floor cludge, but she will have to squat, and douche, repeatedly, before she retires for the night, creeping quietly to her bed recess to think on whether she was right to make this premature surrender, or if she has thrown away something better kept safe.

After Donald had died, sleep had been for Agnes a refuge, a safe, warm place of unawareness, unfeeling. Not that she didn't dream about him, she did, often. Corporeally, metaphysically, he was gone, she was under no illusions about that, but he continued to potter around her subconscious, further in the distance each time, as though seen through mist or smog. When she slept, he'd come back, unable to find his socks.

I need to get my socks Agnes love, he'd say, they won't let me back in without them. Where've you put them?

And she'd run around the house, rummaging through

drawers, finally finding them in the washbag, and off he'd go, quite happy.

Or else he was about to go to work and she'd forgotten to make his piece. She would scramble around the kitchen in soothing activity, hastily assembling bread, butter, wafer-thin ham, those Blue Riband biscuits that he liked.

Oh yes, she'd dreamt about Donald. It wasn't him that was the problem. It was Vina.

Vina had never been one to be ignored. She had presence. It. Oomph. Whatever you wanted to call it. An incapacity for blending into the background, even if she'd wanted to. It wasn't part of her make-up. Or was that just how Agnes remembered her? Had she her shy, quiet times? Bad hair days, bloated stomachs? Perfect, pristine in memory, she appeared now. Whenever Agnes closed her eyes, dropped off to sleep, Vina would arrive. Sometimes she'd be there right away, bored, looking for company, as though she'd been scuffing her heels waiting for Agnes to come to bed. Sometimes it would be morning, nearly, and she'd trip in after a night out, smoke on her breath and smelling of warm sweat and Coty, full of urgent, unwelcome confidences. Most often it was the dead of night. The small hours, though if there was a more inappropriate name for something Agnes didn't know it. The hours that dragged on, if you woke, cold and silent. The hours in which Vina's visits were less than welcome.

It used to be reassuring to dream of her. Like photographs of remembered events, animated. The time they took the Waverley to Millport, and she and Vina cycled round the island. They stopped halfway and Agnes smoked her first cigarette, while Vina egged her on. How grown up she felt, between spluttering coughs. A warm day, the smell of seaweed, veering, careering, in their capri pants and plimsolls, while their parents did what? Sat at picnic tables outside a pub on the front? Uncle Jack would have insisted, Auntie Maureen agreed, not to mention Agnes' father. Lemonade, a poke of crisps, and occasional sorties to the swing park would take care of William. Her mother would have disapproved, at first, but she'd have allowed herself to be talked into a shandy, which would go to her head, then give her a headache. Somebody would've been sick on the way back, William probably. Agnes would have remembered if it had been her, and Vina was never sick. No matter what. Constitution like an ox, Maureen said, proudly.

Now though the dreams were different, and they didn't fade when Agnes wakened. Vina might speak, eyes all over the place in fear, lipsticked mouth open, matte against the redness of her tongue, her white teeth. Often Agnes wouldn't be able to hear a thing, Vina's words obscured by a ringing sound like the sea, as if she had a huge, exotic shell pressed to each ear. Vina would grow more and more frustrated, she'd take Agnes by the shoulder and squeeze as she spoke.

Don't Vina, you're hurting.

In the morning Agnes always forgot to check for marks, but when she woke in the night she could feel where Vina's fingers had desperately dug into her flesh.

Sometimes they moved onto her neck, and this, without fail, sent Agnes twisting in her bedclothes as it snatched her from sleep.

Tonight, despite the warm milk, a new dream. She was a child again, twelve years old, sitting at the end of Vina's bed, on that enviable pink satin coverlet, while Vina used an orange stick to push back her cuticles. She'd demonstrate how to make your nails look groomed, if Agnes hadn't any polish (which she didn't, her mother said it looked cheap).

Soak them in water with a splash of sweet almond oil.

The stuff they give you for earache?

That's it.

Then what?

Cutex. Massage it in. Hold your hands still, while I get these raggy bits tidied up. Now, buff them till they shine. Like this.

All fine so far. In a curious suspended state, seemingly awake but unable to move, Agnes thought how well it worked, how lovely the shine was. That she might pop to the chemist at lunchtime for some of that stuff. There was little point in painted nails for working hands. And her hands were like shovels, these days. But then the mood changed, forcefully, as if in response to her lapse of attention. The buffing got faster, and when Agnes tried to pull her hand away she couldn't, Vina's grasp was too strong.

Stop, please, Agnes said. Stop.

The colour drained out of the dream, everything greyed. And Vina, worst of all, she was still Vina, still moving, still holding Agnes by the hand, but not alive. Like the nastiest scene-of-crime photos she'd seen in *True Detective*, but not retouched, real. The choker of bruises, and was that one of her stockings round her neck? The bluing lips, the waxy tinge to her face, paint and powder all gone. The dirt on her bare arms, the black under her fingernails. Her lovely blonde do all rumpled and straggly, despite the hours spent mixing sugar and water, teasing, coaxing, twisting strands around her little finger. Agnes looked down, to confirm that Vina's shoes were missing. Sure enough, one tan nylon, laddered and tattered, both feet bloodied as though she'd walked all the way home from the Gallowgate like that. And there was something that didn't bear thinking about in the uneven hem of her skirt, the hang of her torn slip beneath it, the wincing shiver of her shoulders.

Agnes woke with a start, clicked the light on and looked anxiously around the room. There were ghosts in the bedroom, she knew, shades of other girls who paled before Vina, though perhaps they weren't so different from her either. Agnes' little expedition with Siobhan had gone some way to exorcizing them, but she hadn't forgotten, and would not forget.

3.26 p.m. – Tom and the Darling Woman

Siobhan assumes he's gay. She'd even go so far as to say she knows he is. He wears it like a badge. Out and proud, it should say, on his lapel. Instead he sports what appear to be elongated lederhosen, and looks astonishingly like Tom of Finland. Certainly his moustache, were it not greying, would not look out of place on one of Tom's artistic creations. He looks at ease not only in his brown leather trousers, but also in his own skin. Coincidentally, as he is loading his many white shirts into a machine, the Darling Woman arrives, booming with customary theatrical projection,

Hello darling!

Tom (if that is indeed his name) replies in kind, and they begin a loud conversation of vocal nuance and double entendre which Siobhan tries to ignore, though the other customers are agog. She knows she herself isn't going to escape unscathed, as the Darling Woman finally approaches with her purse.

Hello darling!

Hello darling, Siobhan replies, weakly, out-camped. She likes the Darling Woman, but finds that a little goes a long way with that kind of thing. At least she confines it to her flamboyant greetings. Others do not, and their banter becomes wearing, old-fashioned, somehow. Not artistic or poised, but forced. Siobhan is sure this isn't how all men approach the issue – in the same way that she knows that she herself differs from the short-haired, deep-voiced females who make no secret of their preference – but she realizes that stereotypes make life easier. Everyone knows what's what. You fit in.

Suddenly Siobhan remembers something her mother said, years ago, when she was a teenager. She'd been looking for books for English class at the local library, ended up chatting to a woman at the feminism section, all two shelves of it. Live and let live, her mother said afterwards, but remember that you have to be careful of that kind of woman, sometimes. Siobhan didn't understand. Older women with short hair generally, or only in libraries? Perhaps she had meant just at the feminism shelves. Romantic fiction and childcare would surely have been safe, though Siobhan suspected hillwalking might not.

All girls your age have phases, it doesn't mean anything, her mother had explained, adding, I'm just thankful you're not sporty.

As she watches Tom unfurl a copy of *The Great Outdoors*, Siobhan wonders if he knows he doesn't really fit in, these days, and if he cares.

A sweetener

Catching herself scowling at the retreating arse of the bar-maid, Myrna corrected the curl of her lip. No need to make herself look bad. And there was nothing wrong with the girl, except the way she walked from the pelvis and her apparent unshakeable faith in herself. Damn it, why not just admit you're jealous as fuck? All round the girl, so thick Myrna could almost smell it, was an aura of good sex. She might as well have come over, sat down in Siobhan's vacant chair, lit a fag and said, I have amazing sex every afternoon before I start work. Then my boy-friend meets me afterwards and we fuck until we're sore. Here, look, I've got the bruises to prove it.

Myrna looked away, towards a group of three at a table. The couple side by side, the girlfriend idly resting her hand on the boy's knee, possessive but understandably so, perhaps, given the company they were keeping. Her friend, and single, Myrna deduced, and who, in contrast to the girlfriend's black t-shirt, was wearing a turquoise and white floral print halterneck, cut very low down her back and tied with a fragile white bow behind her neck. She had a natural-looking all-over tan (no mean feat in this climate) and was, Myrna thought, far sexier than the girlfriend. Who was doubtless finding the other's presence a constant reminder that her boyfriend was with her precisely because she was duller. Less likely to divert attention from him, or run away with someone else. Myrna noticed that Halter Top didn't even smoke properly, instead puffing out thick little clouds of smoke which hadn't been inhaled. Why bother, she thought, then lit another of her own cigarettes as if to prove her point.

In retrospect, it had been fortuitous that Siobhan had phoned and invited her out. She hadn't been planning to return the call, but Siobhan's tone of voice as she spoke to the voicemail had been pure schoolteacher, and Myrna had always been a good girl at school. Did what she was told.

Myrna, I know very well that you're there. I need your help. I want to go to a bar tonight and drink absinthe, but I don't know where to go. You said you weren't working, so please call me back.

What else could she do? It was so unlike Siobhan, but she was changing, slowly but surely. Even now, Myrna could see her over at the bar, talking to someone, laughing as the barmaid drizzled water through sugar and into their drinks. It had only taken a little more persuasion, the recollection of a place none of her old friends went, that they'd consider to be for older people, despite the fact that many of them were over thirty, and only felt younger because they were sleeping with those in their early twenties. It was mutual too, this doing of favours. Siobhan would not be going out were it not for her, and Myrna would otherwise be spending a night in with a bottle of wine. Two bottles, actually, she couldn't risk not having enough, not when her only company was to be soap operas and maudlin tunes. And absinthe was a nice drink, one that embraced you firmly like a lover, pulled you into its world. Myrna looked down into her glass. A good idea right enough, and a chance to wear her new shoes. More ill-gotten gains and, she surmised, not just ill-gotten by her – but she might as well get the use out of them.

It was always a bloody wrench handing the agency fee over, she found, especially after a tough night. But Belinda was cunning, she could spot when Myrna was pissed off, was quick at sweetening her up with a high-spender or two. Yesterday Myrna had stormed up the stairs to the office, ready to pack it in once and for all, ready to go and get herself a proper job. And Belinda had made her hang on before she answered the door, timing it perfectly to allow a tiny element of indecision, of nerves, to squeeze in, as Myrna stood on the landing, waiting. When she finally did buzz Myrna in, Belinda was on her mobile, smiling that big wide open smile, motioning Myrna to the chair where she'd sat to be interviewed, all those weeks ago, while she herself returned to the hallway to finish her call in private.

She breezed back into the room, all apologies.

What can I do for you Celia?

Money for you. Here.

Belinda didn't open the envelope and count it on the

spot the way she usually did. Instead she just said thanks, and waited for Myrna to speak.

Look, I need some time off.

She remembered the line Belinda had spun her about inappropriate behaviour, remembered telling her about the night she'd visited Siobhan, telling her that she'd been sucking the man's flaccid dick for twenty minutes to no avail before she ended up crawling about a corridor floor scraping together the nine pounds seventy-two pence he had thrown at her. Belinda had been gushily sympathetic, then told her,

If you can't take the heat you should stay out of the kitchen.

I thought the bedroom was the place for whores.

But you're an escort. There's a difference. A financial difference, apart from anything else. If you're willing to give that up because of one bastard, you've let them win. But I've got plenty of other girls who can handle it.

The implication being that it was Myrna's fault, the overt message that Belinda didn't give a fuck. Then it was all sweetness and light and the best clients, the easy ones, the ones with the real money. This time Myrna wasn't going to back down, and she said so.

Oh, that's a shame. I had Mr Anderson lined up for you tomorrow night.

Well, I've got my period. I can't.

Again? It seems like only a fortnight or so ago that you had it last.

It's irregular, okay?

Myrna didn't say that she had cystitis and wanted to give it a few days to clear up. Besides, she had it because of her last client, she deserved a holiday.

I'm sorry. He was asking especially for you. And I thought he was a good tipper.

I'm just not up to it right now.

Okay, my love. That's fine. You've been working hard. Actually, that reminds me, I've got a present for you. Call it a bonus.

Oh yes, Belinda was cunning. She knew how to twist Myrna round her little finger, when to give praise and sympathy and when to withhold it. She went out the room, came back with a carrier bag, which she offered to Myrna.

What's that?

Don't sound so suspicious! Open it. I like to reward my best girls occasionally, and you, Celia, are one of my very best girls.

My name isn't Celia.

I didn't think for a moment it was, but let's stick with it for now, shall we?

Myrna looked in the bag, withdrew a box.

You are size five, aren't you? Belinda said.

Yes.

Well, don't you like them?

Yes but . . .

But nothing. I knew you liked your shoes, and money can be so impersonal. You know how many miserable hours you'd slave away in a call centre to buy a pair of those. You and I are the same, in that way. We couldn't do a normal job.

Myrna could have kicked herself for being so easily won over. It was only when she got home that she'd noticed the slight wear on the soles, the tacky patches left by large sale stickers, the creased leather of the straps. Belinda's feet were about the same size as her own, Belinda also liked clothes, accessories, shopping. And Belinda was not generous, or thoughtful. She was a manipulative bitch. At least Mr Anderson had tipped well. Myrna had been drinking off his tip all night, and hardly made a dent in it.

Siobhan was approaching, edging round tables as if it was a more complex task than it looked. It probably was. Myrna hadn't tried standing up for a while, but she thought it might be easier said than done. She smiled, knocked back the dregs of her drink. She was having fun, she noticed, suddenly.

How slow was that? Two more minutes and I'd have sent a rescue dog.

A St Bernard with brandy?

Of course.

Funny, my extremities are getting numb.

Do you think that might be the absinthe?

Makes the heart grow fonder.

Aye, and the bad puns grow worse.

Santé.

Less of that shite. Fuck the lot of them.

Who?

All of them.

Okay then, fuck the lot of them.

Myrna's favourite toast, and she only now realized it had slipped out of usage, as those who used to shout it out began to eye up engagement rings and pay into pension plans. To which there was only one response. Myrna looked Siobhan in the eye,

Fuck the fucking lot of them.

As they were leaving, Myrna glanced over to the bar. A young man, dishevelled, was perched on a stool, getting served even though the bell had gone ten minutes ago and the bar staff had started their gentle mantra of finish-up-your-drinks-and-start-moving-outside-now-PLEASE. Sure enough, there was the sexy barmaid leaning over and kissing him, touching tongues and surely it was impossible at that distance, in that noise, but Myrna was sure she heard a sharp, *sotto voce* whisper,

Ten minutes, can you wait that long?

A moment of weakness

Woozy but nice, the balmy night air surrounded Siobhan. She turned her face upwards, let the weak summer smir revive her. Sounds – a taxi door slamming, voices, the purr of passing traffic – seemed more rounded. This had been a good idea. And Myrna had been on fine form, like the Myrna she'd first met, fun Myrna. Not that Siobhan had a problem with her new job per se. She'd always thought it better to sell your body's labour than to be obliged to think. Loading washing was fine, as stacking shelves and stuffing envelopes had been in the past. And yet there was a difference between boredom or paper cuts and – as Myrna had described earlier – going down on your hands and knees on a wiry hotel carpet, naked in front of the mirror, while some stranger pulled your hair and called you names as he repeatedly slammed himself into you from behind. Even if he was paying you a hundred and fifty pounds to do so. The day before, in the launderette, Siobhan had noticed Myrna sitting at the desk, meticulously picking off her nail polish, scattering the counter with brittle fragments of gold.

What's the matter with your face the day? Agnes had said.

Nothing.

Doesn't look like nothing.

I'm just . . . tired, I suppose.

Well you'd better clear up that mess.

The expression on Myrna's face stuck in Siobhan's mind, until her plan to enjoy a proper night out and at the same time cheer Myrna up had been born. And Myrna certainly looked cheered, as she emerged from the bar, peeling the cellophane from a fresh pack of cigarettes, and asked,

What now?

Siobhan shrugged.

All the pubs'll be shut, Myrna said.

That's okay, Siobhan started to say, but Myrna caught her arm,

Look, across the road there!

What?

That guy from the launderette. The one who's always asking people out.

Arm in arm with the woman?

Exactly. He's finally got a bird and it's too late at night for her to be on day release.

I don't really know him.

Don't worry. Must tell Agnes though, remind me. Wonders will never cease.

They started walking up the road, until Siobhan said,

Where are we going?

Good point. No idea, but I don't really feel like going home yet. Anything to drink at your house?

Yes. Come back for a little while, if you like.

But not to stay over, Siobhan was thinking, not this time. She had other plans for later on, when she was alone. Under her clothes, borrowed pants of aqua lace sat low on her hips. Fine and soft, with a little red rosebud on the waistband, she could feel them creeping gently between her buttocks as she walked, secretly spreading assurance upwards through her body.

Her success in the bar made her temerarious, greedy with alcohol, but free. Undoubtedly free. The aniseed of the absinthe was still on her tongue. Tastes didn't often give her colours, but she'd been right about this. Not the alcoholic symphony of Des Essientes, perhaps, but pronounced nevertheless, the same even indigo colour of the north sky, like dense pigment soaking into thick, porous paper.

The Cosmopolitans Siobhan made once back in her flat didn't have the same effect. They had no colour but the pretty pink in the glass, which Myrna tilted to admire as she topped them both up, sloshing some over her skirt in the process. Siobhan, meanwhile, sat with her legs splayed over the arm of the couch, toenails uncharacteristically carmine, a record she'd once liked, and discovered she still did, on the turntable.

Siobhan?

Mmhmm?

Can I ask you something?

You're going to anyway, so go for it.

Are the blues blue?

That wasn't what you were going to ask, but now you mention it, yes, of course they are. And they ripple, like the hair on a mermaid.

Myrna giggled, a hair's breadth away from coy, her voice slipping from rich purple down into lilac, pale and sweet.

No, it wasn't what I was going to ask.

So?

Soooo . . . are you, you know?

What do you think?

I think yes.

Yes what?

Yes you are.

Am what?

You know.

Even as she was about to reply, a voice in Siobhan's mind warned: don't do it. Don't go an inch, not even a millimetre, further down this particular road. Agnes had a phrase that summed it up – there'll be tears before bedtime. Or in this case, tears on waking up. She couldn't, *mustn't*, try out her atrophied flirting skills on Myrna, just because tonight was the first time in weeks she'd seen her smile without looking like she was lifting weights that were too heavy for her. Easy to say, but not so easy to do, now that Myrna was closer, too close, and abruptly Siobhan felt the burden of their combined loneliness and met her halfway.

Not a twinge, nothing, except a shoot of guilt that had nothing to do with Myrna, but which prompted the image of The Girl, Auerbach, to materialize in her imagination, The Girl she'd been fantasizing about for so long. Siobhan reached out and cupped Myrna's face in her hands and opened her mouth to her kiss. Then more than a twinge, an ache, a need, and she pulled away, quickly. Myrna's eyes had brightened and she looked shiningly eager.

Oh Myrna, I can't.

What?

You're my friend.

I don't understand.

It's a bad idea. I just . . . can't.

Why not?

She wished she could spare Myrna that last, desperate, attempt. The depth everyone hopes they'll never sink to, even as they do, when they transform themselves from a pleasant regret, remembered and wondered about, into something pitiful.

It doesn't work that way.

How does it work then?

You're not interested in women.

Clearly that matters.

Siobhan couldn't think how to make it better. To say there was someone else was worse than a cliché, because the someone else wasn't with her in any tangible way. And it brought with it inescapable connotation that this vague other person was better, better than Myrna, who didn't want sympathy or advice, or even to sleep with Siobhan, but to anchor herself to something she didn't know she needed until it started sliding away.

You kissed me back.

Yes.

You must have wanted to.

Sorry wasn't good enough, not for this. Siobhan didn't know what to say, so she didn't say anything.

Myrna got up, stumbling on the edge of the rug as she reached for her jacket,

I'd better get going.

Stay. Stay for a cup of tea at least.

Siobhan couldn't stop herself from adding,

I'm sorry.

Whatever.

Myrna?

Myrna turned and looked at Siobhan, and now the expression was balanced precisely between hurt and hate,

What?

You're my friend. No matter what.

Yeah. See you around.

Siobhan felt as though a trapdoor had opened on a stage, and she'd fallen back behind the scenes. Her clothes had become a costume, her confidence a sottish act, transparent to any audience. She'd been kidding herself that there was anything more to it. The illusion had dissipated, and she'd been thrust back into her everyday life, only to find a room she felt obliged to tidy before bed, and the beginnings of what would turn into her worst hangover in years.

Burning up

It was hot. One of those days which took the city by surprise. Sunshine belted off the gum-speckled pavements and heat haze gathered around the cars on the main road, while patches of sunburn gently peeled on the shoulders of teenage girls and men with lager cans. Global warming perhaps, in any case it was not what people were used to here. Agnes had been around long enough to know that heat made people funny. She only wished she could put whatever was wrong with her down to the weather.

Her capacity for rage surprised her. It would well up inside, hot and venomous and eager. She had started thinking about her cholesterol, after being battered with statistics by Margaret, who was an inveterate, not to mention inefficient, weight watcher. But really, the feeling Agnes got in her chest when she was angry seemed more likely to keel her over than any amount of fried egg rolls. The customers bore the brunt of it – Sally had been snapped at for overfilling her machine, Darren for paying with a twenty-pound note – but Agnes tried, and sometimes failed, to keep a lid on it with the girls.

Something was going on there, she'd lay money on it. Myrna hadn't been herself for weeks. She went about lacking definition, as though she was wrapped in layers of clear tissue. And Siobhan, well, Agnes had always thought of Siobhan as the sensible one, with a pitying kind of approval. She recognized some element of herself there, a certain reserve, an inability to let go, which seemed a shame in someone still young. But Siobhan was not quite the same either, with her new clothes and odd moods. Once she'd even arrived half an hour late, bleary-eyed and exuding the sour whiff of too much alcohol the night before, and that was not like her. The one time they'd been out for a drink together she'd lit up like a Christmas tree after two gin and tonics. Agnes had an inkling that love was rearing its head there too, and she hoped it wasn't ugly. Which brought her back to Myrna, and the festering suspicions which she didn't want to dwell on. Agnes shook her head. Probably just the heat addling her brain. She turned back to the accounts, which Jean had phoned and requested out of the blue, and by yesterday, as though Agnes just sat there all day twiddling her thumbs. Soon the figures were swimming before her eyes and she fell prey to a whopper of a headache.

She was not, therefore, in the mood when Mr Jarvie started his nonsense. A regular customer since the death of his wife some months before Donald passed away, they had commiserated over the small, specific particles of grief which coruscated in the larger, and largely unvoiced, emptiness of their bereavement. Listening to *The Archers* alone, even though he disliked it intensely (all mooing and middle-class affairs); cooking stovies though personally she could take them or leave them (the tendency to wateriness, you see). That kind of thing. For his part, Mr Jarvie had suddenly discovered that the world was full of questions he'd never previously had to ask. Agnes had been happy to stop for a cup of tea and offer advice on timing for recipes and care of cutlery, whilst privately wondering how he had sailed through life without any comprehension of the effort that maintained a spotless home and put meals on the table at appropriate interludes. She remembered his wife, a neat woman but a nippy sweetie. Maybe she had cause to be. You never knew.

Agnes hadn't caught his drift at first.

I've no time to stop and blether today. This isn't a cafe you know.

I didn't mean a coffee here.

What's that? – Agnes was wrestling with a double duvet which refused to come out of its bag – Siobhan, come and give me a hand with this.

I didn't mean a coffee here, Mr Jarvie repeated.

Right, I've got a hold of it now, just give it a good tug. What's that you're saying about coffee?

It doesn't have to be coffee. We could go out for a drink one day, perhaps. After you've finished work.

Get that phone would you Siobhan?

She turned back to Mr Jarvie, and said, in a tone which her mother would have been proud of,

Eh?

A drink, one evening.

Oh for heaven's sake, don't be so bloody ridiculous.

What's ridiculous about it?

Come on. Just because we're both alone doesn't mean we should get together. And in case it hadn't occurred to you, Donald and Anne are scarcely cold in their graves. You may not have any sense of propriety, but I have.

I didn't mean . . .

Oh, I know fine well what you meant. Bloody typical.

I'm sorry if I . . .

We'll hear no more about it. Now are you going to take that washing away from under my feet or not?

Chastened, he hurried off. Agnes called after him,

Try the tea dances. I hear they're a right meat market.

She turned to Siobhan, who was hovering nearby,

What?

Nothing, Siobhan said, shrugging. I just thought maybe you were a teensy bit hard on him.

Hard on him? He wouldn't know what had hit him if I'd been hard on him. No idea of respect, that's the problem. One-track mind, the lot of them.

Agnes waved her hand towards the customers sitting by the window, as though they were all likely to be closet sex maniacs.

I think he just meant to be friendly.

Friendly!

Well, even so, it was only coffee.

Hah, that's how it always starts. Besides, he's too old for me. I may not look it, but I don't get my bus pass until next year. And do you know where he lives?

Siobhan shook her head.

Albert Street, Agnes said, and nodded emphatically, as though offering the incontrovertible piece of evidence that would turn any jury.

What's that got to do with it?

Nutters, the lot of them. Sorry, *eccentrics*. Half the eccentrics we get in here live in Albert Street. It's always been like that, even before care in the community. He stays in the same close as the one-legged transvestite and that old bat who believes she's the princess Anastasia.

She showed me her mole once.

Yes, she does that to everyone sooner or later. Anyway, you can't tell me that makes him normal. Goodness knows what's going on under the surface.

Vina is falling, she knows it. Nobody ever told her it would be so difficult, to keep hold of herself. He's a catch, apparently. She has overheard other girls talking in the toilet queue. Good-looking, and what a suit. They whispered that he was in a gang, which only adds to his lustre. And now she's broken her own rule, and danced four times in a row with him, and more. Enough to attract their disapproval. A snide comment uttered loud, an attempt to trip her obvious, but unsuccessful. And does she care?

She pushes him away, under pretence of needing to powder her nose, but what she really wants is a little space away from her own body, its desires. Besides, she does not want to accrue a reputation, and the way his hands drift over her hips will be noticed, and commented on. Though she wonders what there is to worry about. There's Jeanie from kitchenware, canoodling with some young fellow, wedding ring tucked away in her purse, out of sight, out of mind. And good luck to her, Teresa says, laughing. Have you seen her man?

When Roddy leads Vina to the fire escape for a breath of fresh air, she follows. Once there they kiss. As his hand slides between her legs, the last thing on her mind is being a good girl. When he offers to walk her home, ardent, she agrees.

There was one way to get rid of a temper, and that was to work it off. Despite the heat Agnes set to, and piled on all the service washes they had. By the time the boy arrived, the one with the sweat stains under his arms from toting his heavy sports bag around, she was too puggled to tell him to bugger off. Siobhan, who had finished the best part of a big bottle of water (imagine paying money for water, there were some things Agnes would never get her head round), slumped down beside her at the desk.

Good afternoon ladies, I wonder if you've got a minute to save yourself a bit of money?

Agnes made a half-hearted growling sound, but let him get on with it. Sometimes they did have bargains those boys, if you weren't fussy about where they came from.

Okay now ladies, either of you got children, no, you're not old enough are you? Ideal for your wee nieces and nephews or just for your own feet I have top-quality pad-dling pools here . . .

Oh come on, Agnes said. Neither of us want a paddling pool.

Aha, you're going to drive a hard bargain, I can see that but it's the only way to be in this day and age isn't it? Well, for the man in your life, and you can't tell me a pair of lovely ladies like yourselves don't have men in their lives . . .

Agnes looked at Siobhan, shook her head in exasperation and shouted,

Next!

After disposable barbecues and miraculous lawn fertilizer he finally managed to sell them a small battery-operated fan each, and, grudgingly lumpen, they went back to work.

Needless to say, Agnes wouldn't have dreamed of confessing the repercussions of Donald's dirty little secret to Mr Jarvie. She hadn't even discussed it with Margaret, who might have understood how she felt. Margaret, whose husband of thirty-one years had left her for someone else, taking all her trust with him. Younger, of course, which was silly, because younger women weren't interested in being wives any more. Agnes hoped it would backfire on him, but Margaret said no, he seemed happy (spitting the word out, as though this was equivalent to him contracting syphilis). Even the children, the eldest of whom was almost the same age as the new girlfriend, had been to visit the couple in their new house.

It was the pay rise that did it, Margaret explained. Flash car the warning sign, then the full mid-life crisis, very undignified. Agnes agreed. At that age, women left the marital home for themselves, men for someone else. And so Margaret was lonely; Agnes herself, though not yet sixty, hadn't begun to imagine the future. She found it easy, therefore, to tell her friend where to stick it when she started harping on about it not being long until they'd be able to go to the tea dances. If hefty emotional blackmail was applied, Agnes succumbed to an occasional game of bingo in what had been the old F&F dancehall, but she considered bingo to be somehow akin to admitting defeat. Expensive too, even with those specials on the alcopops. She usually left feeling low, except for the time she and Margaret won fifty quid between them. A little went a long way sometimes. Nor had she minced her words when singles night at the Plaza had been broached. Not even for moral support, no way. She was in no hurry to start courting again, and wasn't sure if she ever would be. Agnes wafted her fan around her face, felt herself cooling down. If only it was as easy to stay that way.

One's a wish

This could be what attracted people to extreme sports, this feeling. Siobhan had never fathomed the appeal before. But the risk and the high, the long, glorious comedown after, until it became imperative to do it again. That she understood, now. Another, less savoury analogy presented itself on the pages of *True Detective* (not that she'd seen it lying about the place lately). Serial killers experienced the same feeling – although they, unlike Siobhan, retained their trophies. Perhaps if she kept what she'd taken, just once, she wouldn't need to do it again. But she was by nature honest, inasmuch as her own moral code prohibited actual stealing. Borrowing was acceptable. Never to do it again, that thought was not to be borne. Quite the contrary. Somewhere at the back of her mind, in a place as uninviting as the murkiest corner of the cupboard under the sink, was the tiniest suspicion that what she was doing might not always be enough.

Today, it was a kimono-style top. A change from underwear was, Siobhan felt, necessary. The first flush of sexual abandon was, as well it might be, ecstatic, but she needed to balance it with respect. It wasn't just physical, she told herself, definitely not. She could see the top scrunched towards the bottom of the basket of clothes, waiting to go in the first free machine. A flash of chinoiserie. Probably viscose, and you had to be careful with viscose, even in a wool wash. It would need drying flat. She'd lay out towels on the table, spread it over them. Reshape while damp. And it should smell more eastern, perhaps she could add a drop of essential oil to the rinse water? Ylang ylang, sandalwood, something like that. She would not, under any circumstances, masturbate. The shrill of a machine on its final spin, almost time, almost time. It would, of course, fit her, this top, for although The Girl was taller, they weren't dissimilar in build. The smoke from a customer's cigarette caught Siobhan's breath, and her cough turned into a sneeze, then another.

Aha, one's a wish, two's a kiss, Agnes said, in passing. They were busy, that day, with Myrna off for a long weekend. Not that Siobhan was thinking of Myrna; in her excitement she had forgotten any traces of anxiety left by their night out. They had been drunk, that was all. These things happened, and then they were fine. Siobhan smiled, her mind on more important things. She was going to get away with it again, she knew she was. Her nose started itching with another sneeze.

Bless you, Agnes said.

What's three then?

Let me see, oh, a disappointment. One's a wish, two's a kiss and three's a disappointment. Sorry. Any more in there?

That's it I think, Siobhan said, as a woman called over to her,

Scuse me hen, your dryer isnae working. One pound in coins I've put in now and it still hasnae budged.

So she had to get the key, and open the drawer, and dislodge a jammed twenty pence with a crochet hook. By the time she'd done all that, she turned to see that her basket of clothes was gone. Agnes had loaded the machine. Soap was swirling in the window and Siobhan could just make out a sodden dragon, a red-ribbon tie. She had missed her chance, and there wouldn't be another until when? Next week? Longer?

For the rest of the day, the weight of her failure grew. It didn't seem right that when Auerbach decided to put on her pretty new top, she would find it crushed, shrunken perhaps, the fabric harsh without softener. Siobhan looked wistfully at the empty laundry bag, considered, then dismissed, the notion of borrowing something once it was clean and dry. On impulse, she grabbed the scissors from the desk drawer and furtively cut the string which attached the name label to the zip. She tucked it in her pocket. Better than nothing, this keepsake arrow of green cardboard, large, lazy letters from a fibre-tip pen spelling out the name, Auerbach.

It wasn't really the weather for it, but Siobhan felt in need of further consolation, and decided to walk the long way home via the botanical gardens. Everything was glazed with a trembling drizzle of rain. Soon fat drops of water were bouncing off the taut green leaves of rhododendron, with determined orange thunks. One hit Siobhan right in the eye, making her glad that her excursions into make-up hadn't yet encompassed mascara. When she saw a sign advertising a book sale, she thought she might as well shelter from the rain there as in the glasshouse, which would be thickly humid with steam. Siobhan liked second-hand bookshops, they were always quiet and peaceful, with no music departments or clinking-clanking coffee shops to distract her browsing. So she trawled the battered sci-fi paperbacks and the hardback firsts, the cottage gardening and the history of trains. Nothing to tempt her there. At a table of illustrated volumes in ornate bindings, which she couldn't possibly afford, a man was trying to sell the stallholder a small pile of books.

I'll take this, and this, and this one, but I'm afraid the condition on that's just too bad. It's really been in the wars, hasn't it?

Can I leave it here anyway?

The stallholder shrugged, counted out a few notes and handed them over. As soon as the vendor had gone, she muttered to her partner – do I look like a garbage disposal unit? – then ducked out of the hall and returned, minus the book.

As Siobhan was leaving, sure enough she saw a flash of brown leather in the bin by the door. She quickly picked it out by its broken spine and hurried away with it tucked inside her jacket. *Flora of the Coastal Regions of Scotland.* She'd had a notion of finding some old illustrations to frame, so she wiped a bench dry with her sleeve and sat down to have a look. No wonder the dealer didn't want it. The few remaining plates were faded and damp-speckled, too tatty even for Siobhan to turn into shabby chic. She found one illustration, *Campanula rotundifolia*, that might be salvageable. *Armeria maritima* looked as though someone had spilled coffee on it, and as for *Convallaria majalis*, she didn't want to get too close to whatever it was that obscured the flower head. She crinkled on, past black and white illustrations thoroughly felt-tipped by some young child, until she came upon two pages thickly stuck together by a seeping stain. A corner of tissue poked out the side. Someone had pressed a flower. Siobhan peeled the aged sheets apart, slowly, delicately. Between the tissue paper, waxy petals. Once fresh and white, now faded near sepia. Orange stamen, as far as she could make out. Unusually shaped. A white iris, perhaps? Her nostrils caught the faintest of scents, and Siobhan arced her head closer. A familiar perfume, and then unmistakable. This flower was an orchid.

Siobhan slipped the book into her bag, and walked to the crest of the hill, on the other side of which lay the gate that would take her the quiet route back to her flat. Suddenly her eye caught a figure she recognized in the distance, by its walk more than anything else, a loose-limbed lope of comfy shoes and confidence, of ease within the body. Siobhan hurried down the steep hill, then broke into a trot, which turned into a run, until she was haring as fast as she could towards the road. When she rounded the corner she halted, panting, leaned against a wall, her t-shirt sticky with sweat, scanned the street. Too late. The Girl was nowhere to be seen.

It was the first time she had spotted Auerbach away from the launderette, out in the world. Proof positive that she had an existence outside imagination. Siobhan felt exhilarated, then, abruptly, horribly disappointed, the way a child might if told after opening each window in turn on an advent calendar that Christmas had been cancelled. Testing illusions was silly after all, like playing donkey with fine-bone china. What would she have done, had she caught up with Auerbach? Spoken to her? Hardly. You didn't run after people you didn't know in the street just to say hello, I wash your clothes. Another thought dawned. This street was long, stretching the length of the main road, but shielded by trees. She had lost her quarry, yes, but it must've been because The Girl had gone to ground. Entered one of the houses on this terrace. Which wasn't too far from where Siobhan lived. Sandblasted Greek revival to her blackened Babylonian folly. A slight detour, and she could walk this way to and from work. The way she felt, as if this girl was her muse, did not make sense. Not when she didn't translate her feelings into anything external or lasting. But if she kept glimpsing Auerbach outwith the launderette, perhaps eventually Siobhan would adjust to the reality, come to prize it as highly as the fantasy.

4.07 p.m. – George

The smell can be a problem, especially on a day like today when it's warm. But what can she do except wait until he's gone then whizz round with the air freshener? He's modest at least, not like some of the others. When they're high on the drugs, that's when you have to watch. Take everything off if you're not careful, and Agnes won't have it. This one puts his heavy coat back on over yellowing long johns and semmit, furtively slides bare feet back into his boots so that nobody can see them sock-free, naked. That's his system, to wash the few clothes he owns in layers. It shows self-respect, Agnes thinks, to try and maintain some standards even in reduced circumstances. She doesn't like to see that much hair on a man, but doubtless he'd find a way to shave if he didn't want that long, brown beard. Kids call him Jesus, she's heard, they always do with his sort.

She wonders where he sleeps. He's not in the hostel for the alcoholics, she's sure of that. Her nose is finely attuned to the reek of drink, and the measures taken to conceal it. This one is teetotal, she'd put money on it. Instead, he walks. She's seen him in the early morning when she goes to the tube; on the south side when she was visiting Phemie; and in the east, over at the Barras, when he nodded hello and she got the curious feeling she'd been favoured by someone special. He must know the city inside out. She always takes care to say good morning, and he always replies, we'll have fine weather today, or I fear there'll be rain later. He's polite, and was well spoken once, though his voice has rusted with lack of use. He must beg, she supposes, though she's never seen him when the streets are busy, and all the others are out on the pavement. She'd like to ask him if he's okay, maybe even offer him a cup of tea or a couple of quid for some lunch. But she feels a little shy, doesn't want to be rude.

Agnes knows he puts some customers off, but who are they to be snooty? He pays, just like them. Well, that's not strictly true, but he always offers her the money, a huge handful of coppers usually. It's her that never accepts it. She's kind to those down on their luck, much kinder than to those on the up and up. She respects struggle, and hard times, and despair. They are the currency of life, after all.

When anything was possible

Agnes had found the first one at the bottom of the wardrobe, in the stripy box Donald's wedding shoes came in. It was a few weeks after the funeral, and she'd built herself up to tackling his clothes. She wanted them sorted, bagged, handed in to Margaret's shop. Never a pleasant job, clearing up after the dead, but it had to be done. It was rather touching, discovering the shoebox. Imagine holding on to them all those years, she'd thought, opening it to have one last look at the polished black leather dress shoes (and choosing not to remember that their second outing had been her Uncle Jack's funeral). Then she glimpsed something else, tucked under the tissue paper which lined the box. The dated, unreal colours of a magazine, once lurid. A girl with blonde hair, as bottle blonde as Vina, though once she'd thought that was natural. Agnes slipped it out, flicked through the pages. Not so bad, really. Interviews with actors and writers, reviews, even recipes. She didn't look at the centrefold. A stag present, perhaps. From his friends at work. But Agnes had read the true-life tales in her magazines, and she knew these discoveries never came alone.

Once started, she couldn't stop. Every drawer. The hall

cupboard. Donald's tool kit. Each yielded its cache, until she was sure she had them all. Perspiring from the exertion of the search, she didn't know where to take them. Not the bedroom, or the dining room table, not anywhere they'd sat or lain together. Finally, finding it hard to hold on to the slippery pile, Agnes perched at the top of the stairs, let them slide onto the landing. A dozen in total, the most recent dated just six months before. She didn't flick through it, the headlines were enough. As were the contortions of the girl on the cover, with her blonde hair and shiny parted lips, her skewed underwear and, the indignity of it, her lack of pubic hair. Agnes sat there for quite some time, with *Penthouse* and *Razzle* and *Playbirds International* around her feet. Tried to imagine Donald walking into a shop and buying these, didn't try to imagine anything else. Hopefully not the local shop, where she was known by name, hopefully somewhere far away from their home. Something must have made these particular issues worth keeping, while others weren't, but Agnes did not want to know what it was. Too rainy to burn them in the garden, too risky with the neighbours. She'd have to wrap them in black bags, make sure they were well hidden before she put them in the bin shelter. When she finally looked up from the floor the light from the window had faded. Older and a good deal wiser than the girl Donald married, Agnes found that her hurt turned quickly to anger.

Flushed and excited, this is the first time Vina has felt this way. The smell of perfume and sweat, hair lacquer

and wooden-floored mustiness is, she thinks, the smell
of freedom. And fun. She is high as a kite, swirling
around amid the sprinkling of mirrorball lights, which
seem to glamorize all they touch so that even her skirt
and top appear as lovely as the net petticoats and beaded
cardigans around her. This is her medium. She finds
herself chewing her gum in time to the swing
trumpeting from the band, feels the floor quivering
under the feet of the dancers, how many, a thousand,
more? There had been a queue to get in, when she and
Teresa got off the bus in Alexandra Parade, but it was
worth the chilly wait. More than worth it.

When she is asked to dance (which is often), she
acquiesces, and takes to the floor happy and smiling,
scarcely able to hear what her partners say, such is the
noise and bustle. But never more than one dance per
person, this a suggestion of Teresa's, who is keen that
nobody gets the wrong idea about her young workmate.
Fat chance. When Vina is in the powder room, Teri
urges her own fiancé to drop a subtle hint to a fellow
she doesn't much like the look of, him being both the
worse for drink and old enough to be Vina's father.
Liam's hint is far from subtle, but has the desired effect,
and Vina emerges, freshly lipsticked, to a field clear for
more suitable partners.

Sitting on the bus home, downstairs as instructed,
within sight of the driver, she believes her evening to
have been perfect.

*

Had Donald felt shame? Agnes did, against her will, and it was months since she'd found the magazines. To compensate she decided to feel no guilt in indulging her own whims. She would go to a department store and buy herself something to wear, and for once in her life, bugger the cost. She took Saturday morning off, went into town, returned to work empty-handed.

Where are the bags then? Myrna asked.

Didn't see anything. And the prices, you wouldn't believe what they were after for stuff no better than you'd get in Marks.

You need to look harder. You'll always find something if you look hard enough.

Maybe.

Agnes didn't say that nothing would have satisfied her, that the problem wasn't the shops or the clothes or even the money, it was the passing of time. She'd been shopping for an impossibility. Her dream Saturday.

A fantasy not revisited since she was fifteen, but remembered with brilliant clarity. She and Vina going shopping together, happy Vina, full of life. In her mind's eye, Agnes would metamorphose, grow closer to her cousin in height, age and friendship. They'd take the bus into town, go up to Daly's on Sauchiehall Street. Sometimes Agnes even let herself imagine girls from school in front of them, Susan and Ina May, the popular ones, who laughed at her frumpy clothes. The doorman (for they had such a thing, it was an upmarket store) would look them up and down, then say he was sorry, perhaps they should try Paisley's on Jamaica Street. As Ina May opened her big mouth to argue, he'd ask them to stand aside and say morning ladies, as he ushered Agnes and Vina past. Even now, so many years later, the idea gave her pleasure.

They'd start in perfumery and make-up. Vina had a ceramic jar of powder from Lancôme. The best stuff, worth the extra money, she'd said, opening the tub to let Agnes smell it. Then going mental when she sneezed, sending a soft perfumed cloud rising into the air. Today Agnes would not be clumsy. She would buy lipstick with a French name. *Rose subtil. A cor et à cri.* Roberto would do their hair, flirting as he spritzed and tweaked and gossiped. Agnes strongly suspected that Roberto might actually be plain old Robert, but it was quite the thing for hairdressers to affect a continental name, so she was prepared to suspend her disbelief, at least for the time it took to be properly styled. She tugged at the back of her short, fifty-something hair, remembered the thick childhood plait that she'd imagined lopped off with one fierce snip. Agnes had yearned for one of those short styles that were coming in, not curly like Vina's but straight, backcombed up at the crown and set with lacquer. With a fringe, down to just below her eyebrows, so she wouldn't look like such a slaphead. Her mother used to say fringes weren't nice, the implication being that girls who wore them weren't nice either.

Agnes went through the back and made toast and cheese for her lunch, when what she really fancied was a prawn Marie Rose open sandwich and a bottle of Coke in the restaurant at Daly's, followed by an expresso in a tiny wee cup. It had taken hard work to learn to take her coffee black, but she'd persevered. She couldn't go back to milk, even now she was too sensible to care if it looked sophisticated or not. There was, she knew, a catwalk in the middle of the restaurant, with fashion shows at lunchtime. That's when they'd decide what kind of outfit to get for that night. Because of course they'd be going out, out dancing. The Locarno or the Plaza? She couldn't decide. Definitely not the Astoria, or as Vina called it, the Widow's Paradise. She wouldn't be seen dead there. Agnes understood the Plaza to be posh, with its huge chandeliers and illuminated pillars, but Vina seemed to favour the Locarno. The band on a revolving stage and everything.

Excuse me, I need to get my stuff out of the spinner. It's finished.

Sorry, I was away with the fairies there, Agnes said, getting up and reaching for her supermarket loyalty card, which she slipped under the lid of the spinner to lever it open. The customer unloaded it, held up a top in disbelief,

This is torn. Look. It was and your machine's gone and torn it.

Did you put a towel on top on your stuff, tuck it in?

No.

Well, what do you expect then? It needs something to hold it in place.

But . . .

Agnes shook her head, indicated the notice behind her, about the patron's own risk. Interrupted before the best bit, she couldn't properly regain the vision that had been swimming round in her mind, until it had become almost real. How she'd longed to unwrap those gorgeous tissue-wrapped purchases, dance round Vina's bedroom, as they held garments up against each other, leant over the dressing table copying make-up from magazines. In preparation for a night when anything was possible. How long had it been since Agnes had experienced that feeling, that anything was possible? And then, of course, the same image, the one that the years did not fade.

Vina, beautiful, glamorous Vina, on the front page of the *Evening News*, smiling out at the readers in her Sunday name, Lavinia Ann MacIntyre. Smiling at Agnes. A bittersweet expression in her eyes, the same expression that Agnes saw these days, week in, week out, on the faces of disappeared schoolgirls and missing mothers. She knew it was hindsight, projection on her part, but she couldn't quite shake the suspicion that it was this expression, this Marilyn Monroe sadness, that attracted the abducters, the rapists, the killers. It was not a comforting thought, although she was only too aware that she herself did not possess this quality. It never had been and never would be part of her. Unlike poor Vina.

Like getting a crossword clue you've been staring at for ages, it suddenly struck her that Myrna reminded her of Vina. The conversation she'd overheard the other day, between her and Siobhan, when she was too awkward to go in and get a cup of tea. First time in years she'd felt too shy for anything, ridiculous. Something about the girls' voices though, that confidential tone. She knew that Myrna could be a right one for kissing and telling, it sounded like she could keep one of those trashy magazines going in real-life stories single-handed. Not that spilling the beans on a conquest was anything new. Agnes had heard things from Vina that'd made her ears burn. Mind you, what had her mum and Auntie Maureen talked about, over their endless cups of tea? At the time she had always assumed it was boring, adult stuff, but now she wondered. Things didn't change that much when you got older, and when you got married, well. Upstairs, sitting on Vina's bed, on that slippery satin quilt, listening to her records, songs by bands Agnes hadn't even heard of yet. Vina telling her stories that made her want to squirm, stories she'd remember in her bed at night, crossing her legs tight and trying to get to sleep. Vina up against a wall on her way home, not letting them go all the way or they wouldn't come back for more. Leaning forward and touching Agnes' arm as she whispered,

And what do you think I felt when he pressed up against me?

What?

You *know* what.

Vina had giggled, conspiratorially, but Agnes hadn't known, not then. Not until she was married, really. Sometimes she wondered what Vina had been thinking, why she had liked telling her these things, when she was too young to understand.

Feeling empty

Myrna felt cheated. Belinda's patter about the theatre and the opera had been, in a word, shite. No real surprise there. But increasingly Myrna wasn't even getting a meal out of it. Often the client would ring direct, give her a time to meet in a hotel bar, safely after dinner; sometimes Belinda would just text her a name and room number. Rationally, Myrna thought that she had no reason to feel irked, given that her job existed largely to prevent those who couldn't be bothered going through the whole date and conversation caboodle. Guaranteed result, no hassle. That would make a classy slogan for a business card. But after the night she'd just had, she didn't feel especially rational, and what's more, she was ravenous.

After a brief diversion during which she poured herself a glass of icy Chablis and drained it in three gulps, Myrna sank down in front of the fridge, opening her dressing gown to the blast of cold air. Why did it have to be so fucking hot all the time? She ripped open a packet of Parma ham, extracted one fine paring, soft and silky it melted on her tongue. Unable to stop herself, not even to delay gratification until the food was on a plate, she followed it with another slice and another, until it was all gone. She bought nice food, now she could afford it, taxiing to 24-hour supermarkets where nobody knew her to form opinions about the contents of her trolley. Hungry for something more substantial, more satisfying to chew, she unwrapped a ripe wedge of brie, tore off a chunk and lowered it, oozing, into her mouth. For once her moan of pleasure was entirely genuine. She ate and ate until there was nothing left to take her fancy, then slumped on the couch, full, her stomach tight and invincible. She wished, idly, for some chocolate to round off her appetite, took refuge in a fresh pack of cigarettes, and resettled herself with them, Jacques Brel, and the rest of the Chablis.

Perhaps she'd queered her own pitch. Been too efficient, erased any element of wooing. She wondered if it was the same for the other girls. There was no contact between members of Belinda's workforce. A safety measure, Myrna assumed, wishing she'd taken Bernadette's number so she could find out. It seemed a very long time ago, that day she'd spent with Will. It was curious – she'd never have predicted it – but she missed sex. Not what she did for work, which was generally mechanical and relatively passion-free (not just for her, but for the client too. She often wondered why they bothered, when they could just have a wank like everyone else. It would be more personal). No, it was the uncertainty she missed, the does-he-doesn't-he, the raw, fumbling passion and the hope. The laughter when things went wrong. Now it was her job to make sure things didn't go wrong.

Things always seemed worth more when they cost

money, she knew that, and anyone who worked with money, who made it their be all and end all, wanted their money's worth. The city trader who'd complained that she was wearing tights rather than stockings. The solicitor who said she needed a Brazilian. And tonight, the marketing exec who seemed to think she was made of Plasticene. Over there. Now move. Not that way. Slower. Faster. Over a bit. Don't do that. Do this. Not like that. Like this. And always further, more. That was the problem with pay-as-you-view in hotel rooms. It gave them ideas. They paid, they viewed, and then they wanted to pay and do. And thanks to Viagra, it took three times as long.

At the same time as being fed up with her job, Myrna knew she was good at it. And it was a long while since she had felt good at anything. Small solace really, when slowly she was making an enemy of her body. Breasts that hated being squeezed, nipples that chapped, that she never now touched herself, unless to apply soothing balm. Worse, her vagina was becoming so temperamental that she seemed forever to be smearing herself with cream, or inserting a pessary, or dissolving sachets in water to drink, all in between eating copious quantities of live yoghurt. The only part of her genitalia that remained unaffected was her clitoris. Nobody had yet expressed any interest in that. Every so often she masturbated, tentatively, in much the same way that she checked the battery in her smoke alarm. Siobhan was right, she wasn't a lesbian (and the remembrance of that night made her cringe), but all the same she'd started to imagine, sometimes, that a woman was kissing her there.

Myrna, who didn't believe in love but wanted it none-theless, knew that she'd never now be on level footing with any prospective partner. She would always have a past. She wouldn't be able to go for an evening out (not that she could remember what that was, if it didn't involve four-teen vodkas and a lick of coke or a cash transaction), with-out the worry that she might see one of her old clients. She would never shake the fear of being discovered, exposed. And where on earth did you find someone who didn't mind something like that? All her own fault of course, for not turning back, for making that bum decision to spend the rest of her life under a large neon arrow that said Whore!

Yes, something had to give, but Myrna wasn't a quitter. It wasn't going to be her. A holiday would be nice, first of all. (She'd started saving, furtively, and finding the bank prone to absorb everything she paid in, she had reverted to the old cliché, under the mattress.) Somewhere warm, and quiet, where you could swim in the sea and never meet anyone from home. Somewhere for growing fat and brown and sleek, and leaving the past behind. If she just bagged a bit more money. Having made payments on her store cards Myrna had been given more credit to spend, so spend she had. She told herself that you had to speculate to accumulate, that she earned more when she was wear-ing nice clothes and make-up, but really she liked having these things, at long last. It was a pity that she had as much debt as when she started the job. There was only one thing for it. Take the bigger payers. Volunteer for the special clients. The more hung up they were on what they wanted to do, the more they paid to do it. It was the shame, and quite right too, as far as she was concerned. If she could just get Belinda to put her forward for a few more of those, she'd be raking it in. The liberated were a pain in the ass, sometimes quite literally.

Talkers, on the other hand, were useless. They never tipped as much, believing perhaps that they'd embarked on some kind of friendship, which then made them embarrassed about handing over cash. Myrna had thought they'd only moan about how their wives didn't understand them, but she was wrong. They talked about problems with their teenagers, the decision of whether to put their slightly senile father into a home, the guy at work who was making their life hell. The sex was the least of it, but they never did without, and were always grateful, or pretended to be. Even so, Myrna didn't like them. The one tonight had been a talker, and she had listened in utter tedium for two hours until he actually bored her pants off. She reached for her wine glass at the memory of it. Most clients she felt nothing for, and some she hated. But the ones she hated paid so well, and what else was there to work for but money?

She was going round in circles, that was the problem. It was as if she had indulged in some overenthusiastic pruning. She had severed her friends, lopped off her love life, taken the secateurs to career, ambition. One shoot of green growth remained, the launderette. Siobhan and Agnes and the launderette. Except now her friendship with Siobhan was under threat, thanks to her own drunken stupidity. Maybe it was something physiological, some variant strain of nymphomania. They said men were ruled by their libidos, but hers was a tyrant, always had been. There was some expiation in subduing it through her work, a smidgen of revenge.

Myrna poured another glass of wine, drained the bottle this time, and went through to her bath. Just as she was about to get in, the clip-framed poster on her wall fell with an almighty splashing crash, filling the water with broken glass. Myrna screamed, she got such a fright, and before she could help herself she'd sunk down onto her heart-shaped bathroom mat and started to cry. It was the clearing-up she couldn't bear, she told herself, as she sobbed into a length of toilet roll. She just couldn't bear to clear up the mess, not at this time of night.

4.45 p.m. – Jean

The bell on the door dings but Myrna doesn't look up until she hears Agnes say,

Oh hello Jean.

Jean says hello, how are you, and ignores Myrna completely. Her accent suggests that she has done better in life than she would've been expected to, and the effort of keeping it up strains every vowel. She's getting on a bit now, Myrna thinks, not that she can remember a younger version of Mrs MacPherson. She tries for a moment to imagine her in her prime, in the sixties perhaps, mentally replaces the navy trouser suit and Van Dals with a minidress and knee-high boots, whittles the waist back into shape. Jean's coarse hair is already backcombed into a lesser species of beehive, sandy blonde and bouffant and stuck with pins, as though speared by Lilliputian hunters.

Myrna tugs at her tabard, itches to take it off. She hates wearing the thing, but Agnes has made her aware that Mrs MacPherson expects – demands – neatness and order and that includes tabards. They've cleaned, and tidied, and sprayed with air freshener, washed the windows even, inside and out, as the visitation is out of synch with the window cleaner's day, and there were great grimy smears across the glass. The place gleams, and even the customers seem to be sitting up straight and keeping their belongings shipshape.

Yet something is amiss, Myrna has a sixth sense for such things, or maybe it's just experience. This is no social call, no routine check. Mrs MacPherson is here for a reason, that much is apparent even in the way she walks, in each firm, determined tread of sensible, wide-fitting footwear. The feeling has communicated itself to Agnes too, who ushers her boss into the pristine kitchen with a new and uneasy deference which makes her look suddenly as though her uniform does not fit properly. She has, Myrna knows, tallied the accounts and delineated the profit and loss for this very occasion. The launderette is doing well, or as well as can be expected.

Even if you're not busy, look it.

Myrna's been given her instructions, but nevertheless she sinks down onto the bench by the window and swithers over whether to risk a swift cigarette while Agnes and Jean have their meeting. She looks around to ascertain that nobody is about to require her attention, then extracts the pack and her lighter from her pocket. Whatever's coming, she'll have to wait and see. After all, what's the worst that can happen?

Strange little games

Myrna was sitting with her feet up on the bench by the window, blowing occasional and haphazard smoke rings. The swiftest of glimpses through the glass was enough for Siobhan to register that she looked terrible. The last time she'd seen her, the absinthe night, Myrna had been aglow, even as she took umbrage and stormed out. Now she seemed sunken into herself. Siobhan opened the door, quietly said hello. Myrna took another draw on her cigarette, continued looking up towards the polystyrene ceiling tiles, where an oval of smoke drifted apart and then disappeared. Siobhan dithered, briefly, then walked on, through to the back shop, where Agnes was making tea.

Just in time, want a cuppa?

That'd be great, thanks.

No point in asking madam out there, Agnes nodded towards the door. Her face has been tripping her all morning.

Oh.

Don't know what's the matter with her. She hasn't been herself lately, have you noticed?

Maybe. A bit.

Does she talk to you?

About what?

Whatever it is that's bothering her.

No, not really.

Well, I'm a bit worried about her, to tell the truth. Maybe she's not well.

I don't think it's that.

Oh?

I don't know though. I hope not.

You and me both hen, but it's none of our business I suppose. Anyway, she's worse than useless today, and I'm going to be stuck here finishing these alterations for an hour or two yet. Was it busy out there?

Not really.

Always quietens down when the students have gone home. Anyway, you'd better go and deal with the customers so she doesn't scare the ones we do have away.

Okay.

Siobhan wished she didn't have to face Myrna. Agnes was wrong, it was her business, partly at least. Myrna didn't so much as glance in her direction, yet Siobhan felt as though invisible rays of scorn were penetrating her skin. She wondered if the two girls waiting on their washing could feel it, but they were gossiping eagerly in a language she couldn't identify. She waited until they'd folded their dry clothes and left, with a cheery thanks which fell flat as a pancake in the palpably chilly atmosphere. The crushing sensation of being back at school came to Siobhan, as though she'd been paired with the person in the class who most disliked her, and they were compelled to work together for an entire period. She steeled herself, then said, softly,

Myrna?

Blank. Siobhan tried again, a little louder,

Myrna?

What?

This time the response was swift and steely bright.

I'm sorry if I offended you. I didn't mean to.

What?

You know, the other night.

Oh for fuck's sake Siobhan, I've got enough to worry about without getting caught up in whatever strange little games you're playing.

I didn't . . .

Just forget it, okay?

Siobhan nodded. She didn't know what to do. She wanted to leave, that moment, to swing out the door and head home as fast as her legs would carry her. She imagined tucking herself up on the couch with a mug of tea and something sweet, sinking into her latest book. She could make all these unpleasant, inconvenient feelings clean disappear, in the company of the Weimar wannabes in their heavy beaded dresses and faux flapper pearls who flocked to Babelsberg, all cupid's bows, dreams and desperation.

Looking over from the safety of the desk she thought she saw a glint on Myrna's face as the light caught it, a sheen across her cheekbone as though she'd just wiped away a fat, glittering tear. But Siobhan couldn't be sure, and she wasn't going to risk talking again. There were other things in Myrna's life, that was for sure, things far outwith her own ken. She should make up, she thought. Clear the air, reconcile with hugs and kind words. If only she knew how to go about it, how to return things to the way they were. Siobhan felt that time had edged on, that a clockwork mechanism was ticking away seconds and minutes that could never be regained. She wondered what Myrna had meant about games, if she had guessed the secret that Siobhan could not bear for anyone to know. And if she might, in her anger, feel moved to do something about it.

5.31 p.m. – Ryan

A ned. That's what she'd call him. What anybody would call him, himself included, surely. Why else would he wear the uniform? The shell suit bottoms tucked into the sports socks. The trainers laced, but undone. The white baseball cap far back on the head, with the skip up in the air. An amalgam of sportswear, on someone who does no sport, not since he used to play football in the street after school. When he went to school. Siobhan can't see his hands, they're clasped on his knee, but he will almost certainly be wearing a sovereign ring, or perhaps one with the initials of a football club in pure, nine carat gold. Peer pressure, or an expression of something more.

He could be part of a young team. Sometimes the metal shutters of the launderette are emblazoned, overnight, by the HYT or the SYT. They will walk miles, to make their presence felt in rival territory. Like dogs pissing on lampposts, Agnes says. Once Siobhan arrived to find that the Toi had passed that way in the night. She thought they'd disappeared a long time ago, settled down, told their grandchildren that the razor scars happened when they fell off their bikes. Perhaps they'd reconvened, roared through the streets again, for one night only, before returning to beds made cosy by electric blankets and foot-twitching dreams of running battles down on the Green. Agnes remembers them from first time round, though it was the Fleet, up her way. She says it's a nonsense that things have got worse. Except when she has to scrub graffiti off the shutters. Then it's grumble grumble grumble, the youth of today.

Anyway, this ned is different, Siobhan thinks. His face is different. Not handsome, no, but arresting. His skin is pasty and if she was closer to him she'd see the pitted remains of acne scattered across it, the scabs where his razor has nicked a pustule. His eye sockets are deep, and dark-shadowed, his hair a short, straight fringe under that jaunty, ludicrously angled cap. But there's something in his attitude, the perfect symmetry of his pose, that eyes-closed expression, the sunlight streaming through the window behind him. He looks calm, and sad. Serene. Is that a ridiculous thing to think, she wonders? She isn't religious, but that countenance, it wouldn't be out of place in an Ecce Homo. As though all the sufferings of the world have been visited upon him, have driven him to rest in this tawdry sanctuary. To sit with his eyes closed, while his clothes spin round and round until the stain of the world is shaken from them.

Siobhan decides she'll take her morning break, let Agnes serve him when he comes up for the spinner. She doesn't want to hear his voice, in case it matches his clothes rather than his face. A slack-jawed whine, the colour of rancid butter, would deflate her imaginings in an instant, sully them. If she leaves now, who knows, maybe he *has* worked miracles. Raised the dead, and himself risen.

Zero tolerance

As soon as Agnes saw Myrna she knew. Felt it in her water. Myrna had been wearing shades when she arrived, which wasn't unusual until you added it to the hair around her face and the physical sidestepping, an intricate, nervous dance which prevented Agnes getting a good look at her. The cowed movement of someone who's had the stuffing knocked out of them. Agnes had seen it too many times before, and it wasn't a time for sympathy.

Dump him.

Myrna turned with a curious open-mouthed gesture, which lost the last consonant of the word,

Whaa?

Agnes took in the carefully applied make-up, the marring darkness around one eye that it couldn't quite hide.

He won't change.

Myrna scowled,

It's not what you think.

Listen to me, Myrna. They never do. It's never once, and it's you that's got to stop it. I know what I'm talking about.

Myrna shrugged wearily,

Yeah, whatever.

You've not been yourself since you started seeing him.

Myrna went through to the kitchen, flicked the switch on the kettle and eased herself into the chair. Agnes followed her.

I'll make the tea. I know you're thinking I'm an interfering old bitch, but if you'll just listen for a minute . . .

I don't want to talk about it.

Well have a think then. You can report him you know. Folk do that now.

No.

Oh, did he apologize, did he? Say he didn't know what came over him? Say it would never . . .

Agnes could you just stop it, all right? With all due respect you know fuck all about it and I didn't come in just so that you could get on at me all fucking day.

Taken aback, Agnes held her hands up, palms outward. She had never seen that expression on Myrna's face before, or heard her use that tone. It was a sneer. As though the personality of someone snide and unpleasant had suddenly inhabited her body, twisting her lip and narrowing her eye.

Okay. Take your time, there's no hurry. It's dead out there.

Maybe she'd been a bit hard on the girl. Myrna wasn't even married, for God's sake. It used to be more difficult. Depending on your real or perceived social milieu it was either shameful and unspoken, or related almost competitively to those that would understand, having been subject to the same. Her mother, for example, would have gone to

any lengths to conceal it, whereas during that hellish
stretch in the factory Agnes had worked with women
who'd compared injuries, told stories as if it was normal –
because it seemed unavoidable (and in some cases
inevitable). A different, more voluble, kind of desperation.
Times had changed now, hadn't they? It was easier to say.
Or was it humiliating, because you should know better?
Agnes was disappointed in Myrna, truth be told. She'd
had her down as a fighter. Funny, she'd assumed the girl
must have been putting it about a bit, the amount of
phone calls and nights out she seemed to be having. Must
have got the wrong end of the stick. They didn't start that
kind of nonsense too early on, instead waiting until they'd
chiselled away at a bit of confidence, blocked a few escape
routes. It was never as passionate and spontaneous as they
claimed. Yes, she had been too hard on Myrna. Maybe
there was more to this than met the eye. Gently did it. She
would try again later, when it was quiet.

Curlers removed, Vina runs her fingers through her
hair, and pins it into waves around her face. A spray of
lacquer, another for luck, and it's time for her make-up.
She consults a picture in the cinema magazine lying
open on her bed, sponges a light coating of pale pancake over her face, adds powder and blush, pencil and
mascara, lipstick. When she reveals the transformation
to her parents, her mother is reserved in her praise.
Vina chooses to focus on her father's untempered
admiration instead.

What a bobby dazzler, he says. She's so grown-up looking.

Yes, replies Maureen, she is, isn't she?

Nevertheless, she comes to her daughter's aid in the taming of an obstinate curl, spits on her hanky and wipes a smirch from under her eye.

Take care, she calls, as Vina clip-clops down the stone stairs of the close. Take care.

Look hen, I might've gone a bit over the score earlier. S'all right.

It's just that I've seen it all before. A black eye this week then a cracked rib the next, a month later your arm's in a sling, and on and on it goes. And that's only what shows on the outside. It doesn't stop. Look at Sally.

She's a fucking junkie.

Less of that, if you don't mind. She might have her problems but that doesn't mean she deserves it.

The sheer bloody arrogance of youth, Agnes thought, but then didn't we all have faith that there were some things we would never become? She paused, the better to give Myrna a chance to think on what she'd said, and sure enough, she turned contrite.

Oh I know that. Sorry. And look, don't worry, it won't happen again.

Just you make sure it doesn't. Or if you can't, I'll go round and tell him where to go.

Myrna smiled.

Thanks.

I might be old but I'm not past it yet.

I know that. But it's under control.

That's the Myrna I know talking. You can't say fairer than that. But if you need any help . . .

Just trust me, okay?

Okay. Oh, and Myrna?

Yes?

Going to make it up with Siobhan while you're at it? I don't want to know what's going on with you two, but the atmosphere in here would turn milk, and it's doing my head in.

Myrna rolled her eyes, but nodded. Thank God for small mercies, Agnes thought. She knew she'd have to tell the girls about what was happening, and sooner rather than later. They had to start planning for the future. Odd how something so long expected could come as such a complete surprise. If it had happened a few months previously, she'd have felt easier in herself. Siobhan would cope, surely, though she seemed settled enough. But no matter what Myrna said about things being under control, they obviously weren't, and Agnes didn't want to add to her worries. Of course, neither of them should have been working in the launderette in the first place, they were clever girls, who deserved to be off having proper careers. Agnes pictured them with briefcases, marching through automatic doors into glass-fronted offices full of computers.

More to the point, what was she herself going to do? Wait around to throw herself on the mercy of the new owners, even supposing they wanted to keep the place as it was? The alterations were pin money, useful, but not enough to get by on. People changed their shape to get into clothes these days, not vice versa. Hemline tucks alone weren't going to pay her bills. First refusal indeed, that had been a fucking joke (and Agnes didn't usually even think that word). After her long and faithful service. Someone could do with taking Jean down a peg or two, the way she was carrying on, speaking as if she was lady bountiful at a charity gala, when what she was doing was putting three people out of their jobs. Besides, Agnes knew fine well that the MacPherson family had started out six to a bed in a slum tenement in the roughest part of town. Like father like daughter, and all he'd ever amounted to was a ned in a good suit. She sighed. She thought she'd felt angry before, but now it was positively volcanic, bubbling away under the surface, desirous of eruption.

Collision course

Myrna slouched towards Siobhan like a recalcitrant teenager.

I'm sorry, she whispered.

What about?

Myrna widened her eyes, nodded, as if to say, don't be stupid, you *know* what about.

Oh. That. Yes. But don't be. It's me who should apologize. I didn't . . .

I know.

Will we forget it happened?

Deal. As long as that doesn't mean we can't go out and get drunk together again.

I'd love to.

Good.

Myrna?

Uhuh?

You're not, you know, ill, are you?

What? Why on earth did you ask that, has Agnes been havering again?

No. I just started worrying.

Oh no, no chance of that. Careful's my middle name.

Good, I'm glad. But if you were, well, I meant what I said, about you being my friend. If you ever . . .

Myrna held out her palm in a shut-up gesture,

Don't go all Trisha on me now. I know you're my pal. On second thoughts, let's seal it with a hug. A platonic hug, mind.

Agnes walked in, looked startled to see them, shook her head as though what they did was beyond her comprehension anyway, and walked out again.

Anyway, Myrna said as she put the kettle on, I'm not going to be doing this much longer.

No?

No. I've been trying to save up. I want to go to Australia. I've got a friend there, Magda. She's always on at me to come and visit. She'll be able to fix me up with a job if I want to stay for a while. Not like this one, I mean in a bar or something.

That sounds great.

Yes, it does doesn't it?

Myrna laughed, wondered whether it would happen. She'd been mulling over her debts, and how she could skip out on the repayments. A clean break was what was required, or in other words, a runner. Arrive as a tourist, figure out how to become a local and make a fresh start. Learn to think of herself as fresh again too. Siobhan was smiling at her, looking pleased. Myrna hoped she'd give her something to be pleased about, rather than a postcard from some Sydney lapdancing bar. She splashed milk in their tea, handed one cup over.

Thanks. Let's have a toast.

I don't have a hip flask, sadly.

A tea toast.

Well, it ain't Veuve Cliq, but okay. What to?

Your future.

Isn't it bad luck to drink to yourself?

Well, if it makes you feel better: fuck the lot of them.

Fuck the lot of them, Myrna echoed, as they clinked mugs.

Agnes stuck her head back round the door, and said,

Am I the only one who does any work around here? Delighted as I am to see you two talking again, break time's over. So if you've finished with the caring and sharing, I need to talk to you.

Something was coming, Myrna thought, whooshing towards them like the errant asteroid in a disaster movie. Except this being real life, strategic deployment of an atomic warhead might not save the day. Siobhan followed her out into the shop, where they sat down by the desk and looked at Agnes expectantly.

You know how Mrs MacPherson dropped by?

Myrna nodded. This kind of thing was always marginally less agonizing with a cigarette, but she'd left hers on the kitchen table. Plus, it might wind Agnes up even more if she lit up and started puffing away.

Well, she's selling up and moving to Spain.

What does that mean? Siobhan asked.

It means she's selling up and moving to Spain, Myrna said, and unless I'm very much mistaken we're fucked.

279

The new owner intends it to be a family business, Agnes said. So yes Myrna, we're fucked.

What about you? Siobhan asked.

I've to come in and meet him, show him around. And I'm welcome to grovel for my job while I'm at it.

It should be yours, this place, you've kept it going, Siobhan said. Nothing works as well when you're not here. The machines play up, as if they miss you.

Don't be daft. It's kept itself going. But that's nice of you to say Siobhan. It's just a shame I couldn't have afforded to buy it. Not that Jean gave me much of a chance, she had it all sewn up before she deigned to mention it to me.

So how long have we got? Myrna asked.

Until a week on Monday.

Not wasting any time then.

No. Look, I'll understand if you don't want to come in, and I'll still pay you the week's lying time.

Before Myrna could speak, Siobhan said,

We'll be there. We're in this together.

You need to think of yourselves now girls, I'll be all right.

Myrna, who could not remember ever having turned down money for nothing before, found herself agreeing.

Siobhan's right. We'll do our shifts as usual. Besides, a lot can happen in a week.

Agnes smiled.

You're good girls, both of you. If it was up to me . . .

Myrna nodded, abruptly. The asteroid had hit, and she

was reeling in the shock waves. That line she'd spun Siobhan about Australia. She hadn't even phoned Magda yet, had no idea if the invite still stood. The launderette was her grounding. She needed it.

6.00 p.m. – Irene

The girl looks around the empty launderette.

Hello there dear, Agnes says, just the usual, is it?

It's quiet today.

You wouldn't have said that if you'd been in here earlier. I was run off my feet.

Well, I've got time to spare. I'll do it myself, for a change. Anyway, this is my last visit.

Aye?

I'm getting a washing machine of my own, finally.

You've timed it well.

Oh?

Mmm. I wouldn't be surprised if there weren't a few changes here soon.

The girl looks perplexed.

Nothing for you to worry about. We're being bought over. So don't be surprised if there aren't any familiar faces next time.

Really?

Agnes nods,

It's the girls I feel for.

The girls?

Myrna and Siobhan.

Ah. What will they do?

That's the question, isn't it? Anyway, that's £1.80 the now, and do you need twenties for the dryer?

Please.

As the girl reaches to hand over the money, a diamanté bracelet slides out from under her sleeve and sparkles brightly in the fluorescent strip light.

That's a pretty bangle. Looks like an old one too, Agnes says.

Thanks. Yes, it is. Belonged to my grandmother, apparently, though she died long before I was born.

Something niggles at Agnes, but the phone rings and she gets caught up in a complex conversation with a tradesman who is prevaricating about the refund she's demanding for the so-called repair of a machine which is still not working properly. By the time Agnes has waited on hold, and spoken to the boss, she's forgotten all about whatever it was, and the girl's washing is done.

Oh well love, good luck with the washing machine.

Thanks.

Another one away, Agnes murmurs as the door closes behind her. A nice girl too, even if there is something about her she can't quite put her finger on. She's not even sure it's a bad thing, just something. She goes over to tidy the magazines which are messing up the bench, and her eye catches a bright square of paper on the floor. A Polaroid. The girl must have dropped it. Agnes holds it at arm's length (she's forgotten her reading glasses), then shrugs, none the wiser, and wedges it into the corner of the noticeboard by the desk. If she wants it, she'll come back.

Full circle

Agnes overheard the beginning of the phone conversation by mistake, and wished she hadn't. She couldn't stop herself from listening to the rest.

Botanic Hotel, okay.

. . . .

8.30 pm, is that for dinner?

. . . .

Fuck's sake, sorry, I mean, that's fine.

. . . .

Doesn't matter. Should I ask for him at reception?

. . . .

I'll go straight up then. Room 41, did you say?

. . . .

(41, Agnes thought, 41).

Yeah, cheers. Okay if I drop the money off on Monday?

. . . .

And goodbye to you too, have a nice fucking day, Myrna scowled at her mobile, and slammed it down on the table.

It could only mean one thing, Agnes knew, and she was far from happy about it. The moodiness made sense now, as did the bruises. When Myrna turned and saw her boss hovering guiltily in the doorway, she raised her eyebrows as if making it clear which of the two of them should be ashamed, then picked up her jacket and walked out, without saying a word. Agnes didn't move. Her mother's voice rang in her ears, mind your own beeswax. That room number though, why did it ring a bell? There was a horror movie she'd seen once, with a haunted hotel room. Maybe that was it. Not that Agnes was easily scared by such things. She didn't particularly like to think of herself as down to earth, her feet planted firmly on the ground, but that was what she'd become, with such success that she could not imagine another way to be.

Siobhan was emptying the contents of the desk drawers into a bin bag when she noticed the Polaroid. A tree, growing into several trunks of smooth bark, flitters of leaves a little like bamboo. Not native to this country, she thought, pulling it away from the noticeboard for a closer look, though the grey sky behind it suggested it wasn't too far away. The shape of the branches was distinctive, familiar. Siobhan traced them with her fingers, felt the reverse imprint of writing on the surface. When she turned the photo over, she saw written in confident pencilled letters: *Gingko biloba*. And underneath: 7.30 p.m. Letters she recognized. That slope to the right, the easy, definite strokes. Her stomach took a sudden rollercoaster lurch. The Bs, the A, she had seen them before. She didn't have the laundry label with her to compare, but she was sure it was the same.

Agnes?

Uhuh?

Can I get away fifteen minutes early please?

What?

At quarter past. I just remembered that . . .

Siobhan, I know about Myrna.

Siobhan's expression was transparent, as she tried to decide what to say, whether she could deny everything convincingly.

It's okay dear. I know what she's doing. I overheard her on the phone.

I haven't tried to do anything about it.

You never can. Not until . . .

What?

I meant, people have to make their own mistakes, don't they? And sometimes it's only after they've made them that they realize.

She's going to stop soon, she says.

Aye, well, I won't hold my breath. Oh, I don't know, she'll not listen to me. Anyway, you'd better get yourself together if you're wanting away.

Siobhan nodded, went through the back. Agnes looked up Myrna's number in the book and dialled, psyching herself up to be shouted at. The tone turned stereo as Siobhan came out of the kitchen holding the ringing mobile at arm's length, as though it was an especially pungent sock.

Myrna's left her phone.

Damn and blast that girl.

What's wrong?

Nothing, it's probably just my age. Siobhan, do you have a mobile?

No, why?

Well, will you do me a favour?

Uhuh. If I can.

Keep this one with you tonight, and leave it switched on. No, don't ask me why because I can't explain it. Just do what I say, please.

Okay. What . . .

If I call you, will you come?

Yes, of course, but . . .

Right, that's fine then. Now forget about me, silly old bag that I am, and get on and enjoy your night.

It wasn't until after Siobhan had left that Agnes suddenly figured out why that bloody room number was haunting her. Aimee Gallagher was murdered in room 41 of the old Ossington, she was sure of it. Months before she'd started her mourning book for Vina, or imagined that she would ever have cause to do such a thing. She thought of that last picture of her cousin, from *True Detective*. Vina pouting for the camera; Vina, who never wore black, in a tight black jumper with a wide, deep vee and a sparkly brooch at the shoulder; Vina whose glamorous, dancehall death had far more piquancy than that of poor Aimee Gallagher. Nevertheless, the streets and cafes had buzzed with talk of the murder in room 41 for weeks, only to be eclipsed when the story got out about Ringo Starr getting a knockback when he tried winching a girl at the Locarno. Agnes had thought a lot about how a murder like that, in a hotel for goodness sake, could go unsolved. It was as improbable as someone being killed outside the busiest nightspot in the city, on a Saturday night, and nobody seeing anything suspicious.

No back lanes for Siobhan tonight, as she marched up the main road towards the Botanicals. It was an evening full of potential, when even a rusty Portakabin was made beautiful by the rosegold light of the fading sun. Of course she had wild ideas, that The Girl would be standing under the tree, waiting. That there would be a message tied to a branch, telling her how to proceed, transforming her life into a French film. Despite her misgivings, Siobhan didn't slow her pace, or stop to think that there might not even be such a tree in the arboretum. That the time might not have referred to this evening, rather than any other. That the photograph might have been dropped by accident, and have nothing whatsoever to do with her. Hope alone was enough for her to keep walking, determined to let nothing make her late for this, her chance.

Agnes was not used to walking the streets so late, and felt nervous. Crossing the main road quickly, she cut into a cobbled lane. The kind of place you were not meant to go on your own, in evening time, if you were a woman.

Vina has grown into herself, quite suddenly. Her body fits her again, after months of uncertain lumpiness. The bleeding too, a badge worn with pride, rather than an uncalled-for nastiness. Knee socks and semmit have gone, replaced by stockings and a brassiere, resilient and putty-coloured now, but hinting at a silky future. And with this confidence an inkling as to the physical act which might make sense of these things, an urge to experiment which has already led her to the lane behind their tenement flat with a boy from the year above at school.

Rich with fresh experience, she quizzes her little cousin.

There must be someone you've got your eye on.

Agnes pauses for just an instant too long and Vina pounces.

Nobody at all? Bet you've never even been kissed.

Yes I have.

Don't believe you.

Have too.

Who was it then?

Frank Keenan. He walked me home from the Guides dance.

Vina whistled,

Well, you're a dark horse, aren't you? Was he a good kisser then?

Okay I suppose.

Tongues and everything?

Agnes thought of movies, where lips were pressed

together and the camera panned round so you couldn't see what was going on, and then the actor and actress stayed very still for a while.

What?

Aha, got you! You haven't, have you? Tell me truthfully.

No. Never.

Do you know what to do?

Kind of.

Show me. On the back on my hand.

Vina's hand smells of soap. It is quickly apparent that no, Agnes does not know what to do. So Vina says she'll show her, if Agnes promises – on her mother's life – not to tell.

I promise.

Say it all or it doesn't count.

I promise on my mother's life not to tell.

Shut your eyes then.

And she leans in, presses her lips against Agnes' and opens her mouth gently, enough to ease in her tongue, which tastes of the pear drops they've both been eating. After a few seconds she pulls away and rubs her hand against her mouth.

Of course, it's different with a boy. A hundred million times better.

Agnes nods. She doesn't see how anything could be better, ever, and it shames her.

Siobhan looked at her watch, a minute to go, and no sign

of the tree. She had seen it before though, she knew she had. She started to run; past children being told it was time to go home and arguing for five more minutes; past an old man sitting on a bench, dressed for winter, who raised his lager can to her and nodded; past a couple strolling, arms around each other in obvious exclusion of the world. Right up to the summit of the hill she ran, and down the other side, until finally, not far from the gate, she spotted it. Breathless, she pushed the boughs aside to check the plastic identification tag, *Gingko bilboa*. Seven thirty-one, and nobody else in sight. Siobhan stroked the bark gently, then pressed her palms hard against it, as if to feel the movement of sap. And still no one came. The photograph had been dropped by accident. It was not a sign for her to read.

Agnes survived her short cut to emerge into another lane, where the hotel had a back entrance. She had almost forgotten it was Saturday night, and was surprised when she heard music, then saw taxis turning in the car park up ahead. Guests arriving at a function, people shouting into mobiles outside the revolving doors, the whole place was hopping. Arrows pointed to a wedding reception and a work party, on pay weekend as well. Agnes slipped through the throng to the lift, and pressed the button for the first floor, then looked at herself in the mirror. She wasn't the sort of person people remembered, if they saw her outwith her own territory, the launderette. Here, her skirt and blouse and dark cardigan made her nondescript, a member of staff arriving for a late shift.

Siobhan walked back to the top of the hill, collapsed heavily on a wooden bench, and considered the view over the gardens. The seasons had quickened this year, and the paths were beginning to gather occasional fallen leaves and spiky, premature conkers. She could see the tree, its bark catching the light, and beyond that a wrought-iron fence, then the dim hum of traffic queuing at the big junction, and further, in the distance, the pinnacles of high-rise blocks. Siobhan leaned back on the bench (no memorial this one, brand new), closed her eyes and let the warm, quiescent breeze lull her. She thought of her life like speeded-up footage of a flower opening, then, seconds later, withering away. If there was no launderette, there would be no more contact with Auerbach. No more sneaking, pilfering, replacing. No more holding, caressing, loving. Her days would lose their texture. She worried they would empty completely.

The thick carpet of the corridor blanketed any sound Agnes' feet might have made, as they moved to the rhythm of the syllables of Myrna's name. Myr-na, Myr-na, Myr-na. She thought of Myrna at work, before all this started, singing along to the radio, the time she'd been carrying on and had grabbed Agnes by the hands, moved them up and down to the music, saying, come on, like this, dance. Dance. By the time Agnes reached Room 41 another name had muscled its way into the pattern. Vi-na, Vi-na, Vi-na. Vina whispering, laughing, vibrant. Looking as if the world was her oyster. As if she could do anything if she put her mind to it. Poor pretty Vina, with her stocking round her pale neck, all stiffening blue veins and dirty-looking bruises.

Siobhan had been there some time before she felt the planks of the bench sink under the weight of someone else. For a second she considered pretending to be asleep until they had gone, but it was she who should be going, home to her house and her books and her loneliness. She opened her eyes, looked round, and could not quite believe her own calm.

You dropped this, she said, handing over the photograph, which had been in her hand all along, no chance of hiding it. In the launderette, she added. Better to be more specific. Less like a stalker.

Thanks. I heard it's been sold.

Yes.

What will you do?

I don't know. Move on, I suppose.

The Girl nodded. Siobhan felt as if she'd been superglued to the seat. They sat in silence for a moment longer, then Auerbach asked,

So are you Myrna or Siobhan?

The Girl's voice made her name sound immaculate.

Siobhan, she replied.

I'm Irene.

Siobhan nodded. She could feel confession coming, knew she shouldn't say anything – but what did she have to lose? She was leaving the launderette, it was over. Resigned, she said,

I've got something to tell you.

Agnes had absolutely no idea what she was going to do. She stopped outside the door, looked at the small brass letters. 41. A DO NOT DISTURB sign was looped round the handle. She put her ear against the white-painted surface, couldn't hear anything. No keyholes to peer through now, only swipe cards. Agnes hadn't known that they had electronic locks on the doors these days. It was a very long time since she'd been in a hotel, not since the Rothesay trip, their anniversary, oh, three years ago. She could knock, of course, pretend to be the maid, but the sign also specified NO SERVICE PLEASE. Or go to reception maybe, say she thought there was something wrong. Beg for help.

Becoming aware of a faint humming noise, Agnes looked left and right along the corridor, up at the light fitting above her, then finally followed the sound down to the lock of the door. The panel showed a flickering green light, the source of the noise. Brrrrrr, it went, a bit like when the door seal broke on the Wascators. Brrrrrr. A green light, not red. In Agnes' mind, Vina smiled, the same urgent smile she used with that first cigarette, the make-up they pinched from Woolworth's, the time she made Agnes

prove she knew how to kiss. Go on, she was saying, go on.
Do it.

Irene laughed,
I know.
What?
I've known for ages.
What?
She was doing it again, Siobhan realized, going all
monosyllabic. Get more words out, she told herself, try a
sentence:
Are we talking about the same thing?
I hope so. I dread to think what else you've been up to.
Siobhan had never been a blusher, but then again, she'd
never been pre-empted to a revelation quite like this
before. Her cheeks burned scarlet.
I figured it out quite quickly, I think.
How?
The different smell. I'm very sensitive to smell.
But you kept coming back. You didn't mind.
A realization, dropped flat into Siobhan's conscious-
ness.
You didn't mind, she repeated.
Couldn't you tell from my eclectic underwear collec-
tion?
I didn't imagine for a moment . . . not that, anyway.
The blush was out of control now. Siobhan felt as
though her beaming face must be illuminating the whole
park.

I went on special trips to buy it, the silk and lace and bows. It became quite a little hobby of mine. I wanted to see what you'd magpie towards next.

Did I ever surprise you?

Mmm. Once or twice there was nothing gone, and I didn't know if it was because you weren't there, or you didn't have a chance, or you'd got fed up with the whole thing.

Did you always know it was me?

Yes. It had to be you, really.

Siobhan nodded.

Would you have said anything, if I hadn't come here today? If I hadn't found the photograph?

But you did.

Yes.

Irene laughed,

Sorry, I'm being mean. Of course I'd have come back. But I really did wonder what you'd do next. If you'd find me. I knew you came here, I'd seen you.

I saw you here as well, once. You were walking down that way, but I was away up here.

Once?

Yes.

I must have seen you, oh, three times at least. I thought we'd have to speak, eventually.

Suddenly valorous, Siobhan asked,

So, what happens next?

Oh, I've got an idea.

*

Agnes reached out and pressed the handle down, gently, gently, then pushed. A creak, that was all it would take for her to be discovered. She waited a second, then another. Nothing. She pushed the door a little more, edged around it into the room, eased it back into place. She was standing in a short corridor, the wardrobe on the left. The masking noise of running water to her right, the shower in the bathroom, the door closed. Myrna was going to go absolutely mental. Maybe she should turn back right now, quit while she was ahead. But still that fear, that strange, inexplicable certainty. What to do, what to do? Agnes crept forward a step, saw a mirror up ahead, with the bed reflected in it, a figure, just one, lying down. A familiar mop of hair, the head at a peculiar angle, and only in her slip. Myrna was lying there – not sleeping, because she was in the wrong position, unnatural, the bed in disarray. One of the bedside lamps had been knocked to the floor, Agnes saw, and moving closer still, something else, something dark on the white sheets.

No thought of anyone seeing, no thought of anything at all except that Siobhan couldn't believe that finally, after so many weeks, The Girl was kissing her, and it wasn't the same as she'd imagined, it was better. It was real. Her hand rested on Irene's hip, and slowly she stroked it up and into the curve of her waist, up further, pulling her closer, and further, pushing against the weight of her breast and realizing that she wasn't wearing a bra, feeling her own eyes turn opaque with lust.

Oh, Siobhan said, pulling away, becoming aware of the park again, the dusk, the chill in the air.

What?

Nothing.

Irene reached out, trailed her index finger up the inside of Siobhan's thigh, making her gasp as she tightened inside in response, then said,

Come on, my house is two minutes away.

The sudden absence of noise stunned Agnes. The shower had been switched off. She saw a bottle of champagne, unopened, on top of the minibar, grabbed it and pressed herself against the wall, holding it above her head as she waited. A cough from the bathroom, male, and she could feel sweat breaking out all over her body and her heart thudding in her chest, surely he'd hear it. Go back, run for it, don't, don't, don't, and the thought of Vina, in the one situation she couldn't handle, no one to help her, no one to stop her being used and thrown away. The bathroom door creaked open and Agnes took a deep breath, felt Vina's cool hand on her arm, and slammed the bottle down hard on his head. He didn't shout, which surprised Agnes, insomuch as she was able to be surprised at that moment, but he fell with a crash.

As she lay on her back on the thick white carpet of Irene's drawing room conversion, Siobhan just had time to notice that in the kitchen area (slotted neatly under the worktop) was a shiny, new washing machine, before her mouth became filled with the taste that went with that sweet, familiar scent of arousal.

Agnes stood there, frozen, clinging to the neck of the bottle. Worried that the cork might explode, she tightened her grip.

> Radio Luxembourg is blaring, and Vina and Agnes are dancing on the kitchen rug. Vina teaches her little cousin to jive, or at least to copy her movements in an approximation of jiving. When 'Love Me Do' comes on they squeal as though just infected with Beatlemania, and sing along, twirling round and round. Vina, big for her age, catches her cousin around the waist and lifts her clean off the ground, dips her to the left, then the right. When the music stops, they leap onto the recess bed without touching the wood of the floor, and Vina pulls the curtain shut behind them. This is her den, her safe place, and there she tells Agnes of all her bright and shining hopes for the future.

His hands moved, then he lifted his head, and reached for the chair by the desk, clutched it as though to pull himself up, and Agnes didn't look at his face but thought of Myrna, and there was only one thing she could do.

Yes, said Vina, clear as day. Oh yes, do it now!

Agnes raised the bottle again, and shut her eyes as she smashed it down.

Siobhan had her mouth on Irene's nipples, her fingers pushed deep into her cunt, when the phone in the pocket of her jeans started ringing.

Last wash

Myrna staggered along the lane, her heels catching between the cobbles. It was just as well someone was holding her up, she thought hazily. When had she last got into such a state? She should really have taken a taxi home but then if you're sick they charge you and maybe she was going to be sick. Images flashed through her mind, confusingly she could have sworn that Agnes had been there but imagine thinking that, it was silly, she must just have had a bit much to drink, which wasn't like her when she was working, ah yes, she'd been working, she wondered why she was so dressed up. She'd be fine as soon as she got home and her shoes off and collapsed into bed. Not that this was a short cut to her house, and who the fuck was this person anyway?

Myrna flapped her arms to free herself, and promptly fell over, whacking her knees on the hard stones which should have been fucking agony, but oddly she didn't feel a thing. The person was hauling her arm almost out of its socket, trying to get her to her feet again.

Get up. We have to keep moving Myrna.

Why are we going this way?

Myrna strained to hear her own voice. It sounded as

though it wasn't coming from her throat at all, but from somewhere far in the distance.

Because we don't want anyone to see us. Now come on, it's not far now.

Agnes?

Yes.

But . . .

Just get a move on and don't worry.

Home?

To the launderette. Now try and stand up straight, there's a good girl, we've got to get across the main road. Oh God, would you look at your knees, they're skint raw. I hope no one notices.

When they finally made it to the shop Agnes barked at Siobhan (and what was she doing there so late anyway?) to pull the blinds down and lock the door. Kicking off her shoes, Myrna padded unsteadily through to the kitchen – misjudging the distance and bouncing off the door frame on her way – where she flopped down at the table, just as if she was on her lunch break. Agnes hurried after her.

How are you feeling?

Myrna tried to think about that one.

Fine, she said, and vomited on the floor.

Once Agnes had wiped her face with a wet dishcloth and forced her to sip some water, memories began to wash into Myrna's mind, then seep away again, like the tide slowly coming in. She'd been at the hotel, another no dinner cheapskate, and then, and then . . . blank. She could hear Agnes and Siobhan, talking in whispers,

Jesus Christ, I thought she was gone, when I saw her.

Maybe it's that drug that's always in the papers. You know the one.

Or it could be concussion.

Myrna remembered the headboard on the bed, gingerly felt her head. It didn't seem tender. She wriggled out of her jacket, saw that the tops of her arms were a mass of bruises.

Will she be okay? Siobhan asked. Should we get her to the hospital?

There's something else. There was blood, on the bed. I saw it.

Myrna frowned. Something had happened, now what was it? If they'd only shut up and let her think.

Oh here hen, you'll get cold. I'll put this on you, it's nice and soft.

Very gently, Agnes manoeuvred Myrna's arms into the sleeves of a cardigan and buttoned it up, as though dressing a small and somewhat inept child.

I could go with her, Siobhan said. Make up some story, I don't know, say she turned up at my house.

We'll go together. It's the only way.

No, it isn't.

Myrna jumped at the noise her voice made, not distant now but too close, too loud. She tried to modulate her tone,

Don't do anything yet. I'll be okay. Just give me a minute.

She folded her arms on the table, laid her head down and closed her eyes.

Agnes allowed many minutes to elapse before she finally wakened Myrna – worried despite frequent checks of the girl's pulse and breathing – and it was longer still before Myrna was able to continue her story.

I think he did put something in my drink. But I'll be okay. I'm beginning to remember. We can't go to the hospital.

She looked at Agnes, fearful,

You came to get me. But what about him?

There was an awkward pause.

Oh, Myrna . . . don't you worry about that just now darling.

The sound came back to Myrna, a ghastly crunch of bone.

Tell me.

Agnes slumped down in the chair opposite.

I did wrong.

Myrna reached out and took Agnes' scrubbed-clean hand in her own, squeezed it weakly as she started to speak, her voice low-pitched and dull.

We had champagne. He seemed all right. Then I started to feel really funny. Like I wasn't all there, as if I was watching it on TV. He had ideas, about what he wanted to do. He told me. I said no, but the word didn't come out. So I got up to leave, but I'd gone all floppy. He pushed me with his fingertips and I was sitting down again. I couldn't get to my feet. He kept talking, horrible things. I think he liked that I couldn't do anything.

Oh Myrna, Siobhan said.

Agnes wavered, then took out her cigarettes and offered Myrna one. She accepted, unable to make a joke about exactly what it took for her to be allowed to smoke in the shop. Unsure that she would ever make a joke again. She looked around for a lighter, but Siobhan beat her to it, and flicked open Agnes' Zippo, held Myrna's hand steady until her cigarette was lit. She smoked for a moment, awkwardly, as if it was too strenuous, then looked down at her legs.

My knees.

I'll get the first aid box and clean them, Agnes said. If you're up to it.

Myrna nodded.

It might sting.

Myrna raised her eyebrows, recognized in the gesture a hint of her old sardonic attitude, her old self. Watching as Agnes unwrapped an antiseptic wipe, she started speaking again.

But I had my period, and of course I hadn't been able to go and have a wash. When he saw that, he went crazy, shouting about dirt and filth and I don't know what. Then . . . I don't know. You were there, suddenly, and it looked as if you were dusting. I thought I was dreaming but I wasn't, was I?

I was wiping my fingerprints away. Like they do on those dramas on the telly.

Myrna tried to smile, queasily, but it felt artificial, so she stopped mid-grimace.

And what about the other girl?

What?

The blonde girl.

Myrna stared at Agnes, until her eyes were too tired to keep up with the intensity of her gaze. When she looked away, Agnes spoke.

I don't think she'll be saying anything about it.

Not here, not now, Myrna thought. It was altogether too much. Into the silence she said,

Any chance of a cup of tea?

You shouldn't, I'm afraid, love. If you've got concussion we have to get you to hospital. It's dangerous. Probably not supposed to smoke either.

Myrna rubbed her face, as though moulding it back into shape.

I haven't got concussion. My head's clearing a little bit. The rest of me isn't too hot, but I'll live.

Sweet tea's good for shock, Siobhan said, getting up and filling the kettle.

God, I'm a fool, Agnes said. Under the sink, the old cream soda bottle.

Siobhan read the handwritten label,

Wheel motor lubricant?

Dish it out.

Eh?

It's brandy. For emergencies. I decanted it into that so you pair wouldn't be tempted.

Siobhan poured a generous measure into each mug, and they drank in unison. Finally she said,

I suppose we should make a plan.

Not sure whether she was using the right pronoun, she added,

When will they find . . . him?

Not until they clean the rooms tomorrow, Agnes said. Maybe not even then with the NO SERVICE sign. There was a case in the paper the other week where some poor old sod had a heart attack in his hotel room and wasn't found for a week.

Must've given the girl he was with a fright, Myrna said, quietly.

Siobhan splashed more brandy into the mugs,

So Myrna's the only lead?

I guess so.

Slowly Myrna said,

I could be far away.

Agnes looked at her,

What's that you're saying dear?

Australia. I've got enough money now.

Oh well done, Siobhan clasped Myrna's arm, then turned to Agnes. Though maybe it would be a good idea if you went away for a while too?

No. I'm not going anywhere. If they find me, they find me. I did it, after all. I am guilty.

It won't come to that.

Well, if it does, I'll have to accept responsibility. I hear they've got laundries in prison.

No, hang on a minute, Siobhan said. Myrna, did you not tell me that the woman who runs the agency doesn't even know your real name?

She'll be raging, Myrna said.

Don't worry about her, Agnes said. Listen to Siobhan. Does she know where you live or anything?

Myrna thought for a while,

No. She didn't want to know. All she has is my mobile number, and it's pay as you go.

Clumsily she reached for her bag and spilled the contents out over the table: cigarettes, make-up, condoms, tissues, a fresh pair of tights.

Can you see it? Must've fallen out . . .

No, wait, you left it here and Agnes gave it to me. I've got it. It's okay.

All my numbers, Myrna said. Everyone I know, everyone that knows me.

Yes. But we can get rid of it, Siobhan said, trying to open the case without success, and finally throwing the mobile to the floor, where it landed in two pieces. She extracted the SIM card, and laid it carefully on a saucer, which she stuck in the microwave on high. She turned back to Agnes,

Did anyone see you arrive at the hotel?

Lots of people. It was mobbed. Oh God, switch that thing off, would you, we don't want to blow the place up.

What about when you left? With Myrna? Siobhan asked, opening the door of the microwave and making a face at the smell.

Went out the back way, but I think they were more concerned with the wedding party. The bride was steaming and they'd taken her out for some fresh air, and the staff were trying to separate the best man and his brother-in-law. Football tartan at a wedding, I ask you. Anyhow, I said excuse me and muttered something about taking my daughter home, too much to drink, but to be honest, we must've been the last thing on anyone's mind.

Myrna had a vague impression of kilts and shouting, ivory satin and crying.

Sounds like the perfect diversion, Siobhan said. What else?

Agnes shrugged,

I can't think. What else is there?

Well – Siobhan looked sheepish – em, I think you've got blood on your blouse.

Agnes looked at Myrna,

I've got it on her as well, when I was trying to hold her up.

Okay, Siobhan said, if you look through the bags for something to put on just now, I'll get your clothes loaded up for a hot wash. Myrna's too.

You're on, Agnes said, peeling off her blouse carefully to reveal, without embarrassment, her cross-my-heart bra, before she started helping Myrna to disrobe.

Siobhan, do you think you can manage to get Myrna back to yours tonight?

What will you do?

I'll wait until this wash is done, then go home. As usual.

You shouldn't be on your own.

I'm used to it. Is that okay pet, if you sleep it off at Siobhan's?

Myrna nodded. She was aching all over, too exhausted to argue. There would come a day, she knew, when she would wake shouting and trembling and sweating in the night with the memory of this, but not yet. Her temples started to throb. It wasn't how she'd have planned it, and she was scarcely able to recognize what she was being offered, but it was there nonetheless. A second chance. She wasn't going to let it slip through her fingers. She looked at Agnes,

There's one thing I don't understand. What made you come looking for me?

Oh, that's a long story dear. A very long story.

Close

Myrna is browsing in a super-air-conditioned cosmetic hall, listening out for the tannoy announcement which will change her life. She's done it this time. She really has done it. She's heard of others, who've gone there, knows there's always that kind of work in the bars and clubs, but smiles to herself, suddenly, at the realization that it's teenagers they want. At thirty, she is probably now too old for such things. The thought pleases her, but she purchases an anti-ageing cream in duty-free anyway, along with a bottle of whisky for Magda. She is not ready to give up just yet.

Siobhan is dawdling again, but this time it is because she has someone beside her. She wishes she could slow down time to get every last second out of their togetherness, for who knows how long these things will last? Especially when they walk in the shade of a brutal, unshared secret. They don't hold hands, for they are in public, and neither is quite used to the idea, yet. Breaking the gleam of a shiny glass shop front, a large poster screams: Dry Cleaning, 4 items £12! Ironing, 12 shirts, £10! It's already faded by the sunshine, and starting to peel off at the edges. Siobhan pauses, looks in.

Sally is there. Having recognized a kindred spirit she

311

speaks intently to Jay, shining with chemical animation, silent through the glass. In the corner Darren is leafing through a magazine, which on closer inspection turns out to be the Mothercare catalogue. Waiting by the spinner is Esther, all in rose pink, smiling at Agnes, who returns Siobhan's gaze. Hands on hips as she waits to open the machine, Agnes does not smile, or wave, but nods, abruptly, sees Siobhan mirror her gesture then walk out of view.

It's a pity it has to be this way, but Siobhan is young, like Myrna. Agnes herself is not. They will not speak again, there are no ties, now. The risk is too great. At home her scrapbook has reached a bloody conclusion, with a recent clipping from the evening paper, another unsolved crime. She knows it's foolish to keep it, but she can't bring herself to let go. There's no fool like an old fool after all. She looks around her, nods again. Some things never change.

And Vina? Vina is still dancing, her heels click-clickety-clicking as she moves lightly across the sprung dancefloor. Alone this time, but smiling, her ruby mouth open wide in joy, oh yes, she's smiling.